Magnolia Gardens

Magnolia Gardens

ANNA JACOBS

Allison & Busby Limited
11 Wardour Mews
London W1F 8AN
allisonandbusby.com

First published in Great Britain by Allison & Busby in 2024.
This paperback edition published by Allison & Busby in 2024.

A CIP catalogue record for this book is available from
the British Library.

10 9 8 7 6 5 4 3 2 1

ISBN 978-0-7490-3004-9

Typeset in 11/16 pt Sabon LT Pro by
Allison & Busby Ltd.

By choosing this product, you help take care of the world's forests.
Learn more: www.fsc.org

Printed and bound by
CPI Group (UK) Ltd, Croydon, CR0 4YY

Chapter One

Amanda Denby showed the Calliers round the group of finished units they'd had built in memory of their teenage daughter, who'd been killed in a road accident.

'There's always a need for temporary housing for people in trouble,' Mary Callier said softly. 'Our Louise would have approved of this as her memorial.'

As she drove them to the airport afterwards, Amanda said again, 'You can rely on me to do my best as warden to help the tenants sort out the problems that have made them need help.'

When she returned, she parked outside her cottage, then went across the garden between it and the four units. They'd turned out well and had a lovely view at the other side.

She went round the building and strolled across to the two huge trees in the centre of Magnolia Gardens. It was a charming little park and these two trees seemed to thrive here. So would the occupants of the units, she vowed.

After standing in the shade, smiling back at the units, Amanda sat down to rest on one of the benches for a few minutes. Reaching out, she patted the trunk of the nearest tree. Their beauty always made her feel good.

She hoped the occupants of the units would enjoy them too, as the townsfolk who came for walks here clearly did.

Who would be the first person to live here? She would do her utmost as warden to help them to solve their problems and move on.

Chapter Two

When Linda Prosser was picked up by her partner from work, she could see at once that Frank was furious about something. Her heart sank because that meant he'd take it out on her when they got home. He had become rather violent lately and she was getting worried about her own safety.

He stopped at the shops, not looking at her as he got out of the car. 'I need another bottle of whisky.'

Even worse, she thought. Was it his drinking that had made him change so much this past year? Something had. She wished she'd not rushed into living with him, wished she'd not let him set up joint finances for them.

She was now trying to find a way to leave him safely and with her fair share of the money, because she knew of other women who'd had to abandon everything to get away from their abusive partners. It wasn't going to be easy but she was determined to stick it out till she could escape financially as well as physically.

Then, as Frank was striding towards the entrance to

the small shopping centre, an SUV roared into the car park, followed by a police car with its lights flashing and siren screaming. The SUV driver tried to turn right without slowing down, lost control of his vehicle and smashed into the cars parked near the entrance, landing up lying on its side, rammed partly into another vehicle.

Nearby pedestrians were caught in that encounter and sent flying like human skittles. There were screams and shouts, and at first utter chaos.

The police officers jumped out of their car and one nabbed the driver as he tried to run away while the other ran across towards a man who was lying on the ground, not moving.

It took Linda a few moments to realise that this was her partner. Everything seemed to stand still as she watched the driver being handcuffed and shoved into the back of the police car, and the officer now kneeling beside Frank pull out his phone.

She got out of the car and ran across. Was Frank dead? No, he was rolling his head from side to side and moaning.

The second officer barred her way. 'Stand back, please, ma'am.'

She pointed to the figure on the ground. 'That's my partner.'

'Ah. Then please stand to the side and leave the paramedics clear access to him. An ambulance is on its way.'

So she went back to the car, which was close enough

to have a clear view of what was happening, and sat on the edge of the driving seat with her feet out on the ground.

She realised suddenly that he'd left the engine running but didn't switch the engine off because the heater was blowing warm, comforting air around her. Time seemed to move at a snail's pace as she waited for an ambulance to arrive. She kept glancing at her watch to see that only two or three more minutes had passed.

It took the ambulance over ten minutes to get there. The paramedics ran across to him and one knelt to check him then turned to speak to the other, who hurried back to fetch a wheeled stretcher from the back of the ambulance.

She stayed where she was, not wanting to get in their way.

Frank groaned loudly as they lifted him onto the stretcher then took it across and lifted it into the ambulance.

She went across and spoke to one of them as he stepped back. 'That's my partner. Where are you taking him?'

'The Murrenfield Hospital. Do you have a car?'

'Yes.' Frank didn't usually allow her to drive it but she'd have to now.

'Then you'd be better driving there. Park near the A&E entrance. Now, please move out of my way. He's in a lot of pain and needs urgent attention.'

She watched them leave, then hurried back towards

the car, catching her skirt on a piece of metal jutting out from one damaged vehicle as she ran. To her amazement the engine was still running and her shoulder bag was still on the floor next to the passenger seat.

And this time she was going to be the one who drove it, for a change. As she moved away from the main accident zone, she noticed that the other people who'd been knocked about by the out-of-control car had all left the scene, so must only have had minor injuries. Frank had clearly come off worst of all.

Good. He deserved it.

She didn't want him to die, of course she didn't, but he'd changed so much during the past few months and had even started slapping her around so she hoped his injuries would take a long time to get better.

She drove to the hospital, switched off the engine this time and locked up, then took a deep breath and went inside.

At the A&E department she explained who she was and they took down Frank's details but asked her to wait in a small side room until he'd been assessed.

After what seemed a long time, the door opened and a woman in green scrubs came in to speak to her.

'I'm the duty surgeon. Your partner has a bad concussion and he also needs an operation as he's broken his leg. It's no use you waiting around. He's not at the top of the operating list so it'll be hours before we can deal with him, then he'll be under heavy sedation for a good while.'

'Oh. Maybe I'll go home then.'

'Yes, it'd be more sensible for you to do that. And get some sleep if you can so that you'll be ready to look after him once he's released. But could you wait a few minutes to leave? There are forms to fill in and a clerk will bring you his clothes and the contents of his pockets. We'd rather you looked after those because he won't be fit to do that.'

'Oh. Yes, of course.'

She waited and not long afterwards was given a large paper carrier bag, assured yet again that her partner would be well looked after and told to phone before coming in the following day.

When she went back to the car, she saw Frank's fancy briefcase sitting on the back seat as if keeping watch on her. He hated her even to touch it, so she left it there and dumped the carrier bag on the front passenger seat. She'd go through its contents later.

Now that the worst of the crisis was over, she felt nervous as she pressed the starter button. Frank didn't usually let her drive his car at all, said it was a valuable classic. So she had to make do with her old banger of a vehicle, which was in the local garage at the moment waiting for a spare part before it could be repaired.

The neighbour peeped out of her front door as Linda pulled to a halt outside the house. 'Oh, it's you. You don't usually drive your husband's car, so I wondered who it was.'

Trust Marion Greene to poke her nose in. She and her

husband had moved in a year ago and become friendly with Frank, remaining cool and polite with Linda. She thought of them as Mr and Mrs Nosy Parker. 'My partner has been injured in an accident and he's been kept in hospital.'

The woman looked at her. 'Oh, no! Is he badly hurt?'

'Broken leg, they think. They'll be operating on him later.'

'But you're all right?' She sounded to be accusing Linda of some misdemeanour.

'Yes. It wasn't a car crash. He was knocked down in the supermarket car park by a vehicle being chased by the police.'

'Oh. Poor man. You must let us know when he's able to have visitors, then Dennis and I can pop in to see him.'

Linda didn't contradict that. Somehow Frank had managed to convince everyone that he was a decent chap coping with a rather stupid partner.

It wasn't till she had unloaded the car and made a cup of coffee that she let herself think what this accident could mean.

Freedom.

If she left him now, instead of waiting till the end of the year, as she'd planned, he'd not be able to follow her for a few weeks, maybe longer if the break was a bad one. That'd give her time to find somewhere to live quietly and start a new life.

What's more, she'd be able to access their joint bank account while he was in hospital. He'd created a fuss when she said she needed to draw some money out to buy a new car, since he insisted this was their savings for a deposit on an investment property, not a fancy car for her when she only drove to and from work or the shops.

He'd taken away her credit card and cut it up, telling her only to use their other account and to manage with her present car for a while longer. She'd done that and managed with the car until now.

But it was time to do something about the situation!

As she sipped the coffee, her brain seemed to switch on properly and she began working out exactly how to manage her escape. It was too late in the day to go to the bank, which would be closed. But she'd go there first thing in the morning and transfer her share of the money. Half of the total would be fair because though he earned more than she did, he also spent more of their joint money.

After that she'd leave Lincolnshire for good and hope he wouldn't be able to come after her for months.

On that thought, she got his phone out of his briefcase. She already knew he had it well protected, so that she wouldn't be able to use it. She smiled. That wouldn't stop her 'losing' it, though, would it? Tossing it in a river, perhaps. Ooh, yes, she'd love to do that.

She looked at her own phone. She was quite sure he'd have that monitored so it'd be safer to lose hers as well. She'd just buy the simplest and cheapest one she could to replace it.

He didn't know about her personal savings account,

thank goodness. She'd been setting aside small amounts of money from the housekeeping for a while. It all mounted up.

She'd managed that because the one thing Frank didn't bother to control these days was grocery shopping. He wasn't interested in food, boasted about keeping himself 'trim, taut and terrific'. But she knew he'd checked with a friend that she wasn't spending too lavishly on housekeeping because she'd heard him boasting to their neighbour about that.

Shopping was the woman's job, he always told her in a patronising tone. His attitude and way of speaking to her had grown distinctly sexist over the past year and he'd changed markedly since Dennis next door had introduced him to a group of macho male friends.

Frank didn't seem to realise how old-fashioned he sounded nowadays. Had he ever cared about her? No. She didn't think so. He cared about her cooking skills, though, and only used her as a housekeeper nowadays. Thank goodness he'd moved out of their shared bedroom several months ago, saying he'd been sleeping badly. In fact they rarely even chatted now let alone shared interests.

However, when she'd tentatively raised the idea of them splitting up, he'd flown into a rage and threatened to make her regret it if she tried to leave. He'd thumped her to prove it. And when this happened again, she'd started planning 'the great escape' seriously, even before the bruises faded.

But not without her money. And this would be the

best chance she'd ever have to take it and escape.

She drove to the small local shopping centre, which was still open for late-night shopping, to buy a few personal necessities, including a second-hand suitcase from the charity shop. As she was walking round she saw that the hairdresser's was still open. She caught a glimpse of herself in its window and stopped dead. "Bottle blonde", her mother would have called it. It was Frank's preferred colour for a woman's hair, so he insisted she keep hers that way.

She could see through the window that no one was waiting in the salon and her regular hairdresser was just finishing with a customer so she nipped in. 'Any chance of getting my hair done straight away, Penny? I know it's late, but I'd really appreciate it.'

'It's not that late and it's been a slow day so I don't mind earning a bit more money. What do you want – roots bleaching, shampoo and blow dry, as usual?'

'No. I want my own hair colour back, chestnut brown, or as near as you can get to it, and a shorter style this time.'

'Good. Brown will suit your skin tone much better.'

'I know. But Frank liked it blonde.'

When she sat down, Penny said, 'Did you know your skirt is torn?'

She looked down. 'Oh. So it is. I forgot to change when I got back. We were involved in an accident on the way home from work, you see. Frank is in hospital with a broken leg.'

'Are *you* all right?'

And heaven help her she felt tears well in her eyes. 'Not yet. But I'm going to be. I'm leaving him, Penny, hence the hair change. Tomorrow will be the best chance I'll ever have of getting away safely. Even an abusive partner can't chase someone round the country with a leg in plaster, can he? And by the time he gets fully mobile again, I'll have found somewhere to hide.'

'Abusive? Oh, you poor love.' Penny gaped at her, then gave her a sudden hug. 'Got to confess I don't like your Frank, nor does my husband, but I didn't realise he was that bad. How you've put up with his arrogance for so long, I don't know.'

'He used to travel a lot on business and anyway he wasn't as bad until he changed to this new job and acquired a new set of friends. I didn't realise your husband knew Frank.'

'They belong to the same golf club, but they don't hang out with the same groups of people. Now, let's get on with your hair while you tell me about your plans.'

'I haven't got any plans yet, except to get away, because it only just happened. I can't leave till the banks open tomorrow and I can take my money out.'

'Well, you'll have a nice modern car to get away in, won't you? You're not leaving it for him, are you?'

'I'd not dare take it. He loves that car and I think he'd kill me, literally, if I took it. Anyway, that would make me much easier to trace. I heard him boast to a friend that he's installed a GPS tracker and done the same to my car. He always knows where I am. My car is in for repairs or

I might take it and leave it somewhere en route, but it's so old now they can't repair it till the new part arrives.'

She waited till Penny had finished rinsing her hair to continue, speaking more for herself than for her companion. 'I'm going to use public transport at first. I'll take a taxi to the nearest railway station after I've been to the bank tomorrow and who knows where I'll go from there?'

Penny's hands stilled, then she said slowly, 'I've got a better idea.'

'Oh?'

'It's my day off tomorrow and I've arranged to take Monday off as well so that I can visit my gran and not have to rush back. She lives in Swindon in Wiltshire. I can take you there, if you like, and drop you in the town centre. It'll give you a start on escaping that no one will be able to trace.'

'You'd do that for me?'

'Yes. I'll miss having you as a customer, though, and swapping books to read.' She scribbled on a piece of paper. 'Here. This is my mobile number. Phone me if you change your mind but if you're still leaving just let me know when you're ready to go tomorrow morning and we'll meet in the car park here, round the back.'

'It may take a while at the bank.'

'I can wait. I was going to avoid the morning rush hour anyway. And I'm extremely happy to be able to help you escape.'

'I can't thank you enough, Penny.'

'My pleasure. Now, let's finish your hair.'

An hour later Linda smiled at her reflection. She looked like herself again.

But she wouldn't feel like herself till she got away.

She didn't sleep very well that night but she was so tense she didn't feel at all sleepy as she got ready to leave the following morning.

When the phone rang just as she was about to set off, it caught her by surprise and she jumped in shock. She checked before picking it up and it was the hospital. Should she take the call or not?

Not, she decided, so listened to the message some woman was recording. There had been a delay in operating because of two even more urgent cases so her husband's operation had not taken place until late last night. He wouldn't fully recover consciousness until later today and he wouldn't be thinking clearly till the next day, so though Linda was welcome to visit if she wished, it'd probably be a waste of time because he'd forget what they talked about and she'd have to repeat herself.

She didn't correct them about him being her husband. He often told people that they were married. And the late operation was good news. That gave her longer to get away. She wanted to make sure that even if he sent a private investigator after her, as he'd boasted one of his friends had done to his runaway wife, they'd have trouble finding her.

Actually, if she was very lucky she'd never need to see

Frank again. Now wouldn't that be wonderful?

She decided not to phone Penny until after she'd been to the bank, because sorting the money out might take some time. She'd probably have to see the manager to get the account changed so drastically.

The taxi took her to the shopping centre and she hauled her two battered suitcases and backpack out, paid him and watched it drive away. Then she went towards the entrance, struggling to cope with the luggage.

When someone took one of the suitcases away from her, she jumped in shock and swung round, groaning in relief when she saw it was Penny.

'I didn't phone you because I haven't been to the bank yet. That might take a while. Can you wait?'

'Yes, of course I can. I decided to leave home at the time I'd originally planned so that even my husband, bless his little cotton socks, won't know about you coming with me. What people don't know, they can't reveal to others even accidentally, can they?'

'You're taking this very seriously.'

'Yes. Your situation brought back memories. We had a neighbour once with an abusive husband. He killed her.'

Linda gasped and stared at Penny in shock.

'You should take what you're doing very seriously indeed as well, Linda.'

There was dead silence as Penny stared into the distance, looking sad, then turned back to her. 'So if I can help you now, I'll do whatever is necessary. It'll feel like a tribute to Rina's memory.'

'Thank you.'

'I'm parked in a quiet spot at the back, so how about we carry your luggage round to my car then you go and do whatever you need to at the bank. I've brought a book, so I'll sit in the car and have a peaceful read.'

Linda nodded, touched by this generous help.

As she'd expected, it took a while to sort things out at the bank because she did indeed have to see the manager. He didn't seem to take her seriously till she explained that she was leaving her partner because of his violent behaviour.

When he brought up their account details on his desktop, she was shocked rigid. 'He's taken most of the money out,' she said in a croaky whisper. 'My money's nearly all gone!'

'Oh dear. Legally he had the right to do that, I'm afraid, the way the account was set up.'

'Then can I withdraw the rest?'

'As long as you leave a small amount in to keep the account open, you can take nearly all that's left. We can't close it completely without both of you agreeing. I'm sorry I can't help you otherwise. Do you want to report it to the police?'

'No. I have to leave straight away.'

She was left with only a few thousand pounds instead of the hundred and fifty thousand that her parents had left her.

She walked out of the bank with a purse full of banknotes and the rest of what she felt was rightfully her money transferred to a new account. She'd leave the secret account as it was for the time being. It was with another bank anyway.

'What's the matter?' Penny asked before she'd even buckled her seat belt.

Linda burst into tears and explained between gulping sobs.

'What are you going to do?'

'Get as far away as I can, then start a new life under a new name. Rent the cheapest bedsitter I can find, I suppose.'

As Penny set off, she asked, 'You won't be going back to your maiden name or anything like that, will you?'

'No. I'm changing my name completely. I'm going to call myself Carla from now on.'

'Carla isn't your middle name, is it?'

'I may be stupid at times, as I proved by moving in with Frank, but I do have a few grey cells still functioning. I'll be using a different surname too, one I have no connection whatsoever with. So I'm now Carla Hewitt. Sounds good, doesn't it?'

'Sounds nice. You're quite sure you don't know anyone called that?'

'Definitely not. I picked the surname out at random from the newspaper. And I chose Carla from a book of baby names simply because I like it.'

When they were a short distance out of town, she asked, 'Can we stop after the bridge so that I can throw these two mobiles into the river?'

'Throw *two* mobiles in the river?'

'His and mine. He's bound to have trackers on them both.'

Penny grinned. 'Great idea, *Carla*.'

She asked her friend to call her 'Carla' from then on so that she could start getting used to it, but she found it hard to chat. She was still too upset about losing her money.

When they got to Swindon, Penny stopped in the town centre near a taxi rank and sighed. 'I wish I could help you more, L— I mean, Carla.'

'You've helped me hugely already: not only brought me here, but enabled me to get away without leaving any traces. I'm extremely grateful.'

'You'll stay in touch, won't you?'

'If I can.' She wasn't planning to stay in touch with anyone, not even her kind friend. Better safe than sorry from now on.

She found somewhere to buy a new phone but she wasn't even going to try to reclaim her money, she realised. She didn't dare. She was too afraid of what he might do if he found out where she was.

It was going to be hard to find somewhere to hide, even with this flying start, because she'd have to get a job as soon as she could now. She didn't dare run her money down lower than this in case he found her again and she had to flee.

Chapter Three

It was nearly three months before the interiors of the four units were fully fitted out and ready to be occupied, and extensions to the warden's cottage completed. All the tenants would have lovely views of the park and the two large trees in the centre of this end. By then Amanda was happily settled in the cottage.

However, during that time Warren Padgett was promoted to the position of manager of the council building department, and had proved a thorn in her flesh. He immediately started reorganising 'his' department and making his presence felt in a variety of annoying ways.

He seemed to have set his sights on the trust as well and she suspected that he was trying to find a way to take over its administration. His initial target was the selection of tenants and he made it clear during his first meeting with Amanda that he did not approve of homeless people from *outside* the valley being given priority for places ahead of local people already on the council's waiting list for housing.

Two more meetings showed that he didn't approve of anything else she was doing, either, and someone tipped her the wink that he was sneakily lobbying councillors about passing new bylaws that would help him to take over the trust from this amateur female who was (he told everyone) so inefficient.

She doubted he could do anything legally because she prided herself on her ability to write watertight contracts and she knew she was managing things efficiently, but he could and did slow down progress on the council signing off on the buildings. In fact, he was an absolute pain to deal with.

Today was what she hoped would be the final meeting with him about the units and unfortunately her return to the valley was delayed by heavy traffic.

Padgett was already waiting for her, scowling of course, with Corin standing nearby. The usually friendly architect wasn't even looking in the other man's direction let alone chatting to him, but fiddling with his phone. That said something about the general mood of their encounter. She knew whose side she was on. If you couldn't get on with Corin Drayton there was something wrong with you.

When she got out of her car, Padgett made a big display of glancing at his watch and tapping it before she could even begin to explain what had delayed her.

She retaliated by giving him a beaming smile, something which, as she'd already found, made him visibly uneasy.

'Sorry I'm late, Warren. Traffic problems.'

'You should have made allowances for traffic delays. This is a busy time of day. And, as I've said before, Ms Denby, I prefer that we address one another formally. This is a business meeting not a social event.'

She smiled. 'I'm just not a formal person, I'm afraid.' She turned to the other man. 'Hi, Corin. Lovely to see you again.'

He came across and plonked ostentatious social kisses on each of her cheeks in turn, taking his time about it. This made Padgett wince again.

'Always lovely to see you, Amanda *darling*. You're looking rather tired.'

'It's been a busy week finishing everything off.' She turned reluctantly back to Padgett. 'Ready to go round again, Warren?'

This would be the second 'final inspection' they'd made. He'd found two unimportant faults during the first one and had insisted on another complete inspection once they'd been dealt with. She'd agreed only because it seemed likely to be quicker to do that than causing a fuss about his uncooperative behaviour with the town council.

He scowled at her. 'My staff and I have already checked the houses.'

That made her stare. 'How did you get in without keys?'

He avoided looking her in the eyes as he replied. 'The council always retains a master key to any new developments it's dealing with, in case something goes wrong. The key opened the doors of all the units so we were able to have a good look round this time.'

She opened her mouth to protest and he held up one hand like a traffic cop in a movie.

'We always do this with public housing. We didn't want to waste our time hanging around waiting for you and anyway we didn't think you'd object to us going inside. It *is* our job to supervise local building projects, after all.'

'I do object. Please don't try to gain entry to these private premises again. This is *not* and never will be public housing. There is a reversion clause in the trust's favour if you close them down.'

She waited in vain for a response to that. He treated her to another scowl and continued talking at her.

'Everything *seems* to be in order this time, Ms Denby, though since you didn't gain council approval for your choice of builder there will have to be regular, ongoing checks of these premises to ensure that they do not deteriorate and continue to meet local standards.'

'There won't be any further checks, I assure you. I checked and you don't do that to other private housing so I'll make a major legal complaint if you try to do it to the trust's dwellings.'

He stiffened visibly. 'Of course there will be ongoing checks. Someone has to keep an eye on the safety side of buildings in this valley. That is well within my remit.'

'For council properties, perhaps, but the trust owns

these units and as its CEO, I shall be dealing with their ongoing maintenance. If any problems arise, I shall call Corin in.'

'I must insist—'

'You can't insist on anything. The rules were legally set in place before you even came to work here when the trust first acquired the plot of land. It will take care of its own tenants and building maintenance from now on. All the council needs to do is receive the rates money paid on the units. Read the contract again if you've forgotten the terms and don't hesitate to ask for help if you don't understand any of the long words.'

He breathed deeply and started to say something but she turned back to Corin. 'If you're ready now, you and I will do a final inspection to satisfy ourselves that there is nothing else that anyone can complain of.' And, she thought, to check that nothing had been tampered with, but though she was tempted to say that, she didn't want anything else to cause delays.

'Happy to do that,' Corin said.

Padgett breathed deeply. 'I shall join you in case you have any queries about council regulations, though I have already put it on record that this project is being conducted in a way that I thoroughly disapprove of.'

She ignored him and unlocked the rear door of the first unit. She couldn't stop Padgett trailing along behind them without creating a scene but she locked the doors of each unit carefully as they left and didn't address any remarks to Padgett until an hour later, when they went to stand in the residents' summer house and barbecue area at one side of the small garden at one side of the units.

'Did you find any problems, Padgett?'

'Not at the moment.'

'I didn't think you would, so I brought the final document with me and I'll ask you to sign it here and now. We can get your assistant and Mr Drayton to act as witnesses.'

'But I don't—'

'If you are unwilling to do this, I shall make a formal complaint to the council *immediately* about your lack of cooperation and charge for the waste of my time.'

'I'll sign it for now but you can be quite sure that I'll be keeping an eye on those units.'

'From a distance only.'

'As needed,' he corrected.

We'll see about that, she thought, but didn't bother to argue.

Once the document had been signed, she said, 'May I have the master key back, please?'

From the smirk on his face as he handed it to her, she guessed he'd had a copy made.

She put it in her bag and turned to Corin. 'I owe you a coffee, my friend. How about I pay my debt now?'

'Good idea.'

She walked quickly across to her cottage before her annoyance with Padgett made her do or say something rash that she might regret.

Corin joined her at the front door and they stood watching Padgett fuss his way into his council vehicle and watch them without making any attempt to leave quickly.

She said in a low voice, 'I'm going to get all the locks changed this afternoon and every person who moves in will be told not to give copies of their door key to anyone, especially people from the council.'

'Very wise.' Corin glanced back over his shoulder and chuckled. 'He looked like an outraged turkey, don't you think? And now he's shouting at his poor clerk. How the hell did he get hold of a master key?'

'I don't know but it won't happen again. I'll use a different locksmith this time, one from outside the valley.'

She made them a cup of coffee and sat down next to Corin with a sigh. He grinned at her. 'I was lost in admiration at how well you kept control of your temper today.'

'It was touch and go at times. What is wrong with the man? I've never met anyone so negative.'

'He's empire-building and wants control over everything he can grab. Some bureaucrats are like that. Though I must say we've never had one in Essington as bad as him.'

'And yet his deputy has been nothing but helpful. I wish she'd got the job.'

'Well, our direct association with Padgett is now officially over. You should tell the tenants to contact you directly if they have any problems with the council, and to have nothing whatsoever to do with him or his minions.'

'Don't worry. The situation will be made very clear to them.' She paused to consider the situation for a moment then snapped her fingers as she thought of something else. 'We'll add an electronic keypad as well as a lock to each unit, using a system to which we'll have an override for, of course.'

'Good idea. And feel free to call me if you need any further help. There will be no charge for my services because I greatly admire what the Calliers have done here. I think their trust really is going to help people experiencing difficult situations in their lives.'

'I hope so. I can start looking for tenants in earnest now. I've already put the word round and got a couple of possible leads to follow up on.'

Chapter Four

Carla found a cheap hotel in Swindon for the night and got online with the new mobile phone she'd bought to plan her itinerary for the next day. She felt nervous, though there would surely be no way Frank could track her down now, even once he was able to get around again. She was so grateful to Penny.

She wondered how he'd manage when no one could find her and hoped he'd have a lot of trouble sorting out his own care during his convalescence. Presumably he'd have to pay someone to do the housekeeping.

She wondered whether to buy a cheap old car because fares on the railways were horrendous unless you booked trips well ahead, but she came to the conclusion that it'd be better to manage with buses for the time being.

Then she decided that she needed to change her name officially, so had to stay in Swindon till that was done. She found an even cheaper hotel for a day or two and ate sparingly, trying to conserve her money.

To her relief she discovered that there were special

provisions for women in danger of assault from former partners who'd become abusive, so she managed to do all the paperwork necessary very quickly and would be able to make contact online with the authorities from then on. At least the new laws meant Frank wouldn't be able to trace her through official channels, whatever he did.

It was hard travelling with three pieces of luggage, but they contained all she owned in the world now so she didn't want to get rid of anything.

She decided to get the local newspapers from places to the west of Bristol and scout around for a job, preferably one with accommodation included.

She found a job as a barmaid at a country pub in a village she'd never heard of, thanks to her experiences years ago as a student, and when the owners found out her situation and lack of transport, they came to interview her in Bristol while they were visiting someone there.

To her relief they offered her the job together with a tiny bedsitter and storage for her suitcases in the attics free in return for some after-hours cleaning of the bars.

After a few days they complimented her on her hard work and lent her an old banger of a car that had once belonged to their son to get around the neighbourhood in. They even seemed to understand that she needed to get out from time to time. She'd forgotten how reasonable and helpful most people could be.

She didn't enjoy this sort of work but decided that she

would put up with it for the time being because what she really needed was some quiet time to change back into a single person. And it didn't hurt to be able to live cheaply and save some more money.

She had no idea what she would do with her life long-term. That would have to wait till she found somewhere to settle permanently.

But long walks in the countryside and drives to nearby beauty spots seemed to give her a start at finding herself again at least. She'd eventually go back to doing something more interesting, even perhaps start another cake-making business. Well, she hoped she would be able to do that.

Not yet, though. She still felt as though she were a convalescent. She hadn't realised how much Frank had controlled her life until she left him.

And until other people started giving her compliments about her work she hadn't realised that he'd also made her feel insecure and lacking in modern skills.

Chapter Five

Brett Powell knew the change he'd been dreading all year was about to happen when his foster mother told him his social worker was coming to have an important chat with him that evening. His heart sank. He'd been transferred to this foster carer only three months ago when the one he was with fell seriously ill. He wasn't looking forward to yet another move.

And where was he going to move to? He knew that when you turned eighteen you were considered an adult and they moved most young people out of the care system then. It had been his eighteenth birthday last week. Not that anyone here had so much as wished him happy birthday.

He'd bought himself a small bar of chocolate but that was all. He didn't dare spend his meagre savings. It was all he had if they threw him out.

His previous social worker had given him some leaflets about this coming change a while ago, saying they contained valuable information for later in the year when he turned eighteen. He'd tried to read them but as usual the words had started blurring together after a minute or two, especially the longer ones, and he'd abandoned the effort, contenting himself with struggling through the summary page.

Couldn't the system even give him a week or two's leeway without harassing him? They knew he'd been actively looking for a bedsitter but hadn't found anywhere he could afford yet, not on the social security payment he'd receive till he found a job. What more could he do? He had no family left to help him.

Ms Vernon didn't waste time asking him how he was. 'You must have guessed what this meeting is about, Brett?'

'Yes.' He glanced across at his foster parents, who were sitting at the other side of the room and thought it prudent to say, 'I shall be sorry to leave here.'

He wouldn't really be sorry. Indeed, he'd have been happy to leave if he'd had somewhere decent to go to instead. But he didn't have anywhere and had no idea what to do next. He was absolutely terrified of being left homeless and having to sleep rough.

The Shearers hadn't ill-treated him but they usually took younger children and they'd only agreed to provide a stop-gap placement for him when his previous foster father had a sudden heart attack.

Brett had also been forced to change schools at the same time because the one he used to attend was too far away now and came under a different local authority.

They'd have allowed him to stay on for the last few months of the school year, but he had no way of getting there and back each day as there was no public transport going anywhere near it.

That double change had made his life even more difficult than usual.

'Any luck about finding yourself a full-time job, Brett? I know you recently found a part-time shelf-stacking opportunity at the supermarket, but that's not enough to build your life on, is it? You really should get some qualifications.'

He looked at her wearily and said it again. 'I told you before that I'm no good at exams or the sort of studying that gets you into colleges.'

'Your former teachers told me that too, but the one I spoke to in your new school didn't think you were trying as hard as you might have done. He thought you could definitely have improved your skills if you'd bothered.'

He guessed, no, he *knew* that would be Mr Barton, who was a grumpy old sod and didn't believe dyslexia existed, let alone severe dyslexia. Brett stared down at his hands, not knowing what else to say or do. *If in doubt, stay quiet* was one of his rules for avoiding trouble.

'Well, as it turns out, I have a suggestion that may help you.'

He waited. It'd probably be another temporary place to stay, a hostel maybe. Which would be better than nothing, admittedly. What else could she do for him at this stage? There weren't any full-time jobs round here for unskilled young people like him, nor were there any affordable bedsitters. He'd tramped the streets looking for jobs and accommodation, had tried everywhere he could think of, but since he didn't have a car and the bus services were poor, he couldn't search any further afield.

'There's a charitable trust that may be able to help you. It will find you a temporary place to live and help you sort out a job. It's at a place called Essington St Mary.'

'I've never heard of it. Is it far away?'

'It's in a small town in Wiltshire, about an hour's drive away from here. Your family came from that county originally, I gather.' She looked at him questioningly.

'Yes. But they're all dead now.'

She couldn't have read his file properly if she didn't know the rest, but this was no time to quibble so he filled in the details. Again.

'My parents worked on a farm in Wiltshire till I was eight, then my mother died and my father couldn't cope with looking after me and his new job as a truck driver so I was put into care. I never saw him or heard from him again, but the social worker told me he'd died of a heart attack.' He hadn't missed his father because as a long-distance truck driver he'd never spent much time at home. It had been his mother who did everything.

He waited. He did a lot of waiting with this social worker, who spoke slowly to him with regular pauses, as if giving him time for what she'd just said to sink in. He could always tell when people thought him stupid. She certainly did.

That had annoyed him when Ms Vernon first took over managing his care, and he'd told her several times that it was written words he had trouble with, not what people said to him. But she hadn't changed how she spoke to him, so probably didn't believe him.

Now, he no longer cared what she said or did. Or about what Mrs Shearer thought either. If this trust could help him, he'd not be seeing these foster parents again and probably not this social worker either, with a bit of luck.

Ms Vernon started speaking again, so he tried not only to pay attention but to show that he was doing so by nodding occasionally.

'There's a project run by a trust in Wiltshire set up in memory of a girl who was killed in a road accident. Her parents have built a row of four residential units for people who can't find accommodation and are going through a difficult time in their lives. The manager is willing to consider you for one of their units and will try to help you in other ways too once you get there. We've never placed anyone with them before because it's a brand-new set-up, so I wasn't sure about it, but given the urgency of your situation, I think it's worth risking it in your case.'

He stifled a sigh. These people in Wiltshire would want to interview him first and he was no good at formal interviews. But you had to play along, so he asked, 'What do I have to do to be considered?'

'You have to chat to their lawyer.'

So he said that again, too. 'I'm no good at interviews.' He knew it'd be a waste of time even going to this one but he didn't dare say that. He'd learnt to seem willing to do anything. And he was willing. He always tried his hardest. He just wasn't very clever.

'Luckily this isn't a formal interview. It'll just be you and this lawyer having a chat. I've spoken to her on the phone a few times and she seems really nice.'

He didn't know what to say to that. An interview by any other name was still an interview as far as he was concerned.

'You have to give this a really good try,' she said slowly and emphatically. 'You're nearly an adult now and have to learn to control childish nerves and get on with things.'

'However kind this lawyer is, I'll still feel nervous. I can't help it.'

Her voice grew sharper. 'You really don't need to be nervous with Ms Denby, Brett. I found her absolutely charming and I'm sure you'll like her too.' Another pause, then, 'Give it your best try, hm?'

'Yes, of course I'll do my best. My very best.' And he would. Only his best was never good enough.

'Right then. I'll pick you up tomorrow morning at nine o'clock and drive you there. Essington is about an hour away from here.'

'I'll be ready.' As usual he tried to look on the bright side. It'd be a day out if nothing else and he loved looking at the countryside.

'And dress nicely.'

How was he to do that? His clothes were all too small for him and looked tight and shabby, but he didn't dare complain about them.

His foster mother chimed in. 'I'll make sure he's well turned out.'

As she was showing the social worker out, he heard Mrs Shearer say, 'Don't give him any drinks on the way to the interview or he'll spill them down himself. He's very clumsy.'

He was only clumsy when he was nervous, he thought indignantly, and Mrs Shearer would make even the king nervous!

She came back and said brightly, 'That's good news, isn't it?'

In other words, she was hoping to get rid of him.

'Yes, it is. Very.' He spoke as cheerfully as he could then went back to his room to try on his best clothes. They seemed even tighter than last time because he'd grown a lot lately. He was over six foot now.

Why did people still say six foot even though everything had been metric for years? he wondered.

He hung his best clothes up again then went to

stand by the window and gaze out at the back garden. He'd have liked to help with it but Mrs Shearer didn't trust her foster children and they were forbidden to go anywhere near her precious vegetables.

Chapter Six

By nine o'clock the next morning, Brett was dressed in his best and feeling so nervous he hadn't been able to eat much breakfast.

'You'll be all right, Brett,' his foster mother said. 'Just do your best.'

'I'll try.' But his best wasn't usually good enough for people in authority, however hard he tried.

Ms Vernon parked in the drive and sounded her car horn, so he hurried out to join her.

She studied his face. 'Nervous?'

'Yes.'

'Ms Denby is really nice, I promise you.'

'Yes. You said.' But interviews weren't nice and nothing could make them pleasant, in his experience.

The drive would take at least an hour and he had to ask Ms Vernon to stop the car half an hour into it, then go and throw up his breakfast under a hedge.

She shoved a box of wipes at him when he got back in the car, but at least she didn't shout at him. 'Clean your face with these. I do wish you'd believe me about how nice Ms Denby is.'

'I'm sorry. It's me that's the problem. However nice she is, I'm rubbish at interviews.'

He leant back, closing his eyes, letting his stomach settle down again. Well, more or less settle down.

It was some time before Ms Vernon said anything else, then she touched his arm. 'The satnav says we're near Essington. You might like to open your eyes and look round in case you're lucky enough to come and live here. The town is apparently at the foot of a long, shallow valley. The main road up it is Larch Tree Lane, which goes right to the top, but stops at a dead end there. We're not going up it today. We're meeting Ms Denby at her office in the town centre.'

'I see.' He nodded as well as speaking to show he was listening but then realised she was looking at the road ahead, not at him.

'She'll talk to you then take you to see the units. This Magnolia Gardens place is apparently a little park on the outskirts of the built-up area and she suggested I go into town and have a look round, then pick you up from her office when she phones me. Is that all right with you or do you need me to stay with you?'

'It's fine by me.' It would be a relief not to have to perform in front of her as well as this stranger, actually. If the stranger really was nice, it might even be easier. Now, there was a thought!

She went back to driving in silence and he stared out

of the car window. The town centre surprised him. It was really pretty and more like a large village than a town. He'd only seen photos of places as pretty as this before, couldn't remember ever visiting one.

Pity he wouldn't be coming to live here. He really liked the look of it.

They parked outside an old-fashioned house just off what seemed to be the main street. The house turned out to contain offices, not living spaces. Ms Denby came out to the reception area to greet them and took them into a room at the back.

Ms Vernon embarrassed him straight away by saying, 'Brett's very nervous, I'm afraid.'

He could feel his face going hot.

The woman smiled at him. 'I don't usually terrify people.'

Then she turned back to Ms Vernon. 'I'll phone you after Brett and I have finished our chat and had a bite of lunch to eat.'

When his social worker had left, he waited, numb with fear, for the lady to begin firing questions.

Instead, Ms Denby took his hand and held it between hers, then patted it gently with her top hand. 'I don't think I've ever seen anyone as nervous as you are at this moment, Brett.'

When she let go, she smiled at him and it was a really lovely smile, which made him feel a little better. 'Would you like a can of soft drink before we leave? The water has only just been switched on at the units and it's coming out a bit rusty still. They're finished but still unfurnished, by the way.'

He suddenly realised how thirsty he was and how bad his mouth tasted. 'Yes, please. I'd love a drink because I've not had anything since breakfast. It doesn't matter what it is.'

She got out two cans, lemonade and ginger beer. 'I like them both so you choose whichever you prefer.'

He took the ginger beer, which was his favourite drink and it seemed like a good omen. When she opened her can and took a long swig, he did the same. He loved the tanginess and his mouth now tasted much better, which was a small relief at least.

'I'll tell you a little more about the units before we leave, then we'll drive over and I'll show you round one of them.'

She explained about a girl being knocked down and killed, then the parents building a row of units in her memory for people who were desperate for somewhere to live.

'That was kind of them.'

'They're lovely people but very sad still. They've gone to live in Australia near their son now.' She waited then asked, 'Any questions?'

'Is the rent high? I won't have a job, you see, though I will look for one, I promise. Only, the social security money isn't very much and jobs are hard to find when you don't have any experience or training.'

'You won't be charged any rent at all till you find a job. That's part of the deal.'

He was so surprised it was a minute or two before he could speak. 'Really? I've never heard of that before.'

'Yes, really. The Calliers aren't short of money and they don't want the people who live in their units to be stressed. Anyway, let's go and look at one then have a casual chat. *Not* an interview.'

She removed the squashed can from his hand, tossed it into a wastepaper basket then patted him again. Which made him realise how long it had been since anyone had actually touched him.

'I shall keep saying it till you believe me: I'm not going to interview you at all, Brett, just chat. And I promise not to bite.'

She might be nice, but he still felt shuddery inside and was sure she'd find more deserving people than him to live in the units. That would make it worse because he loved the look of the town. He sighed about that as they walked out to her car.

They drove up Larch Tree Lane from the town centre then turned right off the main road onto a side road that curved round some pretty, older-looking houses. It led eventually to a dead end where there was a parking area, a garden and summer house and a long, new-looking building.

'These are the units,' she said. 'They're in a row.'

They weren't posh but they were nice to look at, seeming friendly though he couldn't work out why. There were parking spaces at the street side of the units with numbers painted on the ground, two for each unit, as if guests were expected. There were a few more parking places without numbers at the other side of the space. Ms Denby left her SUV in one of the unmarked ones and got out of the car, so he did too. She didn't move so he didn't either.

'We're going to look at Number 2 today. It's only just been finished so it smells of paint, I'm afraid. The units all look out onto the park at the other side and this summer house is for the residents to use.' She pointed across the car park. 'Will you mind living close to other people?'

'Not at all as long as I have my own bedroom.'

'You'll have a whole unit to yourself.'

'Wow, that'd be wonderful.' He followed her across to Number 2.

'You have your own entrance. I can't call it your front door because it's at the back of the unit. Your living area is at the other side and has sliding doors opening onto a small garden and beyond that is the park itself, which has a path round it that people walk round.'

'I'd love doing that.'

'The units' gardens haven't been planted yet. The trust is going to give the tenants some money to buy plants for their own outdoor spaces from the local nursery. They thought people would like to choose their favourite plants and shrubs to look out at.'

'That'd be lovely – choosing your own plants, I mean. I really like gardening.'

'Do you? So do I. What's your favourite flower?'

'Peonies.'

'I love those, but I like roses even more, especially white ones.'

She led the way to the second unit. The entrance door had frosted glass panels with coloured glass round the edges and a pattern in the middle. It looked really pretty. She unlocked the door then stepped to one side and gestured to him.

'You go in first, Brett. It's a very simple layout: there are two bedrooms, one large and one small, at the car park side with a bathroom between them. The living area and kitchen look out onto the park. There are built-in wardrobes and cupboards in the bedrooms so the unit might be small but it's very practical to live in.'

'It seems quite large to me for one person. I've only ever had a single bedroom and shared facilities. A lot of the time after I first went into care I had to share a bedroom with another boy.'

'Well, if you come here the whole unit will be yours. Three of them are this size but Number 4 at the end is slightly bigger. Go on inside. Take as long as you like to look round. I'll sit in my car and read the newspaper. Come for me when you've finished.'

She gave him another of her lovely smiles and made a shooing motion with one hand, so he went inside on his own. He might as well look round it, though he doubted he'd be so lucky as to be invited to live here. Pity. There was a really welcoming feel to the whole group of units.

He went straight to the front of the living room and

peered out. It had such a lovely view. There were two big trees in the middle of this end of the park, magnolia trees she'd said, and clumps of what he presumed were smaller trees and bushes here and there, though they looked like green fuzz at that distance with his eyesight. He sighed. It must be so nice to see the world clearly, whether close to you or far away. He had to close one eye to get a clear view of anything.

How lovely it'd be to live right next to an open space, almost like being in the country. He couldn't imagine anything better.

He went back to look at the kitchen, pretending he was coming to live here and could eat what he wanted every single day. He'd buy a cookery book and learn to make new dishes. He might read slowly, but recipes were only short.

Then he went into the larger of the two bedrooms and the bathroom, which had both a bath and shower.

Oh, what a lovely place this was!

He so wished he could live here.

When he'd finished looking round he went reluctantly out of the entrance door because he didn't like to keep her waiting for too long. He was about to walk across to join her when she got out of her car and gestured to him to stay where he was.

'Let's go and walk round the park as we chat. That'll be much nicer than sitting in a car.'

'OK.' Here it came, an interview.

As they went inside, she locked the back door of the house carefully from inside. 'You can't be too careful these days. Am I right in guessing that you'd rather be out of doors for our chat?'

'Yes. I would.'

'So would I.'

She took out a remote from the top drawer in the kitchen and showed him how to use it to lock the sliding door at this side of the unit, then led the way outside and across the grass.

'The park is called Magnolia Gardens, obviously because of these two big trees in the middle. Aren't they lovely?'

'Gorgeous.' He couldn't resist reaching out to touch one of the leaves.

She pointed across to the side of the park on the opposite side to the units. 'There's a snicket over there which leads to Hawthorn Close. That's a street of really pretty older houses lined with hawthorn trees that are over two hundred years old. When they flower in the spring they look as if they're waiting for a bride to walk along under them.'

'It must be beautiful.'

'It is. So much so that most of the houses and all of the trees on that street are heritage listed and the town is very proud of them. Tourists come from miles away to see them when they're in bloom. If you're on foot, the snicket is the best way to get onto Larch Tree Lane from the units and there's a bus that runs up and down it from the town centre, which is only a fifteen-minute walk away if you don't want to get on a bus.'

'What's a snicket? I can't see it very clearly from here, I'm afraid. I don't have good eyesight.'

'Oh, sorry. It's an old-fashioned name for a footpath between two buildings or hedges. In this case hedges mainly.'

'Thanks.' He looked round and drew in a deep breath of the lovely fresh air. He couldn't get enough of air like that.

'How did you like the unit?'

'It was lovely. The park and unit both *feel* really nice, too,' he ventured.

'I agree. I gather you don't have a driving licence, let alone a car?'

'No. I'd like to learn to drive but I don't think I can see clearly enough to be allowed to.' He shrugged. 'I couldn't afford lessons or afford to buy a car, even if by a miracle I did pass the test. I've only been able to get some part-time weekend and evening work so far.'

'Ms Vernon said you don't enjoy studying.'

He was sick and tired of people assuming he was lazy and worried that she would think that of him too, so his words came out more sharply than he'd intended. 'That's because I have trouble reading. The nicest teacher I ever had told me I'm dyslexic and she said I can't help having difficulty reading. She booked me in to see a specialist about it, only I kept having to move foster homes and change schools so there was never time for me to get to the head of the queues and actually be seen by a specialist.'

He paused then said it: 'My present teacher doesn't even believe dyslexia exists. He says I'm lazy. I'm not, Ms Denby, really I'm not. The letters jiggle about when I try to read and it's really hard to see them clearly.'

She stared at him, looking shocked. 'I can't believe any teacher can believe that, not these days when dyslexia is a well-documented condition.'

Brett could only shrug. It was too late to worry about it now that he had left school.

'So you've never even been properly tested or tried something like coloured lenses in your glasses to help you read more easily?'

'No. I haven't even had ordinary glasses. One of my foster mothers said I was a borderline case, so it wasn't worth getting any.' He sneaked a glance sideways. Was it possible she actually believed him about not being lazy? That'd make a change.

'If we gave you a place here, would you agree to be tested for dyslexia and to accept professional help in dealing with it, if necessary?'

'I didn't think there was much they could do about it.'

'There is but some people respond to treatment better than others. Would you get tested for us, Brett, if we thought it might help?'

His voice came out fiercely again. He didn't usually let himself speak angrily. Well, too bad. 'If there was some way of helping me deal with it and making me able to read better, I'd grab the chance with both hands, I promise you.'

Then he realised something and added in a choked whisper, 'Do you mean I might have wasted all these years, absolutely wasted them, when something could have been done to help me?'

'I'm afraid so.'

His voice broke when he tried to speak. 'I'd try anything – of course I would. I'd *love* to be able to read easily like other people do and not be so *stupid*.'

'It's not stupidity if you can't see the words in the same way as other people see them.'

She gave him another hug and kept hold of him, so he found himself hugging her back, not wanting to let go. He couldn't remember when he'd last been hugged like this. Not since his mother died, that was certain.

When she pulled away, she reached up to pat his cheek. He was taller than she was.

'Are you hungry yet? Only, I had a really early start and I'm absolutely famished.'

'I threw up on the way here, so I'm hungry too.' Brett broke off, surprised at himself for confiding in her.

'Nerves or something you ate?'

'Nerves.'

'We'll go and get some food then. I know a great café. Tell me one thing: I don't make you nervous, do I?'

'No. Not at all now I've spent some time with you.'

'Good. Then we'll be safe eating together. It won't make you throw up.' She gave him a nudge and a cheeky grin. 'And by the way, you don't make me nervous, either.'

And he found himself joining her in laughing at that. Wow. He wished everyone was as easy to talk to.

The café was just right, neither posh nor scruffy, and it smelt really good. They sat in a corner next to a window.

She picked up a menu and offered it to him. 'I can recommend their burger and chips. It's what I'd call a posh burger and it's delicious. But if you want something else, just check out the menu and say.'

He closed the menu without trying to embarrass himself by reading it. 'A posh burger sounds great to me.'

'And how about a jug of fizzy water with it to share?'

'Lovely.'

She chatted about other things as they waited, then they ate the delicious food. There wasn't only a beefburger but a lot of salad. He ate every single bit. So did she.

Once everything had been cleared away, she said, 'Brett, I'd like to invite you to come and live in one of our units. This is an official invitation because I'm the one who chooses our tenants.'

He gaped at her, couldn't speak a word, he was so surprised.

'You're exactly the sort of person our units were designed for.' She waited for him to respond, still with that lovely gentle smile on her face.

His words came out in choked-sounding spurts. 'I didn't expect – but I'd absolutely *love* to come and – and live here.'

'Good. That's settled then. I'll have some basic furniture put into your unit to start you off and we'll furnish the place properly after you get here. We have some older, second-hand pieces stored in a warehouse that you can choose from.'

And heaven help him, he felt tears of joy escape his control and trickle down his cheeks. What a fool he'd seem to her!

'Stay where you are for a few more minutes. There is no one close enough to see that you're emotional and you have your back to the room.'

She held out a handkerchief and when he took it and used it to mop away the tears, she waited for a moment then took hold of his hand again. He clutched hers tightly, wished he need never let go.

After he'd calmed down, he said huskily, 'Sorry.'

'Don't be. You have good reason to be upset, the way you've been treated.'

'I'll do my best, I promise you, my very *very* best to keep the place nice.'

'I'm sure you will, Brett. And we'll do our best to help you with your reading and other things that make life easier. When do you want to come here?'

'Would tomorrow be too soon?'

She laughed, a happy little burst of sound that made him smile too.

'It'd be fine, Brett. It's good timing actually, because I've got an appointment the day after. I'll pick you up from Mrs Shearer's around eleven o'clock in the morning. Will that be all right?'

'Perfect. I'll be ready. And – well – I can't thank you enough, Ms Denby.'

'Do call me Amanda. You'll be the first to move in, so I may ask you to help the other people settle in.'

'I'll do anything I can to help. You only have to ask.'

'Good lad. There are a lot of people in this world needing help with this and that. Our little trust can make a difference to a few of them and you're part of it now. That's a good thought, isn't it?'

He nodded and another tear took him by surprise as it slid down his cheek and he had to get his handkerchief out again.

When he'd put it away, she took his hand and he clung to it like a little child. Couldn't stop himself. Needed to hold it just for a while longer.

Not only was the hand warm and soft, and she didn't try to pull it away, but she had the loveliest smile he'd ever seen.

He'd been feeling so lost and hopeless, terrified of the future, and now, all of a sudden, he could sense hope creeping into his life. It was wonderful and yet terrifying to think about things improving so much. He prayed he wouldn't mess things up.

Chapter Seven

Carla finished clearing up the pub and went outside to empty the rubbish. When she heard someone behind her, she swung round quickly and froze in utter horror.

Frank was standing there, smiling in that wolfish way he had when he was about to hurt her.

'Thought you'd got away, didn't you?'

She tried to pull herself together. '*Hoped* I'd got away.'

He was between her and the entrance and took another slow, smiling step forward. 'Well, you haven't got away and you never will because you're as good as married to me now so you belong to me. And you always will, unless I throw you out. If I ever do. I might not, because I enjoy playing with you.'

She didn't wait for him to thump her to scream for help at the top of her voice.

She managed to escape some of the blow from the rounders bat he'd been hiding behind his back. It didn't hit her on the head, but still caught her on the upper arm, which she'd raised to protect herself. It hit so hard she was sure it'd broken a bone.

As she tried to push past him, still screaming, two more blows landed, one on her back, the other on the side of her head. The world seemed to blur around her and she fell heavily, wondering if he was going to kill her. Instead she heard footsteps running away.

She still felt someone beside her so made a huge effort to roll away, putting up the uninjured arm to fend off more blows.

'It's all right, Carla love. It's me.'

The voice was that of the landlord of the pub and she opened her eyes to see him crouching beside her. 'Oh, thank goodness!' She clutched the hand he held out but couldn't seem to pull herself to her feet.

'Who attacked you?' he asked.

It took a huge effort to get the words out. 'My ex. Frank Prosser.'

There was the sound of a siren in the distance.

'When I looked out and saw you being attacked, my wife called the police and ambulance. I picked up the ornamental gun from the bar and ran outside but unfortunately he'd got away. She said he was limping. The police got here quickly but too late to catch him.'

She tried to get up and failed.

'Lie still. Looks like you'll need the ambulance.'

'Thank you.' The world was spinning round her and she wasn't sure she'd managed to speak clearly.

The ambulance arrived shortly afterwards and the

first responders checked her injuries and said she'd need to go to hospital.

When they unloaded her stretcher there, the police followed them inside the casualty department.

She heard one of them ask the doctor, 'Is she able to talk?'

'Give me a minute or two,' he replied as he bent over her. 'What's your name?'

'Carla Hewitt.'

'Can you move your arms and legs for me, please?'

She did but winced. 'Yes, but my right arm hurts badly. Is it broken?'

'I don't think so. But it's going to need stitches because it's bleeding.'

He finished checking and turned to the woman police officer. 'I think she was lucky and the blow to the head didn't land fully. But it glanced off her forehead and she's definitely got concussion, so I need to keep her in for observation for one night, possibly even two. Be quick with any other questions. She needs some stitches.'

'Do you know the person who did this, Ms Hewitt?' the male officer asked.

So she said it again. 'Yes. My ex. Frank Prosser.' She gave them his address and the name of the firm he'd been working for, then added, 'I knew he'd try to come after me when I ran away from him so I changed my name and got a live-in job. How on earth did he find me?'

'You had no former connection with that pub?'

'None at all.'

'He may have planted a tracer of some sort among your belongings. Abusive men do that sort of thing these days. In your clothes, perhaps. On your phone.'

'I threw my old phone away and I've bought mostly new clothes because I couldn't bring much away with me.'

'Handbag still the same one?'

'Oh. Yes, it is. I was doing the cleaning at the pub today, so my handbag should still be in my bedroom there.'

He looked at his fellow officer. 'Phone the landlord. Get that bag and have it checked out ASAP. And ask him to pack all her things and send them to us here. We'll get someone to go through them.'

He looked down at her with a sympathetic expression. 'You can't go back to the pub, love.'

'I was already planning to leave. I had an interview arranged for tomorrow to go somewhere else, a live-in place again.'

'Give us the phone number and we'll contact the people interviewing you to let them know you've been injured. We'll find you somewhere else temporarily, a women's refuge.'

She grimaced, hated the thought of that, but what other choice was there?

The other officer came back. 'The landlord's happy to pack her things and send them here by courier. He says to tell her he'll put the wages owing and her tips in an envelope in her handbag.'

'He's a decent guy,' she said quietly. 'Can someone thank him for me?'

'I'll do that.'

The female officer next to her said, 'There's somewhere she might be able to go, other than a refuge. A friend of mine told me about it. It's a new place so people won't know about it yet. This is the phone number.'

The other one nodded and went outside into the corridor to make another phone call, but he came back shaking his head. 'No answer. I'll try again later.'

'We'll post someone on duty here at the hospital so your ex won't be able to get to you while you're here.'

'Thanks.' But she could feel herself fading again. 'Sorry. I can't – think straight.'

'She needs to rest now,' the doctor said.

'Can you keep someone near her until our guard arrives?' the police officer asked. 'We'll send help straight away.'

The doctor looked shocked. 'You think he'll try to get at her again? *In here?*'

Carla didn't wait for the police officers to answer. 'He'll definitely come after me again. He boasts that no one ever gets the better of him without regretting it bitterly. I've heard him say that several times. And he told me today that I belong to him.'

'We'll make sure you're safe while you're here with us, then.' The doctor turned to the nurse. 'We'd better put her in that little room off the secure ward once I've dealt with her injuries. Can you ring through and let them know she's coming?'

Shortly afterwards, Carla was aware of being wheeled along again. They put her into a bed and she closed her eyes, had to, couldn't stay awake any longer.

When she woke it was to a dark room with only a low light glowing in one corner. She jerked in fear as she saw a figure stand up and come across to her.

'You're safe here,' a woman said. 'You've got concussion so let yourself rest. You'll feel a lot better in the morning.'

'Who are you?'

'I'm a police officer.'

'Thank goodness.'

When Carla next woke it was light and felt like early morning. She felt a bit better but still had a thumping headache. A nurse was sitting across the room but there was no sign of a police officer.

The woman got up to take her temperature and study her face carefully. 'How are you feeling, Carla?'

'Bit better. Head's aching.'

'When your guard comes back I'll get you a light snack and then some painkillers. Yoghurt all right?'

'Yes, but I need to use the bathroom first.'

'I'll help you across. This room has its own bathroom.'

They were kind and there were always other people nearby, but in spite of that the fear never left her as the minutes ticked slowly past.

Later on, a detective arrived to ask her some detailed questions, by which time she'd remembered enough to ask them if they'd cancelled her appointment for the interview.

'Yes. One of our clerks got word to them that you'd been attacked and were in hospital,' the young woman said. 'They said to call back as soon as you can if you still want their help.'

'Why should they help me? They haven't even met me yet. I don't know why they offered me the interview in the first place when I hadn't done a proper application.'

'Well, don't look a gift horse in the mouth. You should phone them. Someone checked them out and they're well thought of, have helped other people.'

'Oh. Did you find a tracker among my possessions?'

'Yes. Standard gadget. It was in your handbag. A couple of stitches had been unpicked in the seam underneath and it had been slipped into the bottom. We checked the bag's contents carefully then transferred them into a scruffy old handbag that had been lying around in lost property at the police station for ages. You'll probably want to buy another handbag when you can to be utterly certain he hasn't hidden another more skilfully. I'd advise it.'

'Thank you.'

'We'll check your other possessions in case he's put tracers on them.'

'I had to buy a whole set of new clothes when I escaped from him so they should be all right.'

'We'll still check. And your suitcases. Try to get a good rest today. They're talking of letting you out tomorrow.'

As if she'd be able to have a good rest! she thought. She doubted she'd ever rest peacefully again unless *he* fell over a cliff.

She shuddered as she remembered how wild-eyed and insane he'd looked when confronting her. That vicious expression on his face had haunted her nightmares for a while. It had seemed as if he was changing – but where would it stop?

She doubted he'd ever stop pursuing her.

She feared for her life.

It took two days in hospital before they would let her leave. Then one of the police officers told her they'd arranged for her and her possessions to be picked up secretly the following day.

When they added that they'd take her out of the hospital in the laundry van so no one could see her leave, that made her feel a little better. But she still worried that even that would not be fully safe because he'd come after her again, she knew he would.

He was one of the most stubborn people she'd ever met.

Perhaps she would escape for a while, but unless the police could prove it had been Frank who attacked her and lock him away, she was quite sure he'd get away with this attack and come after her again. It was much harder to become invisible in a digital world.

A police officer came to bring her things from the pub and to chat, explaining the details of their escape plans.

They'd checked her clothes and other possessions from the pub and her suitcases, then put them in a couple of laundry bags. They were going to send them and her out of the hospital hidden under the dirty washing and there would be other suitcases waiting for her when she was away from the hospital. 'Are you all right with that?'

'I'll do anything that's needed to get away from him.'

'The van always arrives around lunch time to bring the clean washing back and then takes the previous day's dirty washing to the laundry, so if you could be ready half an hour or so before that, you can go out with the dirty washing. All right?'

'Yes, but you haven't said where you will be taking me.'

'One of my colleagues from the abuse unit spoke to someone from a new housing trust. She's going to interview you, and given the circumstances, she's offered to house you in their unit for the time being. You'll be transferred to their vehicle once we've got you away from the hospital.'

Carla nodded, wondering if that would be enough to fool Frank. But surely even he couldn't keep watch on every vehicle going into and out of the hospital?

'No one from the domestic staff will see you being loaded into the van. You may not be very comfortable but you'll be completely hidden.'

'Thank you.'

'It wouldn't hurt to have another rest before you leave, maybe a nap.'

As if she could sleep!

The rest of the time there seemed to pass with excruciating slowness and she was relieved when they came to fetch her.

Chapter Eight

Just after mid-morning the following day, Amanda stood by her car watching Brett bring his things out of the house and stack them neatly in the boot. There wasn't nearly as much as she'd expected. Was this all he owned?

And she'd have to buy him some new clothes quickly. He must have just had or even still be going through a growth spurt. He was tall already and going to be even taller if she was any judge, but he seemed quite muscular, already past that ultra-thin, gangly stage many lads went through.

'Have you said goodbye to Mrs Shearer and thanked her for looking after you?' she prompted.

He hesitated.

'It never hurts to be polite. How other people behave is their own choice.'

She watched him take that in and nod.

'I was wondering about asking her something.' He picked up a paper carrier bag and showed her its contents. 'I've been borrowing audiobooks from the local library. She visits it every week or so and lets me go with her to change my books, said they kept me quiet at least. Would it be an OK thing to ask her to take these back for me?'

'Yes, definitely.' She followed him back into the house out of sheer curiosity to see how he was treated there.

Mrs Shearer looked across at them, not saying anything.

'I just wanted to say thank you for having me here,' he told her.

There was a longer silence than Amanda would have expected, then his foster mother nodded. 'That's all right.'

'I'm sorry to trouble you, but could you take these library books back for me, please? I know you go there yourself or I'd not ask you.'

Another pause, then, 'Yes. I can do that.'

He handed over the bag and she gave such a slight nod it could have meant anything. He looked at Amanda uncertainly.

'We'll be leaving now.' Amanda led the way outside again and Brett followed her. Mrs Shearer closed the front door on them without saying anything else. The woman hadn't even wished him well for the future, or said anything personal. Well, shame on her.

Amanda got back into the car and waited to start it until he'd made himself comfortable next to her in the front. 'Friendly type, isn't she? Anyway, you did the right thing by thanking her.' Though that cold fish of a woman hadn't deserved it.

'I try to do the right thing, because it feels right in my head.'

She gave him a quick roll of the eyes. 'I do that, too. I don't think Mrs Shearer does, though.'

He glanced sideways, a slight smile on his face now as if he'd guessed what she was thinking. 'Her husband doesn't smile much, either.'

'Why am I not surprised? She's a right old misery, but don't tell anyone I said that. Oh, and before we start I'd better warn you that I'm expecting a phone call from another client. She missed an appointment with me a couple of days ago, but someone got in touch with me to say she'd been involved in an accident and was in hospital. From what he told me it's rather important that I speak to her so I may have to stop suddenly to take the call.'

'No worries.'

She set off and couldn't help noticing that he didn't turn to look back. She didn't blame him.

The call came only fifteen minutes later and fortunately she was able to pull over onto the verge to answer it properly.

'Sergeant Greeves from Stinstead Police here.'

She checked the image on her phone and yes, it was a police officer and there was a police car in clear view behind him.

'I'm calling on behalf of a client of yours. First, could

you give me your name, please?'

'Certainly. I'm Amanda Denby.'

'We have a potential client called Hewitt.'

'Yes. Carla Hewitt, I gather. I was told that she'd been in an accident. Is she all right?'

'I'm afraid not. She had to go into hospital because she was attacked and badly beaten. She says it was by her ex, but we can't prove that. We feel she needs help to get completely away from this area if she's to stay safe. Can you help her, do you think?'

Amanda took a quick decision and hoped she wouldn't regret it. 'I do know somewhere for her to stay. Can I speak to her about it?'

'She's still in hospital. She doesn't have a car, so we need to find a way to get her away from there without her being seen by her ex.'

'Oh dear, poor woman.'

'She's due to leave hospital today. Can we bring her straight to you?'

Amanda took a deep breath and continued to follow her instincts. 'Yes.'

'We'll need to agree a place and time to meet you without her being seen because we don't want her ex finding out where she goes.'

She shot a quick glance at Brett, a bit worried about taking him along with her for something like this.

'Tell me where you are in Stinstead and I'll pick her up there. I don't know exactly where the town is but I have a satnav. Give me a moment to look it up . . . Hmm.

It'll take me a couple of hours to get there.'

'Contact me again when you're getting close. By that time we should have worked out a way to do this. Her ex is a cunning devil and claims she's lying. We believe her but can't prove it.'

'OK. See you soon.'

She ended the call and stared out of the windscreen for a moment.

'It sounds as if something is wrong,' Brett said tentatively.

She took another decision. 'We've got to pick up a woman called Carla for one of the other units. I've heard about her from a friend in the police who thought we might be able to help her. She ran away from her abusive partner about three months ago and went into hiding, so he must have found her and given her a beating that landed her in hospital again. *She* said it was her ex but he claims to have been elsewhere and a friend of his backed him up on that claim.'

Brett didn't say anything for a moment. He'd thought he was in a bad position but at least nobody had attacked him. 'That's terrible. I've seen TV programmes about it. What do they call it? Oh, yes, domestic violence.'

'Yes. I need to go and pick her up today. She'll be worried sick and may still be in danger so it has to be done carefully. I'm afraid you'll be in for a longish detour because there's nowhere I can leave you.'

'I don't mind going with you and if he still comes after her, I'm quite strong and maybe I'd come in useful to help protect her. And just so that you understand me a bit better, I know I'm big for my age but I don't fight except in self-defence when someone else starts it. I've had to learn how to defend myself, you see, because of changing schools quite often so always being an outsider.'

'Have you had a lot of moves?'

'Yes. I've never stayed more than a year or so anywhere and before you ask, it wasn't because I behaved badly. Foster parents prefer younger kids, you see, and a couple of them complained that I ate too much.'

That surprised her. The more she heard about his life, the more that poor lad sounded to have been shockingly neglected by the system. 'Well, thank you for the offer of help, Brett, but we'll try not to get into any fights. Let me put the details into the satnav then we'll head towards this Stinstead place, which is on the other side of Bristol. I've agreed to phone them when I'm nearly there and the police will keep an eye on her till then and work out how to get her to us without anyone seeing her being transferred.'

There was heavy traffic and it took them over two hours to get close to Stinstead. He didn't say much but he seemed interested in everything they passed and asked her an occasional question.

Amanda stopped in a lay-by and phoned the police, then was directed to meet them at the police station.

When they got there, she said, 'I'll go inside on my own if you don't mind, Brett. I need to find out exactly what's been happening to the poor woman.'

She pressed something into his hand and gestured

further along the road. 'Go and get yourself something to eat but be quick about it. I'm not fond of fast foods but sometimes it can be convenient to grab something quickly. Keep the change in case you need something else to eat later. I don't know how long we'll be out and about, you see.'

'I don't mind waiting. Do you want me to buy you a snack?'

'Not at the moment, thank you.' She gave him her spare key to get back into the car with, then frowned. 'On second thoughts, three bottles of water wouldn't come amiss. Plain not fizzy, smaller size bottles.'

'I'll get some.'

'I'm sorry this happened just as we were making a start on sorting out your new place, Brett.'

'It sounds to be more important to rescue Carla. I don't mind about the delay, truly I don't.'

Only after she'd gone into the police station did he look down at his hand and give a soft whistle of surprise when he saw the two banknotes. This was enough for him to buy more than one meal if he wasn't extravagant, as well as the water. He was always careful with money and food, had learnt that the hard way when he was much younger and living in a foster home where regular food wasn't a high priority.

At least Mrs Shearer had fed him adequately and on time, even if her meals had been cheap and bland.

* * *

Amanda hurried into the small police station and, after she'd produced proof of her identity, she was taken through to the back to discuss the situation with the detective in charge.

'May I see Carla first?'

'She's in hospital still. Luckily the publican she was working for came to her aid quite quickly, so she wasn't hurt badly enough to be in danger of losing her life but she had concussion, bad bruising and needed stitches in one arm. They have a safe ward there, so we knew her attacker wouldn't be able to get to her, even if he did guess or find out where we'd taken her.'

'She sounds to be in a difficult situation.'

'Yes. One of our officers is looking for a way to get her out of the hospital without anyone seeing her leave and then we'll bring her to you. We're hoping you'll be able to look after her from then onwards, though we will report her presence to your local police, of course.'

'By "anyone" you mean her partner, I suppose. Hasn't he been arrested for this assault yet?'

'He was back at home by the time we found him. When we tried to question him he brought in a fancy lawyer and another man who swore they'd been together miles away at the time of the incident and therefore he couldn't have been anywhere near Stinstead. And his car didn't show up on any CCTV systems. We think he must have stolen one. So unfortunately he got released more quickly than we'd expected.'

The officer sighed. 'We can get a court order that will

allegedly keep him away from her, whether we manage to prosecute him or not, but brutes like him don't always obey court orders, and after violence like that, we prefer to get the victim away and into hiding.' She looked at Amanda. 'You're sure you're all right with having her, given that situation?'

'Definitely. The place I'm taking her to is at the end of a new stretch of street which isn't even on the digital road maps yet.'

'It's not an isolated place, is it? I don't think it'd be safe to leave her anywhere on her own.'

Amanda explained about the units and the fact that Brett would be occupying the one next to Carla and that her own cottage as warden would be just across the garden as well.

'There's some temporary furniture in both units, which will do for tonight, but the trust has more furniture in storage.'

'That sounds good. If you can make your way to the hospital, I'll tell our officers to expect you and introduce you to her. She refuses to leave without meeting you, she's so terrified of him tricking her into going off with someone else. Go to A&E and identify yourself at their reception. I gather they've worked out a way to get her and her belongings out without anyone seeing where she goes.'

Amanda was surprised by all this cloak and dagger stuff. 'You feel the situation is that bad?'

The officer shrugged. 'Could be. There was a battered

wife murdered by her husband near here a couple of years ago, so we've all been extra careful since. Maybe you should wrap something round your hand before you go into the hospital so that you look as if you've been injured.'

'Yes. Good idea.'

Amanda walked slowly out to her car and got into it. She hadn't expected to be in this dangerous situation and didn't set off immediately because she felt it only right to explain to Brett what was going to happen next.

'I don't like to involve you in this.'

'I want to help, if I can,' he said without hesitation. 'And if you don't mind me saying so, I think I should be the one to wrap up my hand and pretend I'm injured. It'll look more convincing because I can't drive and you can.'

He fumbled in his pocket. 'I even have a little sachet of tomato ketchup left from my snack, so I can make my handkerchief look a bit bloody.'

He smiled at her surprise. 'I like murder mysteries. I watch them on TV and listen to them on audiobooks. So I'm trying now to think what the good characters would be doing in one of those.'

'Well done, you. And you're right. It would be better if you play the injured role.' She watched him give a happy little nod. Definitely not stupid, that lad.

He seemed to alternate between boyish and surprisingly mature, like most kids that age. And the more time she spent with him, the more she liked him.

Perhaps his difficult life had made him more mature because young as he was, there seemed to be a gentle strength to him.

Before they went into the nearby hospital, Brett wrapped up his hand and she smeared a little tomato ketchup on one side of the handkerchief, then rubbed in a bit of dirt to make it seem less bright red. He held it up against his chest, cradling it with his other hand.

She stepped back. 'It looks surprisingly realistic.'

He beamed at her, then assumed a solemn expression. 'Let's go.'

At the casualty reception she gave her name and they at once directed her and Brett to the supervisor's office. He frowned at the sight of her young companion. 'Does the lad need attention for real?'

'No. We're trying to look the part.'

He relaxed visibly. 'You're doing it well. Had me fooled, even. I'll take you both through to the south wing.'

They were shown out of the A&E area and taken up in a lift to a locked floor, where they found a police officer on duty outside the entrance doors to the ward.

Once again, Amanda had to produce her ID and explain Brett's presence. She was glad to see that these people were taking no chances, very glad given her own responsibility for Brett as well.

'I'll take you to meet Carla here and then we'll arrange how and where you can pick her up,' the officer said. 'She wants to make sure she can recognise you later. We'll take Brett into the ward as well, then perhaps he can wait near the door while you talk to her privately?'

A nurse had come to greet them in the ward and had stayed nearby, listening openly. 'I'll bandage that hand properly while he's waiting. We can't send him out of our hospital still wearing a dirty amateur bandage. It won't look realistic. This way, young fellow.'

When they were alone, the officer said, 'Just a quick word with you about what we're planning to do, Ms Denby. After you've met Carla, I'll help her get ready to leave then hide her and her belongings in a big container of dirty linen. The usual man is happy to wheel it out and load it into the laundry van. Good thing there's a lifting gadget on the van, eh?'

'Sounds a good idea.'

'When you leave here you must turn right out of the front gates and the van will follow shortly afterwards. There's a small local supermarket just down the road and he'll meet you in the car park behind it. If you park under the trees in the far corner, the van will stop in front of you, blocking your car from view.'

She nodded.

'The driver's going to walk up and down as if he's smoking a cigarette while Carla gets out of the back and slips across to your vehicle. Don't forget to get her belongings too. She mustn't carry anything heavy with that arm injury for a day or two. The belongings are also in the big bin, in two smaller laundry bags, the only ones with red tags. She'll be wearing the same green disposable overalls as the hospital staff. You can throw them away after she changes into her own clothes.'

'You're certainly taking a lot of care.'

'Yes. All very cloak and dagger, isn't it? Trouble is, it turns out her attacker is part of a so-called real men's network that encourages macho behaviour and keeping women under control, so he can get help from the other members any time. Coincidentally a team has been keeping an eye on that group too. We hadn't realised how far some of its members were prepared to go till this violent attack, or that they'd got a lawyer on side.'

'That's shocking.'

'Utterly disgusting, isn't it? Anyway, let me take you to meet Carla now.'

Amanda was shocked when she saw how bruised the young woman's face was. 'Are you sure you're all right to travel, Carla? That looks painful.'

'It is a bit. I'm lucky I got away with only bruising and a few stitches.'

'Is your ex crazy?'

'I'm beginning to think so. And has some equally crazy friends, it seems.' She fell silent, unable to hide a shudder.

The officer said gently, 'Well, now you've met Ms Denby, we'll take you out of here with the laundry to hand over to her.'

'I have a lad with me as well,' Amanda said. 'He's tall and eighteen so nearly a man.'

Carla nodded. 'I'd travel with the devil himself to get

away from my ex. And I know who's coming to help me now, so let's get on with it and do whatever is necessary for me to escape.'

Brett and Amanda walked out of the hospital and got back into her car with him still pretending to favour the now neatly bandaged hand.

'I really shouldn't be involving you in this,' she said abruptly as she started the car.

'I'm happy to help. I think I'd better take this bandage off now, though. It makes it a bit awkward to move my hand and it's rather conspicuous.'

'Good idea. Stuff it out of sight in the glove compartment.'

He did that and turned to her. 'I've been thinking. I should get out and open the door for Carla when we stop while you stay in the driving seat with the motor running in case we have to leave quickly. Once she gets into the back of the car, she can slide down out of sight for the first part of our journey. I'll toss in her possessions any old how. I noticed you have a travel rug. She can cover herself with that.'

He was continuing to surprise her with his intelligent remarks and logical planning. Definitely not at all stupid, this young man. He must have been very unlucky with his carers and teachers to have had no help with his dyslexia over all those years. That made her so angry.

She smiled wryly. Injustices always upset her. At least from now on she might be able to make a difference to a few people who'd been treated badly. That would be enormously satisfying to someone of her age. She didn't intend to spend her retirement sitting around idly feeling useless and watching television as her main occupation.

Once the car had stopped under the trees, Brett opened his door, ready to get out quickly.

It was only a couple of minutes until he said, 'I think that's the hospital van coming round the corner now.'

It drew up very close to them and the driver looked round to check that no one was nearby before getting out and calling, 'You open the rear doors of my van, lad. It's not locked. Try to stay out of sight as much as you can.'

He poked his head back into the driving seat and called, 'All clear to get out now, Carla.'

Then he pulled a pack of cigarettes out of his shirt pocket, lit one and leant against the front of the van to take a drag before starting to walk up and down.

Brett grimaced as the man took a puff in a way that showed he really was a smoker. The small cloud of smoke wafted back towards the car and smelt as horrible as cigarette smoke always did. Even if he'd got money to burn, he'd never take up an activity that smelt so horrible.

He tried to stay out of sight as he opened the rear doors of the van.

When he saw Carla's bruised face as she got out, he

was shocked but tried not to show it. He whispered, 'I'll get your bags. You get in the back of the car.'

She slid quickly into the rear seat.

Amanda saw her passenger wince in pain as she scooted down to crouch on the floor out of sight without needing to be told.

Brett tossed Carla's possessions onto the back seat then covered them and her with the travel rug, before closing the rear door and getting back into the front. Amanda set off even before he'd fastened his seat belt, looking into the other cars parked here and there as they passed them, relieved to see that none had people sitting in them.

She looked in the rear mirror too but the laundry van stayed where it was and the man wasn't watching them drive away. He seemed to be more interested in enjoying his cigarette.

Once they had driven a little way and turned onto a busy major road, Amanda said, 'I think you'll be safe to sit up normally now, Carla.'

'I'll wait a bit longer if you don't mind, just to be sure.'

'OK. Your choice. This is Brett, by the way. He'll be living in the unit next to yours.'

'Pleased to meet you,' Brett said.

'Are you feeling all right?' Amanda asked.

'Very sore still where he hit me. I have to check the cut with a doctor and get my stitches out in about a week.'

'I'll make sure we do that, Carla.'

'And I don't like having a black eye. It looks horrible.'

She couldn't be too bad if she was worrying about her appearance, Amanda thought.

A short time later, Carla said, 'I'm really grateful to you for coming to get me.'

'I'm happy to help you. You haven't had a chance to see it yet, but I'm sure you'll like our unit.'

'I'd like living in a cave if Frank wasn't there,' Carla said bitterly.

'Are you thirsty? We have some bottled water.'

'Ooh, yes. I would like a drink, please.'

Brett passed her a bottle and she got up on the seat to drink it, sitting in a way that kept her head mostly out of sight.

It upset him to hear how on edge she was and how afraid she had been of getting fully upright from her hiding place.

'Are you sure your ex doesn't know about the trust?' Amanda asked.

'I don't see how he can. I didn't know about it either till the police officer responsible for women's safety told me. And I did all my communicating about that online from the new mobile phone I bought after I'd left him, and under my new name, so there can't have been one of his tracers on it.'

She added in a tone of relish, 'I got the friend who originally drove me to Swindon to stop near a river so that I could throw my other phone and I tossed away his with it.'

'Good for you.'

A short time later, Carla said, 'I'll lie down on the seat if you don't mind. I'm rather tired.'

When she didn't say anything for a while, Brett glanced into the back and said quietly, 'She's fallen asleep.'

'Let's press on, then. Unless you need to stop anywhere.'

'I can manage till we get there. The important thing is to keep her safe.'

Chapter Nine

When Matthew woke, he stared round in bewilderment, not knowing where he was. He tried to sit up but couldn't manage more than a slight lifting of the head, he felt so weak.

A woman said in a gentle voice, 'Don't try to sit up without help yet, Mr Woodley.'

'Where – am I?'

'In hospital. You've had severe pneumonia, caused by Covid, but they got to you quickly, thank goodness.'

'I remember feeling ill and thinking I should visit the doctor, but I don't remember going to see him.'

'You didn't. You were found unconscious by the postman a few days ago. He came to deliver a parcel next door and saw you lying on the ground in your front garden. I don't know any other details yet because this is my first day on this ward. I was going to check your records when you started twitching around. Take things gently, please.'

He stared at her in dismay. 'Lying in the garden?'

'Mmm.' She continued to read the notes then hung them back at the bottom of his bed. 'You were lucky. The postman called in the emergency services as soon as he saw you and you were picked up and brought to the A&E by ambulance.'

Matthew blinked and tried to pull his thoughts together but his brain felt woolly and he wasn't sure what to say or do. Then he suddenly thought of something. 'What's happened to my house?'

'When the police found out you'd been rushed to hospital they locked it up. A social worker will be coming to discuss what to do with it as soon as you're fit enough to consider the situation. Though if there's a neighbour we could contact on your behalf who'd keep an eye on things . . . ?'

'The neighbours on one side are new to the area – I don't know them except by sight. And the house on the other side has been knocked down ready to build a bigger one.'

'Oh dear. Well, the police locked yours up so it should be all right. You're looking as if you need a little food and drink then more sleep.'

And heaven help him he could do nothing except have a drink and give in to the drowsiness.

When he woke again, the same nurse was still there. She gave him what she said was a special nourishing drink. It tasted horrible but he managed to drink half of it.

Then she said, 'The police want to know if you have any relatives or friends who could visit your house occasionally?'

'I've only got a nephew now. No other close relatives left.'

'What's his name?'

'Grant Woodley.'

'Do you have his contact information on your mobile phone? You didn't have it on you when you were found. Is it somewhere at home?'

'No mobile. I only use a landline.' His late wife had dealt with all the fiddling about online. In fact, Gillian had loved it. He hated it.

'How about a physical address book, then?'

But he was feeling so desperately tired, he had to let the world slip away again, just for a few minutes.

The nurse left him alone and went to write down the name of his nephew in his file. She felt sorry for the poor man. What a shock for him to wake up here with several days missing from his life. But his colour had improved a little and he looked on the way to recovery.

There must be someone he could call on for help, though, surely?

Though people of his generation could sometimes be very alone in the world. There ought to be some system for connecting them to other people, she always thought, but she had no time to do anything about that, not with three lively kids to look after as well as working full-time.

When Matthew next woke he was feeling a lot less fuzzy-brained. It was a male nurse who came to check on him this time.

'You had a nice long sleep, Mr Woodley. How are you feeling now?'

'Bit better. Thirsty.'

'Like some water?'

'Please. And hungry.'

He had several sips of water then managed to give them his nephew's full address before swallowing a few mouthfuls of some more of that ghastly bland mush.

His last thought before sleep overtook him again was that Grant would surely look after his house for him.

The following day just as they were starting to serve lunch to the patients, a social worker came to tell Matthew that the police had called at the address he'd given for his nephew.

'I'm afraid your nephew moved out of that house a few weeks ago and rented it out to a young couple.'

That astonished Matthew. 'Grant's moved?'

'Are you sure you gave us the right address? Perhaps you have a newer address somewhere.'

'Read that one out to me again.'

He listened carefully. 'No, that's the only one I know. He bought that house three or four years ago and has been living there ever since.'

'Then I'm afraid no one knows where he's gone. The house is being managed for him by a rental agency now and the woman I spoke to there said she thought the owner had gone overseas, but she didn't know where. Can you give us someone else to contact? A friend, maybe?'

'No. I moved here from London last year. I don't know many people these days. They're dying off one by one.' And unfortunately he'd been like a sleepwalker after Gillian died, so had lost touch with others. He'd had to move away from the home they'd shared because the memories of his wife it evoked hurt too much.

'Isn't there even a neighbour you chat to occasionally? The police would much prefer to find someone nearby who can keep an eye on your house.'

'The next-door neighbours at one side moved out a few weeks ago and their house got knocked down. I don't know the people next door on the other side very well, just to nod to. I'm not good at making friends and I haven't made any at all since my wife died.'

Her voice grew more gentle. 'So you're a widower, are you? How long?'

'Two years.' He couldn't hold back a big yawn.

She patted his hand. 'Well, we'll leave it for now, then. The house is locked up, after all.'

He nodded then closed his eyes again.

The following day he felt nearly normal mentally but weak as a kitten physically. The social worker came to see him again in the afternoon.

'Since you have no family to look after you, we think you'd benefit from a few days in a rehabilitation unit, Mr Woodley.'

He was about to protest at that when she added, 'Unless you feel you can cope with looking after yourself, shopping, cooking, washing clothes, etc?'

The mere thought of doing any of that made him want to hide under the bedcovers and whimper. He didn't think he'd ever before felt this weak after an illness. So he said, 'Yes. Whatever you say.'

'All right with you if the police go inside your house to check things and bring some of your clothes?'

'Yes, of course.'

'We'll transfer you to rehab around four o'clock.'

Damn Grant! Where the hell had he gone and why hadn't he left word? Then he realised the social worker was speaking again so tried to pay attention.

'The police will lock up the house for you then their patrols will continue keeping an eye on it every now and then. The neighbour has said they'd take in your mail and keep it till you get back.'

'That's kind.'

He wasn't worried about his mail, because he didn't get much, and if the police locked up his house, it should be all right. But he continued to worry about where Grant could have gone because he'd just given his nephew some money, quite a lot of it, for a joint investment.

He hadn't felt completely comfortable about that, but Grant was so enthusiastic, he'd given in. He hadn't retired rich but his nephew had sworn it was a brilliant, once-in-a-lifetime opportunity. He'd been very persuasive, producing all sorts of facts and figures that had seemed to prove his point. So in the end Matthew had taken the risk.

And after all, Grant was a relative not a stranger,

had always been a nice lad. If this investment made even half the money predicted, it'd be a very nice bonus and perhaps he'd use it to find something more interesting to do with his retirement now that his life had changed so drastically.

He could scrape by without the money if it had been lost, he supposed, but at his age, after a lifetime of steady work, you should be beyond having to scrimp and save. And what if the house needed really major repairs? How would he pay for them?

He yawned and forgot his financial worries as sleep began to take over once more.

It was hard to make plans when you didn't know your position financially, but surely his late sister's lad wasn't trying to swindle him?

He hoped no one saw him shedding tears of self-pity that night after he'd watched other people enjoy the company of visitors. They seemed to trickle out of his eyes however hard he tried to hold them back and it was a while before he could stop.

It had been such a difficult couple of years, what with Gillian's death, the move and the loneliness. But he wasn't going to give in to his worries when he got out of hospital. He was going to concentrate on getting better, then find something worth doing with his life.

Chapter Ten

Brett glanced sideways at Amanda. She was driving carefully but she was looking tired. 'Aren't you hungry? You haven't had anything to eat or drink for hours.'

'Yes, I am hungry. Maybe I'll stop and have a drink of water, but only briefly.' She pulled onto the verge and did that, then returned the half-empty bottle to him and set off again, saying, 'I think we should press on while we can. It's not far now.'

He remembered the town from his last visit and smiled as they drove into it. Essington was so pretty and he'd be able to make a home here for a while at least. Maybe he'd even achieve his lifetime ambition of having a permanent home one day if he worked and saved hard, a home he'd never have to leave. Never, ever!

If Essington was as pleasant to live in as it was to look at, he could at the very least stay in this area once he had a regular job.

Just then Carla woke and let out a cry of panic before

she realised who she was with.

He turned round quickly. 'It's all right, Ms Hewitt. You're safe with us in the car.'

'Oh, yes. Sorry. I was having a bad dream and it took me a few seconds to remember where I was.'

'I'm sorry you've had such a bad time recently,' Amanda said.

Brett kept an eye on Carla and saw that she was sitting up now and looking more alert. 'We're nearly there. This is the start of Essington. The units are just a few streets away on the other side of the town.'

'Thank goodness.' She leant her head against the back of the rear seat, looking round.

They were soon through the town centre and he said in an excited voice, 'This is Larch Tree Lane, the main road up the hill.'

'It's a pretty name for a street.'

'It's a pretty town,' he said softly. As they turned off onto the small side road, Brett couldn't help feeling excited and it suddenly exploded out of him. 'We're here! Look! These are our new homes.'

Amanda drew to a halt in front of his unit, smiling at his excitement. She watched him get out of the car and stand beaming at the row of four neat units, then got out of the car herself.

Only then did Carla follow suit and come to stand nearby.

'This one is Brett's new home and you might like to have the one on that side, Number 1.' Amanda added quietly, 'Isn't it lovely to see how happy he is? That lad hasn't had an easy life.'

The two women watched him move from one foot to the other, turn round to look at Amanda, then look back across at the nearby door, clearly longing to go inside.

'Let's not keep him waiting.' She fumbled in her handbag then got out a key. 'This is your front door key, Brett.'

He beamed and took it from her.

She grabbed his sleeve. 'Just a minute. First, you must never give a copy of the key to anyone else or even lend your key to them.'

They nodded like two obedient children.

'Secondly, we've put in a security system and you'll need to put your own number into the keypad as an added security measure. Dial 000 this first time then enter any three-digit number of your own choosing. After that, 000 will fix it as your password.'

'Do I have to tell it to you?'

'No. I have an override key for the whole system, though I promise not to use it except in an emergency. You shouldn't tell anyone else your security number, not even each other, and try to hide the pad with your other hand whenever you key it in. You'll need both the actual key and the number you've chosen to get in and out. Number first, key second. Don't leave the entrance door unlocked when you're not nearby.'

His smile faded a little. 'Is there a lot of crime round here?'

'No. On the contrary. But the newly appointed manager in charge of buildings owned or managed by the Essington Council is having trouble accepting the fact that this group of units isn't under his control. He's called Walter Padgett and has only just been appointed so is a newcomer to the valley. I've been surprised at how quickly he's tried to take over our group of buildings. He even got hold of a master key and let himself in without my permission. We had to change all the locks.'

'Why would he do that?'

'He *says* it's public housing and therefore in his remit, which is absolute rubbish. Anyway, he has no power to demand entry and don't let him tell you otherwise. Tell him to contact me if he pesters you.'

She frowned. Strange, that interest of his in this insignificant group of units. There had to be some reason for that.

Perhaps it was the position of the piece of land that was of interest, because it stood on the border of Magnolia Gardens. The small park was very attractive and popular with locals. There had been battles fought in the past few decades to prevent the park being sold and the land built on.

Come to think of it, Padgett was the second person who had taken an interest in the trust's piece of land. There had been a man who said he was the agent for a potential developer. He'd pestered her soon after the council ceded the land to the Calliers in lieu of paying them financial damages. He'd known enough about the situation to target her directly and not the council. How had he known that before they'd taken any public steps to design let alone build the units?

When she first moved in someone had thrown a couple of stones through the front window of the old cottage that had been modernised and adapted for her, as if they were trying to make the place unattractive.

She shook her head slowly. Surely a developer would need other nearby pieces of land to make all this fuss worthwhile? Come to think of it, who did own the piece of scruffy land just along the park's perimeter from the trust's block?

Fortunately, their contract with the council had been watertight about who managed what. As a lawyer, she was, if she said so herself, rather good at drawing up contracts.

And Padgett wouldn't get into the units again even if he found out someone's security number, because she'd brought in a locksmith from outside the valley to change all the locks, someone who wasn't reliant on the council's goodwill.

She turned back to Brett, who was waiting patiently for her to say what to do next. His patience said something about what his life must have been like. Lads of his age were not usually noted for waiting so calmly.

'I'm sure you will. Now, go ahead. Make this place yours.' She gestured with one hand and he turned towards his entrance, holding one hand to hide the small pad and keying in a number straight away.

Carla yawned again. 'I'm still a bit dopey, I'm afraid. But I was listening to what you were saying to Brett and I won't forget about the key and the numbers, or Mr Nuisance from the council.'

'Let's stand here quietly for a few moments so that we leave Brett free to do this at his own pace. I'm sure you're not too dopey to enjoy watching his joy as he opens the front door of his very own home.'

She smiled at that. 'No, of course not.'

Brett dealt with the number pad and put his key into the lock.

'Isn't he tall?' Carla whispered.

'Yes. And I don't think he's stopped growing yet. He looks strong too.'

'But he seems gentle and kind as well.'

'Yes. I've noticed that.'

Brett opened the door gently, swiping furtively at a tear as he stepped inside.

'Don't tell him we saw the tear,' Amanda whispered. 'He's not had a proper home since he was eight. Anyway, how about I show you round your unit now and we give Brett time to enjoy his own place in peace?'

'I'm looking forward to seeing mine, I must admit. I've been living in a grotty bedsitter over a pub for the past month or two.'

'Well, before you go in you should know that basically this patio area is public space for all the occupants to share and, we hope, enjoy. That's your barbecue area too. We'll have to have a lesson about how it works, because it's a safety-first barbecue, and then I'll give you keys to that as well. Here's your door key.' She held it out. 'Enter your number in the keypad, then open your front door.'

'I like the idea of the double protection,' Carla said quietly. 'And I like the feel of this place, too. My grandma used to say that people made "stone tapes" in places they used or lived in, leaving their mark on the place. You can go into some places and feel an emotion like sadness for example at times.'

'Well, I hope you firstcomers will make some happy stone tapes as you start off here.'

Amanda followed her inside the unit and they walked round it together.

'These are very safe units in other ways than the entrance, Carla. The glass in the windows can't be broken without some specialist cutting equipment, and if anyone tried to smash it, the glass would just crack and craze. It's tinted so that people can't see in from the park in the daytime – though you'll need to draw the curtains after dark or they'll see you then.'

'How clever.'

'There's an emergency button in each unit, too, in case you need help, either for medical or security emergencies.'

She heard Carla's sigh of relief and added, 'Well, there are two buttons connected to the system actually, one by the entrance door and one on the wall near where the bed will go in the main bedroom. When I'm out, the alarm goes through to a local security firm, otherwise I come running.'

Carla stared at her, relaxing still further. 'That's wonderful. How did you know to put in the safety features? You don't usually get those in rented accommodation.'

'We expect a variety of people to move in and out of these units. Some might have disabilities or trouble in their personal lives, like you. And actually, you won't be paying rent until you're in a better position financially.'

'Really? That's absolutely wonderful.'

'We didn't know what sort of difficulties our people would be coming from, only that they would be in a difficult situation of some sort to qualify for a tenancy. So in the end our architect put security systems into all the units as well as doing other things like making them all wheelchair friendly.'

'I'm relieved about the emergency buttons, I must admit. I can't help worrying about my ex finding out where I am. Frank has built up a network of friends with the same attitudes towards women, and they help one another track their partners or wives if they dare to run away. And it's hard to stay totally invisible online, isn't it?'

'Unfortunately, yes. What's wrong with your ex?'

'A lot. Frank says people are coming back to a more sensible view of the world, one where the strongest are in charge, which usually means men.'

'He's a dinosaur.'

'Yes. But he's also a big man and very strong physically.'

Amanda grimaced and stepped away from Carla to move towards the door. 'I'll leave you to walk round the unit again on your own and I'll wait in my car. After that we'll make arrangements about getting you both some food supplies. There are emergency rations like stuff in tins and packets of biscuits in the pantry. I've put some fresh fruit in Brett's unit, but I wasn't expecting you today, so I'll bring you some across from my cottage. Luckily I have plenty and also bread in my freezer.'

'Thank you. I really appreciate your help and the use of this unit.'

'You're very welcome.'

Brett walked into the kitchen area and opened the fridge door, just because he could. He was surprised to see a little card saying *Welcome* sitting at the front edge of the top shelf. There were tomatoes, celery, carrots and a block of cheese, plus a tub of butter and a jar of jam.

Another sign was stuck to the door of the freezer next to the fridge – *Bread in here* – and when he looked there were two sliced loaves sitting inside it, wholemeal not the soft, tasteless white stuff favoured by Mrs Shearer. There was also a pack of currant buns.

He beamed at the sight of them and took a loaf and one bun out to thaw for later. No one would be counting how many slices of bread or cake he ate here. He could eat a whole loaf for breakfast if he wanted. Not that he would want to eat that much, but he definitely needed more than two slices of toast as the basis of a meal.

He'd never forget how mean Mrs Shearer had been. She'd always set out only two slices of bread at a time and sighed loudly when he asked for more, even though he'd done so at each meal. He'd had to. He'd been ravenously hungry some evenings after the meagre lunches she continued to pack for him to take to school and the equally mean evening meals.

He dismissed those memories with a happy smile. That part of his life was over.

Amanda waited a while longer then went back to join Carla in her unit. 'I just remembered that we'll need to make up your bed.' She got out the bedding and the two of them made short work of the task.

'I'll just check that there's enough fresh food in Brett's fridge to see him through till tomorrow morning. Lads of his age can have very hearty appetites. Then I'll nip across for some more for you from my cottage.'

She tapped on the half-open door of Brett's unit and called out a cheerful greeting.

'I came to check whether there's anything else you'll need to camp out here tonight. We'll have a big buy-in of food at the supermarket tomorrow. Oh, and we have some second-hand furniture in an underground warehouse at the top of the hill and you can take your pick from it tomorrow to finish furnishing your units. We thought the people coming here would like to choose their own style of furniture.'

Both of them nodded vigorously at that and Brett said, 'It'll feel truly our own then.'

'I have to admit that I'm starting to feel rather tired now, so if you don't mind I'll go and get the food for you, Carla, then have a rest.'

'Well, you did all the driving so it's no wonder you're tired,' Brett said. 'There's easily enough food for me to manage on till tomorrow.'

'That's all right, then. Just a couple of other things. You'll have noticed that there's a TV set in each unit. They're rather old but they work OK. I'd guess that they were donated because they're a bit small for modern taste.'

'That'll be even better for me,' Carla said. 'I don't like huge TV sets.'

'I also have some old computers that are still working if you want them. There's Internet access set up here and the details are on cards in the top drawer in the kitchen. So Brett, can you help me to unload the rest of yours and Carla's possessions from my car? She's not to use that arm on lifting anything heavy for a few days. After you've done that, I'll go and fetch the other stuff from my cottage.'

She looked at Carla. 'I don't think you should use your computer to contact anyone from your past, mind. Not even good friends.'

'I know. I'd not dare try it. And I won't join any social media sites, either. Safety is more important to me than keeping in touch with friends at the moment. Until something's been done to stop Frank coming after me, I'll stay incommunicado.'

Brett hadn't moved and was staring at Amanda as if she'd offered him first prize in a lottery. 'You mean I'll get my own computer?'

'Yes. It's only an old one, so a bit slow by modern standards, but it's yours to keep if you want it.'

'*To keep?*'

'Yes.'

'Oh, that's wonderful, absolutely wonderful!'

'I'll drive round to my cottage and bring them and the other things for you, Carla.' She pointed across the garden to one side. 'That's the warden's cottage where I live. You can walk across to it along that path if you need to see me, but I have to carry all sorts of things this time so I'll nip to and fro by car.'

'Do you need any help?' Brett asked at once.

'I'd welcome some at this end when I get back.'

Once their possessions were unloaded, she left them to start unpacking while she fetched the other things.

So we begin, she thought. But she couldn't help worrying a little about Carla's ex. He sounded dreadful.

For the first time in ages, Carla was starting to feel safe and relaxed. It didn't take long to take her two laundry bags of possessions inside the unit before standing outside and watching Brett unload the final boxes of his things.

He had about double what she'd brought and yet if that was all he owned in the world, most people would say it wasn't a lot. He carried it inside easily.

But Amanda was right. He did urgently need some

new clothes. He was already tall, about six foot old-style measurement, she'd guess, with the sort of face and build that said he was turning into a man but wasn't quite there yet.

When he'd taken his last box inside his unit, Carla went back into her own place and closed the door, then twirled round a couple of times in the centre of the living area out of sheer pleasure at having a proper home again, not a tiny bedsitter.

After that she went across to the big window to stare out at the park. What a lovely view! And if the glass in the windows was as safe as Amanda said, she needn't fear anyone being able to break in during the night, either.

She went back to the other side of the house and stood in the bathroom, which lay between the main bedroom and the much smaller one next to the entrance. It was far better than the bathroom she'd used since she ran away from Frank, with both a walk-in shower and a large bath. She sighed in pleasure at the thought of these facilities belonging only to her.

She gave in to the temptation to try out the bed, lying on her back with arms spread out. It was a double, thank goodness. She hadn't liked to lie on it after she and Amanda had made it up, but who was going to know or care what she did now? After bouncing on it a few times, she decided it was just right, neither hard nor soft.

She had to force herself to get up again because she could have stayed there and gone to sleep straight away, she felt so deep-down weary. But that wouldn't have been fair to Amanda, who would be back soon, no doubt.

After tipping the bag of clothes out on the bed, Carla emptied her other bag on the small dining table. She pulled out two or three favourite books, and other personal possessions and papers, then put them on the built-in bookshelves at one side of the room as a temporary measure.

She'd lost a lot of family treasures, thanks to *him*. She'd guess that he'd burnt her old photos. She forced herself to take a deep breath. There was no way to get them back now. The old saying *no use crying over spilt milk* came to mind and she managed not to weep at the thought of her losses.

Would she ever feel truly safe again? Probably not. She didn't let herself dwell on that, either. Maybe he'd stop chasing her.

And maybe pigs would fly.

When Amanda opened the front door of her cottage, she found several envelopes sitting on the doormat. She bent to pick them up, sorting through them to see if any were urgent.

She was surprised to see that one of them was from the building company which had contacted the trust soon after it had taken possession of this block of land. They'd offered to buy it and throw in a similar but slightly larger block of land on the outskirts of Essington for the trust to build a set of six units on.

It had been a low offer, considering the scarcity of

residential building land in this part of the valley, and the other block of land was quite close to an industrial area, too. Had they thought she was utterly stupid and didn't know how much more valuable the trust's block was?

She stared at the envelope, not wanting to open it. If she never heard from them again, it'd be too soon. How anyone could have been aware of what the trust had been set up to do at the early stage they'd made their first offer, she didn't know. She'd had no hesitation in turning it down.

They'd been very rude about that, one man going so far as to tell her to get some advice from a real estate agent in town who was very savvy about business and stop messing them around because she'd do as they wanted eventually, one way or another.

For a few days strangers had stopped her when she went shopping or for walks, to tell her to sell the block, two men and one woman whom she'd never met before in her life. In the end she'd reported this to the police and only gone out for a while by car or with someone else.

She hesitated now, wondering whether to toss the letter in the bin unopened because contact with them had never made her feel good. Surely the annoyances weren't going to start again?

In the end, however, she gave in to the temptation to see what they wanted this time.

She read the letter quickly and, to her amazement, it said that they were still interested in buying the piece of land she managed. Since they'd now bought the block next to the units, it'd surely make more sense for them to buy the units and incorporate both pieces of land into one attractive and stylistically balanced set of houses that enhanced the park instead of looking mean and ordinary as her units did.

There was only one plot of land next to the units and even if you put the two together, they weren't enough to hold a decent and profitable development.

The words *GOOD NEWS* were printed in red and occupied the next line, followed by an offer of a better price than last time. What's more, an even larger block of land further up the valley had now become available where she'd be able to build double the number of units for these unfortunate people.

She stared at the letter, couldn't understand why they were doing this again. What made them think that the trust would suddenly destroy a year's effort, move people out – no, they wouldn't realise that tenants were now living there – and start the building work all over again? That would mean waiting a further year or two to put people into similar units.

She scowled at their damned offer. Apart from anything else, the attractive location here next to a quiet park was part of the package provided for people who'd been in difficult situations.

She reread the letter and this time noticed a sentence mentioning that, currently, changes in zoning were being planned that would make a coherent development in this location even more attractive than previously so the price offered was higher.

What zoning changes? She hadn't heard about the council planning to make any changes and anyway the units were now completed, so should not be affected by any changes in council rules. Was Padgett in cahoots with the people wanting to buy the trust's property? That might explain his aggressive behaviour towards the trust and its units right from the start. If so, who on the council was backing him? He couldn't have been doing it alone because he had no power to vote.

She should have kept a better eye on what was going on in valley politics, but there were only twenty-four hours in a day and she'd wanted to finish building the units and start helping people. And sometimes housing developments were set up in a very secretive manner. She'd have to ask around and see if anyone knew what was going on.

She suddenly realised that Brett and Carla were still waiting for her to return with their food and computers. She'd settle them down for the night, then contact Arthur Keevil and his daughter Jane, and perhaps Ben Thorson too. If anyone in the valley would know what this Hotchkin and Co. were up to, it'd be them.

And if they didn't know now, they would within a couple of days. Both the men might be old and needing to use wheelchairs at times, but there was nothing wrong with their brains, which were sharper than most people's at any age, so they were still shakers and movers locally.

She thought about how this block of land would fit with a development and, with a sick feeling in her stomach, she realised that the only thing that would make a big development here worthwhile would be if this company had been able to buy Magnolia Gardens as well.

Surely the park would never be sold? It was an integral part of the town, used by a lot of people, and had been gifted to the people of Essington on condition that it never be built on.

How could anyone get round that?

Chapter Eleven

When Amanda took much longer than expected to come back, Carla started to worry about whether something could have happened to her. She even went to the door to peer across the back garden at the cottage, but the car was still parked outside it with the boot lid open, so she went back to wait inside her home, standing looking out at the park this time.

She heard a car pull up outside the units and hurried across to the door, stopping to stare at it in shock. How could she have left it open like that? She half-smiled. Wow, that showed she was starting to feel safe here. Only she shouldn't. She wasn't really safe anywhere, just a bit safer.

Amanda got out of her car. 'Sorry to keep you waiting, Carla.'

Brett came out to join them and she beckoned to the two of them, opening the boot to show that it was full of boxes of various shapes and sizes.

'You should put the food away first, then we'll sort

through the rest of the things. Brett, can you take the boxes into Carla's unit, then we'll sort out who is having what before you take away your own share of the contents.' She smiled at him. 'You're the youngest and strongest of us, after all.'

'I'll carry anything you need me to,' he said cheerfully.

'The larger of these two boxes contains some non-perishable food and crockery bits and pieces for Carla and the smaller box contains more bits of food and crockery for you, Brett.'

They left the computers till last. They were older in style and quite heavy, as were the printers.

When Brett had emptied the car, they gathered round Carla's table.

'I just shoved the electronic items into boxes without sorting them out so let's spread them out and do the sorting now. You will each have a computer and printer as well as a mouse and various other bits and pieces. What sort of a computer did you have before?'

'An elderly laptop I'd bought second-hand,' Carla said. 'But I couldn't bring it with me so I left it for the publican. I'm hoping he's hidden it away and not let it fall into my ex's hands. I'll have to rely on him to do that because I'm not contacting him again.'

'Brett?'

'I've never had a computer of my own, and wasn't allowed to use the ones at school in my last place.'

'Why ever not?'

He scowled. 'The teacher said I was too stupid.'

'He's the stupid one if he thought that of you,' Carla exclaimed indignantly.

Brett looked at her in surprise, then gave a little smile as if pleased by her support.

'We'll help you get used to having one, then,' Amanda said. 'For now, go and put this box on the small table near the Internet connection in your unit. It's this one, and the same in all the units.' She indicated it on the wall to one side of the kitchen.

'There's another Internet connection in the smaller bedroom in case someone wants to use it as an office, but no furniture in there at the moment apart from one single bed.'

They exchanged happy grins and did as they were told.

When Brett came back, Amanda had pulled two rather old-fashioned printers out of another of her boxes. 'I'm told that these still work but once again, they're not the most modern types. There are refill cartridges with them too.'

She then indicated two other boxes and two lumpy sacks. 'These contain more household bits and pieces. You won't have many bowls, plates, glasses, mugs and who knows what else? You can go through the oddments tomorrow at your leisure and share them out when we come back from some serious shopping.'

'Serious shopping?' Carla exclaimed. 'With all this?'

'We need to buy Brett some new clothes as a matter of urgency and I thought you'd like to come with us and get your first view of the town centre, then we can go on to the supermarket together.'

'Ah. Yes. I'll enjoy that. It's ages since I did any fun shopping.'

Brett was looking embarrassed.

'You can't help growing!' Amanda told him. 'Your foster mother should have bought you some new clothes well before this. The authorities pay for that sort of thing, but if she didn't bother to ask for any clothing money, that's not your fault.'

'Thank you,' he said quietly.

'I'll come back tomorrow morning, but I must confess that I'm utterly exhausted now, and I still have a business phone call to make.' She paused then asked Carla quietly, 'Will you be all right tonight?'

Carla didn't pretend not to understand what the warden was really asking. 'Yes. The double locks and alarms make a big difference to how I feel, not to mention the smash-proof windows. And Brett is just next door. He'd hear me if I called for help.'

A yawn took Amanda by surprise. 'I'm so tired I think I could sleep standing upright.'

Carla did feel nervous still – how could she not? – but she wasn't going to say so because Amanda was exhausted and about double her age.

They waved her goodbye, then Brett said, 'Um. I don't even know how to set up a computer. When you have time, could you help me do that, do you think, Carla? You sound as if you really know what you're talking about.'

'I do. I've had to use computers a lot at some of the temporary jobs I've done – well, until my recent spell as a barmaid and cleaner. I'd be happy to help you.'

His compliment had pleased her more than it should have done, but she'd had so many put-downs in her relationship with Frank that any positive comment about her skills was like a candle being lit in a dark room. She wasn't stupid. Why had she started to believe it when her ex had told her she was?

And someone must have brainwashed Brett too, because he wasn't stupid, either.

Every time she saw her bruised face in the mirror, or moved her arm awkwardly because it hurt, she was reminded of her ex. Perhaps by the time the bruises had vanished and the stitches had been taken out, her fear of him would have faded too. 'I'd be happy to help you any time, Brett.'

'Thank you.' He hesitated then added, 'You only have to call out if you need me or feel nervous during the night. I may not be good at reading but I'm pretty strong physically and have had to learn to defend myself.'

'Thank you. I am a bit nervous but don't tell Amanda. She has enough on her plate. Besides, my ex can't possibly know where I am yet so I'll surely be all right here for a while.'

That conversation had driven the thought of sleep away, so she said, 'Let me lock up my unit and I'll come and have a quick look at your computer now, if you like. Just to set it up.'

His face lit up. 'Really?'

'Yes, really. If it's going to be complicated, or the connections aren't all there, I'll wait till tomorrow to set it up, but if it's straightforward I'll do it tonight. Have you had much practice at using computers?'

He went slightly red. 'Virtually none. I'm dyslexic and when I had trouble following the printed start-up instructions, my last teacher told me I was too stupid to use one so I had to stand at the side and watch the others. I'd taken my turn at using one in my previous school, and it hadn't seemed that hard, but there were a lot of us in the class and only a few computers, so it wasn't possible to get a lot of practice even there. I tried to memorise what the others were doing at my last school and I remember some of it but I haven't *done* it.'

'You've had some rotten luck with schools and teachers in the past few years by the sound of it.'

He shrugged. 'It didn't help to have a lot of changes of foster carers, and since I started in the country, I had to move long distances to get to new places sometimes. I have a reasonably good memory, even if I'm no good at reading.'

'I'll always help you if you need it. But I think when it comes to computers, it'll fall into place when you start using one.'

She left the lights on but locked her outer door and followed him into his unit, where it didn't take them long to set up the computer. It was all straightforward but she was too tired to do anything except set it up for him to play card games in order to improve his hand-eye dexterity and use of the mouse. Even so she could see that he had difficulty seeing the card numbers quickly and clearly.

When she started to go back to her own unit, he got up and followed her outside. 'I'll just see you into your place.'

'Thank you.' What a lovely, thoughtful person he was.

She unlocked the door, waved goodbye to him, then locked it carefully again.

She went across without putting the light on, drawing the curtains at the park side of the big living space. Then she put a couple of lights on and drew all the other curtains or blinds in the unit.

Only by then, she didn't feel as tired, so she set up her own computer and got online using a new username.

She wished she could contact some of her old friends, would have loved to chat, but didn't dare. Damn Frank! He'd taken so much from her.

She had to blow her nose good and hard, and breathe deeply for a few moments before she could stop crying. By then she didn't want to stay up fiddling with her computer and was glad she was so tired. Surely she'd be able to get some sleep tonight?

She did sleep better than she had for a while, only waking twice during the night when some strange new noises disturbed her, lying wide-eyed till she'd worked out what they were.

She got back to sleep quite easily after the second time because she placed a chair back under her bedroom door handle. She'd asked Amanda whether she could fit a bolt to the inside of her bedroom door, something she could do herself, and been told to go ahead.

In the meantime, it was a good thing there was one old-fashioned chair with a tall back that fitted neatly under the door handle.

She could stand the chair near the bed during the daytime and no one else would know how afraid she still was under it all.

When she got home, Amanda hesitated then said aloud, 'Do it! Stop trying to be Wonder Woman.'

Jane Keevil answered the phone and recognised her voice at once.

'Sorry I haven't been in touch, Jane, but I've been busy getting the units finished and bringing the first two occupants to live in them.'

'That's good to hear.'

'Yes. But now a problem has cropped up, well, a potential problem, and one in which the heritage society might be interested. It might be nothing but . . . well, it's got me wondering.'

Jane immediately said, 'You're too sensible to worry for nothing, so tell me about it.'

Amanda explained about the two offers to buy the trust's land and units.

There was silence, then Jane said, 'I thought we'd stopped that sort of developer poking into Essington's municipal affairs. The name of this company is new so didn't ring any alarms with me.'

'Or me. But it's easy enough to change a company's name, isn't it?'

'Yes.' Jane sighed. 'I thought we'd stopped them with that last kerfuffle about Hawthorn Close.'

'And even our piece of land plus the one next to it still wouldn't make a holding big enough to interest that sort of developer. So why would they spend so much money on buying out the trust?'

There was silence, then Jane said slowly, 'Do you think whoever is behind all this is still making long-term plans to take over the whole park?'

'Could be. That would give them enough land for a very big profit.'

Jane sucked in her breath. 'How could they get anything that important through the council without anyone knowing, Amanda?'

'There's a new guy started as buildings manager. He's an arrogant fellow. Tried to take over our trust already.'

Jane let out a snort of disgust. 'And he refuses to deal with the Heritage Protection Society at all.'

'Why?'

'He told me that amateurs can have no idea of what professional building and development work really requires and he'd not got time to waste on jollying around with our society's members.'

Amanda whistled in surprise. 'Wow! Where on earth did he come from? I'd hoped Madge Barnard would get that job. She gets on well with everyone and knows the valley and its residents.'

'I was told that our MP gave him a glowing reference and on paper he has superb qualifications, so he got the job. Singleton has let the flak from that fiasco about Hawthorn Close die down and is back poking his nose into things. How he got to be the local MP in the first place I'll never understand. He's in the pocket of big business, if you ask me. He's managed to prevent a few projects the heritage society proposed. Dad was going through a bad health patch when the last council elections were held and had to step back from involvement.'

'I guarantee never to vote for Singleton now I'm a permanent resident here.'

'Can you hang on a minute, Amanda? Dad's just come in so I'll tell him why you've called and put this conversation on speaker phone. He'll be very interested in what you've told me.'

Amanda continued to give details of what had happened to her as warden of the trust, and answered a couple of pertinent questions from Arthur, who knew the valley better than anyone, except perhaps for his even-older friend Ben Thorson.

When they'd finished their conversation, it was agreed that they'd keep in touch and share information. Arthur added that he'd have a poke round behind the scenes and chat to one or two people.

'I'll call in on the people in your units too, Amanda,

and welcome them to the valley. We've got some home-made chutneys to spare as local presents, because we had a glut of fruit and vegetables in my allotment.'

'I'm surprised you can still look after it.'

'I pay a young lass to dig it and do the heavy work these days. Donna's as strong as a lad and studying garden management at the local tech.'

'Don't come to see them for a few days or you'll embarrass Brett. I have to get him some bigger clothes and he needs eye tests as a major priority. No one will give him a proper job when he's so badly dressed or can't see to read properly.'

'Isn't he going on to tech education, even?'

'He needs to be tested for what level of dyslexia he has first, but he's happy to do anything I ask. You'll find that he's a thoroughly nice young fellow.'

Arthur stared at her, head on one side. 'How about I introduce him to Norry Thorson? He's a leader in the making with the younger generation, that one is. Sharp as a nail like the rest of his family. Lads do better when they have a few friends.'

'I don't think Brett has had much experience of making long-term friends. He's been moved around too often by social services, just about annually, poor fellow.'

'I'll have a word with Norry, then, and ask him to help Brett settle in. If he's too old to make friends with him, he'll know someone of a more appropriate age.'

Amanda went straight to bed after the phone call ended, but tired though she was, it took her a while to get to sleep. She'd walked into a hornet's nest here in some ways.

Who was behind Padgett? A town hall employee, even a head of a department, wasn't usually earning enough to be involved with big finance.

And though Terence Singleton had never been caught out doing anything chancy, that didn't mean he wasn't corrupt.

Chapter Twelve

The following morning, Brett got up and had a leisurely breakfast, enjoying being able to eat what he wanted without disapproving looks and to watch the morning news on TV as he ate.

He couldn't help worrying about how he was going to manage here, though. He had a little money left, but wasn't certain how he'd buy food and other necessities once that was used up. He wasn't really sure how the social services system worked after you turned eighteen, how much they gave you to live on and what they did about helping to find a job for an unskilled person like him.

Around half past eight, Amanda descended on the units like a human whirlwind and informed him and Carla that they were going into town to register for social benefits, so that they'd have money to live on till they got jobs. After that they'd go shopping for clothes for Brett and food for them both.

'I can't afford new clothes,' he told her frankly.

'I can, though.' She held up one hand. 'Don't worry. It's not my personal money. The founders of the trust provided what they called "settling-in" funds so that we can help people who come here to set themselves up in their new homes. It can be spent in any way I feel they need: food, clothes, study materials. In your case, some of it will need to go on clothes quite urgently.'

He looked relieved. 'What if I keep on growing?'

'If you grow out of the new clothes we'll give them to the charity shop and buy you some more. You're going to be a fine, tall man by the time you've finished growing. I know short people who'd sell their soul for that. And though you're quite tall now I bet you've still got further to go. You'll have the girls sighing for you one day, my lad.'

He went bright red and she chuckled. 'Don't worry. We'll find a way of clothing you decently before the day is through and you'll never need to wear such shabby old clothes again. But first of all let's go and see what officialdom can offer you. Everyone has a right to be supported in times of trouble, after all.'

'I suppose so.'

'And you don't actually have to leave the care system totally at eighteen these days, but can receive help till twenty-one if necessary. Mrs Shearer didn't tell you that, did she?'

'No. She said she only had to have me till I was eighteen. I could tell from my first day there that she hadn't really wanted to take me at all.'

It was the first time she'd heard him sound bitter. Mostly he was very careful how he spoke to and about other people, a type of behaviour he must have learnt when he was quite young to avoid getting into trouble, but a good rule for life.

'Our local social security people in Essington manage things better than that, Brett. I'm betting they'll take one look at you and realise how badly you need bigger clothes.'

'Yes, but—'

'Look, you have a *right* to this sort of help as well as an ongoing living allowance. An absolute right.' She saw him relax.

'Thank goodness.' He let out an involuntary sigh of relief as he tugged his top down again, something he did quite often without realising it, she thought, because the clothes were so tight on him now.

Amanda turned to Carla as they got out of the car. 'The social security people will help you too, but we'll need to inform them that you're being stalked and invoke the secrecy provisions about your personal details. It's a good thing there's a system for dealing with women in your position these days, isn't it?'

Carla nodded, but still looked worried.

Brett first, Amanda thought. His needs were acute.

By the time they came out of the social services department at the town hall, both of the newcomers looked happier. They had ongoing living allowances arranged and Brett had vouchers to buy clothes of all sorts immediately from a shop in the town centre.

The man he'd been interviewed by had been horrified at how badly he'd been treated. 'This is all I'm allowed to give you,' he'd said apologetically. 'But it should provide you with a decent start on getting some proper clothes at least. And there's a very good charity shop where you can get odds and ends cheaply. And make sure you get comfortable sneakers. Those look far too small.'

The man had also been interested to hear about the trust being operational now and had chatted with Amanda about how it selected tenants.

'So Padgett can't nominate people?' he asked.

'Definitely not.'

He lowered his voice. 'I overheard him boasting to someone on the phone as I walked past his office – what a booming voice he has! – that he'll change how your trust operates, and do that quite quickly too.'

Amanda scowled. 'Oh, will he? Well, he'll find out differently if he tries.'

The man lowered his voice still further. 'I'll let you know if I hear about anything brewing. He's an incomer and has played a few nasty tricks already. He's definitely not making himself liked or respected. Madge Barnard would never have behaved in such an arrogant way if she'd got the job, as everyone expected her to.'

Amanda replied to that in an equally low voice, slipping the man one of her business cards. 'I'd be grateful for any helpful information. The people living at our trust have gone through some very hard times.'

The man merely winked and slipped the card into his pocket.

Brett watched them. He watched people a lot. The looks these two were giving one another said that they'd somehow, in that subtle way that he'd seen happen before, become allies.

Then he forgot about that as Carla and Amanda joined forces to nudge him into buying as many clothes as he could for the money. He walked out of the shop wearing new jeans, T-shirt and sweater, and with a hooded windcheater in one of the big paper carrier bags. They felt wonderful.

Amanda had added a cheap tracksuit at trust expense. 'You won't have any clothing to use for simply relaxing in the evenings. See how this one goes. If you're comfy in it we'll buy you another, for when one needs washing. Now, let's lock these in the car boot then get you some footwear, after which we'll go and buy a snack. My treat. I'm thirsty even if you two aren't.'

To his delight she bought them something to eat as well as to drink, so he was able to enjoy a big muffin.

'Right then,' Amanda said as they left the café. 'We'll go and get some basic food stores with the settling-in money.'

By the time they got back to the units, the car boot was full of packages and groceries, and the back seat next to Carla was piled high too.

Both of the two newcomers had tried to manage in the supermarket with meagre, careful purchases, but Amanda had simply tossed other items into their shopping trolleys.

'You two need to stock up completely with basic supplies and emergency items. There is money for that.'

'I don't know what exactly I need to get,' Brett confessed.

'Leave it to me, then,' Amanda said. 'You just push the trolley and nod or shake your head about optional items.'

One of her last purchases in town was a cheap mobile phone for each of them, plus six months' worth of subscriptions to an Internet provider.

Brett held the phone as if it were made of gold, eyes positively glowing with happiness, and she wondered if he'd ever owned one before. She guessed not. He'd had such a deprived life, even in this information-rich age.

It hadn't escaped her notice that Carla had sat in the back seat of the car and slumped down as they drove round, or that she'd tried to stay in the background inside the various shops. How long would it take for her to feel safe enough to behave normally in public? Or would she always feel she had to live life in the shadows for fear of her ex finding her? How sad that would be!

What could they do to protect Carla if her ex did find her here? Amanda frowned. She'd have to ask around about ways to get help locally.

After they'd unloaded all their purchases, she said, 'I'll leave you for the rest of the day, but I'll pick Brett up in the morning at about quarter to eight. I've got an emergency appointment for an assessment of your dyslexia. We were lucky and there was a cancellation or we might have had to wait another week or two.'

She'd didn't say that she'd used her local connections to press for a speedy resolution for the poor lad.

Brett looked at her apprehensively.

'Don't worry. They're really nice people at the reading centre. They've helped quite a few young people in our valley who were struggling to keep up at school.'

He didn't look convinced. 'Well, I'll certainly do my best.'

How had he stayed so kind and helpful after all the difficulties and neglect he'd faced? Perhaps his basic nature had triumphed over adversity so he'd not let things make him uncooperative? How would he cope with any sort of success? That might be hard for him to believe in at first.

By the time Brett and Carla had unpacked and arranged all their purchases and his neighbour had given him another lesson in using his computer, the afternoon had flown by and it was time to cook tea.

They decided to do that separately then each watch their own TV for a while, since when they discussed it, they found they liked different sorts of programmes.

'I'm going to read in bed,' Carla said.

'I've got an audiobook to listen to,' he said, not wanting her to feel sorry for him. 'I bought a couple of them in a charity shop.' He'd heard this one before but it had been extremely cheap. He'd watch TV if there were any interesting programmes on. He could watch what he wanted here.

Nothing disturbed their enjoyment of the peaceful evening as the quietness of that night wrapped around them like a cosy blanket.

Frank was furious when his ex disappeared completely. None of the usual avenues of search led him to her, whether he hunted for Linda or Carla, as she was now calling herself, of all the silly names!

He took some time off work to investigate more carefully and find the place where she'd been working.

It took him a few days to make sure she wasn't still hiding in the small country pub. She'd definitely been employed there for some weeks, though.

He collared the owner one night after the pub had closed, but the sod refused point-blank to give him any information. He waited till the man had gone out to sneak around. There were no other cars parked there so he assumed the place didn't have any guests that evening. Once he'd checked that the owners weren't around, he let himself in through the back door. Talk about security! This place was pitiful.

He checked what were clearly the owner's quarters and just as he was about to leave, he stopped to stare again at an old laptop computer standing on a shelf in one corner. Why was it standing there? Didn't the owners use it? Or had it belonged to his ex?

He managed to get online and check the current

contents of the computer and it had belonged to 'Carla'. But there were only visits to websites, nothing personal about Linda. He had a rather clever friend who could probably retrieve some of the previous information, but since she'd not had it at home he doubted there would be anything useful.

None of the other bedrooms showed any signs of her possessions, so he left, taking care to lock the back door again, but taking the computer with him.

He'd find her. Oh, yes.

She was too stupid to stay hidden from him for long.

Chapter Thirteen

In the morning, Brett woke early, absolutely dreading today's visit to the reading centre. Even dressing in his new clothes didn't lift his spirits for more than a minute or two.

He made breakfast but didn't finish his toast so put his uneaten slice in the fridge. It fitted neatly between two matching plates with the top one turned upside down. He'd considered throwing it away, but could never bear to waste a single scrap of food; he'd gone hungry too often to do that.

Amanda picked him up at quarter to eight and whizzed him into town. 'Cheer up, Brett. They're not going to torture you.'

He wasn't so sure about that.

She left him at the reading centre and said she'd do some shopping and they should phone her to pick him up when they'd finished. A very pleasant woman called Evelyn gave him a series of written tests, at which he proved as useless as always.

She was frowning at him as she watched what he did and the frown deepened afterwards once she'd gone through his attempts to answer. 'You kept screwing up your eyes. Do you have difficulty seeing the words?'

'Yes. I always have had. They seem to jiggle about on the page.'

'Didn't you ever have your eyes tested when you were younger?'

'Yes. We all did in one of my later years at primary school.' He took a deep breath and admitted, 'I did really badly at it.'

'Give me a minute.' Evelyn left the room and he could hear a faint murmur as she made a phone call and spoke to someone.

When she came back, she smiled at him. 'We're in luck. An optometrist friend of mine has a free morning. He was going to use it for some research but he's agreed to test your eyes first if we can go there straight away, because he thinks you might be an interesting case.'

He stared at her in surprise. 'Interesting?' That seemed a strange word to use. There was nothing interesting about being stupid.

'Yes. Come on. I'll walk across town to his shop with you.'

When they got there, Brett hesitated in the doorway, wishing he dared run away. But he'd agreed to do whatever Amanda wanted about his problem, and she'd kept her side of the bargain by giving him his own home, so he took a deep breath and tried to prepare mentally for another humiliating series of tests.

Only it wasn't humiliating this time. Evelyn sat in one corner while the man dealt with him. He was silver-haired and had a gentle half-smile which somehow put Brett at ease straight away.

'Call me Gordon. I don't like being called Mister.'

Quite a few of the tests that followed had nothing to do with reading, thank goodness, but following dots about on a screen and saying when he saw a light flash on and off at the edges of the screen, so Brett didn't find it nearly as embarrassing as usual.

When the tests were over, Gordon said, 'Evelyn, will you call Amanda and ask her to join us? I'll tell you all what I've found at the same time.' He patted Brett's shoulder. 'I think you'll find that it's good news.'

He took them into another room, one without big, threatening pieces of equipment, and gestured to them to sit down. 'I'll join you again once Amanda arrives.'

When she came, he intercepted her in the shop then they both joined Brett and Evelyn.

'I'm really surprised by the results of these tests,' Gordon said.

Brett tensed. What had he done wrong now?

'Have you ever worn spectacles, Brett?'

'No.'

'Did anyone ever prescribe them for you, do you know?'

'I think someone suggested getting properly tested for them when I was about ten, only I moved to another foster home before they could arrange it and the new foster mother said she didn't have time to fiddle about with appointments to get glasses, and in her experience lads my age were forever breaking them. Anyway, she said I didn't really need them as I was a borderline case.'

Gordon's smile faded. 'I'd like to get that woman in here and wring her neck.'

Brett gaped at this tone from a person who had seemed to be such a kind, gentle man.

'You have unusual eyesight, Brett, and you should have had glasses from a very early age, three at the latest. It's no wonder you have difficulty reading and it's going to take a while for your eyes to settle down, but I think if we get you some glasses made as quickly as possible, you're going to be amazed at how much they'll help you with seeing the world around you, as well as being able to read.'

Brett stared at him, then said in a voice which broke as emotion threatened to overwhelm him, 'You mean, I'm not stupid, but have always needed glasses? And that would have sorted out my reading problems?'

'Yes. You need them much more than most people do, unfortunately, because your eyes are so very different from each another. One eye has a focal length in the far distance, way beyond the normal range, while the other focuses at about three metres away. It's hard for them to work together without help. It's no wonder you've had so much trouble with your reading.'

Brett gulped and tried not to let emotion make him

weep, but he couldn't help it. This was so unfair, so very unfair. All his life he'd been cheated! Sobs burst out of him but they couldn't clear the pain away. So much pain.

Amanda stood up and pulled him into her arms, giving him a rocking cuddle until he'd regained control of himself.

Then she turned to the optometrist. 'Order some glasses for him, Gordon. Doesn't matter what they cost, and if there's any way to speed this up, doesn't matter what it costs, do it.'

'I will. Actually, if Brett would agree to one of my colleagues at the university being involved, Riley will be able to speed things up hugely. He'll be fascinated to document this case and it may help others in future.'

Amanda looked at the lad and her voice softened. 'You'll do that, won't you, Brett? Let your story be told, which will help others as well as yourself?'

'Yes, of course.' He blew his nose hard and tried to stay calm, but anger was humming through him as well as pain. He'd been cheated so badly!

Gordon nodded approval. 'In the meantime, I'll give you a pair of high magnification reading glasses, which will help a little. But until we've got something that deals specifically with the differences in your eyes, you won't get anything like the ability to read easily.' He stood up. 'Let's go and choose some frames for your prescription glasses.'

They went out into the shop and he gestured to some rows of empty spectacle frames near one corner of a wall full of similar frames, pointing to the end row. 'These are usually used by men, so I'd suggest you choose something from this section.'

Brett hesitated then told the truth. This was even harder than doing the shopping properly. And it was far more important. 'I don't have any idea where to start or what to look for.'

'We'll ask our Mrs Wolton to help you, then. She can match spectacle frames to people better than anyone I've ever met.' He went to open the door to the back room and called, 'Edith! A customer needs your help.'

An older woman with hair dyed a pale pink and glasses with very fancy twirly frames came out into the shop. She listened to the story of what had happened, gave Brett a hug and helped him choose three sets of frames, one for his main bifocals, another for working on the computer and the third pair simply for reading printed material.

'Can we afford this?' he whispered to Amanda.

'Easily,' she whispered back. 'Isn't it great?'

After Mrs Wolton had sorted out three pairs, Gordon gave Brett some magnifying glasses to wear when he was trying to do close work till his special frames arrived. They did make a little difference, especially if he closed one eye.

As they left Evelyn to return to the reading centre and walked back to their car, Brett said, 'Sorry I was so stupidly emotional, Amanda. I usually control myself better than that.'

'You had every right to be upset. You were badly cheated in the first place by that woman who was supposed to be caring for you, and then neglected by the system that was supposed to supervise your care after your parents died. They can't have checked on your eyesight at all.'

'They didn't.'

'That neglect left you unable to benefit as you should have done from your years of education. It also cheated you out of getting qualifications for an interesting career in the way students usually do. But fortunately there are paths into education nowadays for late developers and I promise that I will personally make sure you get on the right track from now on.'

He nodded but still felt deeply sad. He wouldn't let himself cry again, though.

'I promise you we're going to change your life for the better, Brett. Just let anyone try to get in your way this time.'

He was surprised at how fierce she sounded, as if she really cared about how he got on in life.

When she dropped him back at his new home, she said apologetically, 'We didn't even get round to coming back for Carla and visiting the storage place we use for our furniture. It'll have to wait until tomorrow. We can go there first thing in the morning so that you can choose some personal pieces. Will you tell Carla that?'

'Yes.' But first he wandered inside his unit, put his glasses on and stared at himself in the mirror. He looked different wearing them, more grown up, his eyes seeming bigger because of the magnification. He rather liked this new Brett.

He was so looking forward to trying the new glasses. Would they really make much difference to him? If so, how much?

And what was he doing standing around like an idiot at the fair when he had a message for Carla?

Chapter Fourteen

Matthew pushed the plate away. 'I'm not hungry.'

'You didn't eat your breakfast either, Mr Woodley. Just have a little.' The attendant pushed the tray back in front of him.

He scowled at her and shoved it back so violently it would have fallen on the floor if she hadn't reacted quickly and grabbed it.

'Isn't it about time you told me what's going on? I'm quite *compos mentis* now, you know.'

'You're still convalescing. You need to go easy with yourself.'

'I'm not eating till I've been told what's happened. Clearly something has, from the way people are whispering and staring at me today.'

She hesitated, then sighed. 'I'll fetch the manager as soon as he's free.'

'Good. You do that.'

She hesitated by the door. 'In the meantime, couldn't you just eat a few mouthfuls?'

'Not till after I've spoken to the manager. And please stop trying to hide things from me from now on.'

It was nearly an hour before anyone came to speak to him, even so. And it wasn't only the manager but two police officers as well. What had happened now? Something bad, obviously. Matthew's heart sank and he waited. They both looked young – and worried. It must be something really bad.

He waited till they'd sat down, still trying to work out what this visit might be about that it needed police to tell him. Something about his errant nephew, perhaps? Grant wasn't in trouble with the law, surely?

'I'm afraid we have bad news about your house, Mr Woodley.'

He stiffened. *His house?*

'There has been a fire there and though the fire brigade were called by your neighbour as soon as they noticed it, it couldn't be saved. I'm afraid it's now uninhabitable.'

The silence that followed seemed to echo round him and it was a while before he could string words together. 'What about my car? Did it burn with the garage?'

'There wasn't any sign of a car, so I'm guessing the vandals stole it.'

That was the last thing he'd expected. His voice came out as a mere scrape of sound. 'How could that possibly have happened?'

'It looks as if vandals started it on purpose.'

He could only stare at them in horror. He'd always wondered if vandals knew how much they hurt people who'd never hurt them. But he'd never expected to be a victim of such cruel behaviour.

'It hasn't burnt down completely so you may be able to rescue some of your possessions from one part before the authorities demolish it. Or rather, you may be able to pay someone to go in and do that for you. You won't be allowed to go inside it yourself. Far too dangerous.'

He didn't know what to say or do. He'd lost everything now: wife, home, money. What on earth was he going to do when he left here? Where would he live?

He didn't care who saw him weeping now.

A nurse took over from the police, but it was still a long time before he could stop sobbing.

Amanda woke up earlier than usual the next morning to pouring rain and a sound that she couldn't at first place. When she realised what it was, she threw off the bedcovers and rushed across the landing to check. In the bigger of the two spare bedrooms she found a ceiling leak at one corner and water dripping steadily into the house, presumably from inside the roof cavity. The bedside rug was absolutely soggy underneath her bare feet.

She couldn't at first think what to do, then figured out she'd have to get a builder or someone similar in to check what was causing this. It was way beyond her meagre DIY skills, and she wasn't comfortable climbing ladders, even low ones.

The new cottage had been created by building a wing onto a small older dwelling. Only, she'd been living here for months and it had never leaked before, even in heavy rain. Why was it leaking now?

All she could think of was to put a bucket under the leak and then phone Jane Keevil, who seemed to know everyone in town, and ask her who to call. She hoped Jane was an early riser and she wouldn't be waking her up, but she was desperate enough to do that if she had to.

To her relief, Jane was already up and said at once, 'Oh, you poor dear! Try Barney Murcott and tell him I suggested you contact him. He's taken over some of Belkin's building work but unlike his late unlamented predecessor, he's an honest, reliable chap. He'll not come out to see to your problem himself but he'll know who you could try, or he may even be able to send someone.'

'Do you have his number?'

'Yes. Just a minute. Here you are.'

As soon as she'd ended the call to Jane, Amanda tried the number she'd been given.

'Murcott builders, Barney here.'

She explained that Jane had suggested she call him and told him about her emergency.

He questioned her about the details, then said, 'Well, I'm really busy at the moment because I've still got a lot of jobs left that were started by the former owner of this business. However, my nephew has just come to work with me and he's able to deal with such minor problems even though he's not a specialist tradesman. I can send Rob round to look at it straight away if you like.'

'Please do. I'm desperate for help.'

'He's a real jack of all trades and he'll know whether he's able to repair it safely. Believe me, he won't try to tackle anything that's beyond his skills.'

'Thank you.'

Once the call was over, she ran upstairs with her biggest bowl and found the bucket almost full. She put the bowl under the drip and then tipped the contents of the bucket into the bath.

Barney went to find Rob. 'I've got a job you should be able to handle.'

'Good. I like to keep busy.' He smiled at the plump builder. 'I really am handy and I keep telling you, I won't risk doing anything that might make a situation worse.'

'So I've been told by your boss. I hope the inspector knows what he's doing, sending you here.'

'Please, Barney! Don't say that sort of thing aloud, even when there's only you and me. You never know who might overhear. I have to seem to be your nephew for real at all times, or lives might be at stake. Now, where is this little job?'

'You'll be happy to hear that it's at the cottage next to the new units.'

Rob smiled. 'Couldn't be better for my other purpose, then. What's wrong?'

'The roof's leaking where the new build meets the old, apparently, and it hasn't leaked before. You'll need to take a tarpaulin and that toolkit we put together for you.

I'll get you one of the new tarps from our stores. And whatever you say, I'm coming across to check your work later. I have my good name to safeguard.'

'Bring me some sandwiches then and pretend I left them behind. I mean it, Barney. We have to make sure every detail rings true.'

His companion rolled his eyes. 'I don't know why I allowed myself be persuaded into doing this.'

'Because you know our mutual friend wouldn't ask you if there weren't a danger to innocent people.'

'Do your best, then.'

'I will. My very best.'

They walked across the yard and Barney stood back deliberately to watch him get the van ready and had to admit that Rob seemed to know about tools.

But who'd have thought they needed to do something like this in their peaceful valley? He'd thought when Belkin died things would settle down again.

Who were these people apparently working behind the scenes to ruin Essington's heritage sites?

Amanda had to empty the bucket again before the repair guy arrived, the water was dripping into the house so fast. She took him straight upstairs to look at the leak from inside because she wanted to empty the bucket again.

He took the bucket from her and tipped the water away. 'I'm Rob, by the way.'

'Yeah, yeah. Amanda. But can you fix my roof?'

'I'll have a proper look at it from the outside.'

He ignored the rain, which was less heavy than before, at least, but still enough to keep water dripping into her spare bedroom.

He climbed the ladder and fiddled around, then came back to get the tarpaulin he'd brought. 'Been in this cottage long?'

'A few months. I moved in last year to supervise the building of those units.' She pointed across her front garden.

'Are any of them for rent? I'm looking for somewhere to stay. With the best will in the world, I don't want to live with my uncle twenty-four-seven. We're chalk and cheese.'

'No, the units aren't for rent. They're for a charity trust which provides housing temporarily for people having serious trouble in their lives. I'm semi-retired and have been hired as a warden, to help them in other ways if needed.'

'The units sound like a great idea. Just a minute. I'll go and empty that bucket for you again.'

He'd run off to do that before she could even say thank you, and when he came back he said, 'Go on about your trust. It sounds to be valuable work.'

She'd always thought so. 'Well, it won't change the world but it'll help a series of people in distress. The first two tenants have only just moved in.'

'Can you hang around in case I need anything passing up? I want to do this as quickly as possible.' He frowned at what he found. Was it possible someone had done this deliberately? 'Has it ever leaked before?'

'No. I already told Barney that. And I've been living here for several months, so it would have done. I can't understand why it's happened so suddenly.'

He'd not say anything about it being deliberate till he'd investigated more thoroughly. 'Well, let's make sure it doesn't leak again. Tell me about the people who've come to live here.'

'There's a lovely, orphaned lad who's been let down badly by the foster care system. He's only eighteen, with no family to look after him. We're trying to rectify some eyesight problems for him at the moment. He should have been given spectacles and wasn't. The other tenant is a woman who's been stalked and attacked by her ex.'

She was surprised to hear herself telling him the details. Goodness, he was good at drawing people out. Still, Barney's nephew could only be one of the trustworthy guys or he'd not be employed here in the first place.

'I can't stand stalkers!' he said suddenly.

'Nor can I. But why do you get so upset about stalking, Rob? Men don't usually suffer from it, so with the best will in the world, they don't always understand how badly it affects people.'

'A friend of mine's sister had that problem. Good thing she had her big brother to look after her or the chap might have killed her. He did manage to beat her up once or twice.'

'Our tenant has no family to help her and she's

been beaten up, too. Which was one of the reasons she qualified for one of our units.'

He let out an angry-sounding growl, then gave her a wry look. 'It's not my problem, I know, but if this stalker turns up again, and you or this woman need some physical support, don't hesitate to call me in to help. I'll give you my personal card before I leave with my mobile phone number on it. I'd be happy to punch him into the middle of next week, as my old granddad used to say. That might help to discourage him from ever coming near her again.'

She looked at him in surprise at the vehemence. 'Thank you for that offer. I hope I never need to take you up on it. She seems to have got clean away from him this time.'

'You never know, so the offer still stands. In the meantime, you definitely need help with your roof. I've got a tarpaulin in the van which I can fasten across the part that's leaking, but I'm afraid it's going to need more work doing on it. A few of the tiles at that side are going to need replacing too. Have they been broken for long?'

'I didn't think any were broken. The cottage has only just been renovated.'

'Well, several of them are broken now.'

'Oh, dear! Can you do the whole job for me?'

He looked surprised. 'I haven't even given you a quote yet.'

'I don't care what it costs. I just want it done as quickly as possible. I don't suppose Barney Murcott will allow anyone working with him to cheat a customer and I gather you're his nephew. I've not used his services before but I've heard that he's well respected in the valley.'

'I'll get him to send you a quote anyway.'

She smiled. 'I'm semi-retired and not scraping to get by financially because I used to be a lawyer. Nor is the trust. This warden's role is as dear to my heart as to my wallet.'

'OK. The tarpaulin will give you temporary relief from leaks and I'll see about getting the materials I'll need.' He grinned at her, a very boyish grin from a guy who had to be in his mid-thirties at least. 'I shall enjoy doing a job like this. You get great views over the park from your roof.'

'Thanks. I'll take your word for that. I don't like heights.'

He hesitated then said, 'I'm fairly certain the tiles have been tampered with. Easy to miss. Have you had any work done on your roof since the renovations?'

'No. Definitely not.'

'Ah. Then do you know who might want to damage it?'

She shook her head. 'I can't think who would want to do that.' But suddenly she remembered the builder who'd wanted this piece of land and said, 'On second thoughts, maybe I can.' She explained the situation and Rob began to look grim.

'That particular builder doesn't have a good

reputation. I've heard my uncle mutter about shoddy work when his name's been mentioned.'

'And this goes beyond shoddy work, doesn't it?'

'Yes. You should keep your eyes open for intruders. Pity there aren't any houses close to yours, just the units.'

She watched him pack up and leave, then went to make herself a belated breakfast. If the tiles had been tampered with it must be those people who were again pressing her to sell.

She was busy for the rest of the day and kept worrying about the roof. But she didn't see any signs of intruders and although there were one or two heavy showers, the tarpaulin held and the roof didn't leak again.

The rain seemed to ease off during the evening, thank goodness.

In the middle of the night, however, Amanda woke up to hear the sound of rain beating down hard on the roof again. It was accompanied by the sound of dripping water inside the house, and that sounded exactly the same as it had the previous night.

Had the tarpaulin been blown away? She got up and went to investigate. Not only was water coming in where it had done last night, but coming in more quickly than before.

She went outside and found the tarpaulin lying on the ground and it didn't take her a minute to see that the ropes that had held it in place had been cut and the tarpaulin itself slashed here and there.

She heard a sound in her garden and didn't even try to investigate but ran for the front door. She slammed it shut behind her the minute she was inside in case someone was out there waiting to attack her.

There was a thud as something hard hit the door, then another couple of thuds, which proved she'd been right to run inside. She grabbed her phone and called Rob to tell him what she'd seen and heard.

He said immediately, 'Ropes and tarpaulins don't cut themselves, Amanda. Phone the police and let them know what's happened. I'll come round straight away and stay for the rest of the night. Apart from the fact that these vandals are damaging our company's equipment, I don't like to think of you being there on your own.'

She didn't like to think of that, either. 'Thank you so much. I'd be really grateful.'

When she put the phone down after calling the police, she admitted to herself that she was feeling very vulnerable and worried about how safe the tenants were.

Rob arrived just after the police and joined the two officers in studying the damage. Then he pulled an old tarpaulin out of his van and went up on the roof in the darkness and rain to fasten it in place.

When he came down, he told the police he'd stay all night and they left. She had the kettle boiling to make him a hot drink.

He looked into the house from the front doorway but shook his head. 'I'm soaking wet. I don't want to drip water all over your nice, clean floor.'

'Don't be silly. You can't stand outside in the rain all night. Anyway, you just saved my house from serious damage, so you're welcome to drip away. You can stand on an old towel.'

She didn't wait to argue but grabbed his arm and pulled him inside, which made him give a rich-sounding chuckle and stop protesting. He was such a nice young man, reminded her of her nephew. She locked the front door behind them.

'Now, let me look at you. Hmm. My nephew is about your size and he left an old tracksuit here when he was helping me move in and paint the sitting room. He didn't want it back and told me to chuck it in the bin. But I'm famous for never throwing anything away, so I kept it *in case* it came in useful – and it's about to do just that so it goes to show you never know what you'll need.'

She ran up the stairs, opened the bathroom door and got a bath towel out of the linen cupboard.

'Come up. Rub the wet off as much as you can then put this trackie on. Bring your soggy clothes down and I'll put them in the tumble dryer.'

When she thrust the tracksuit at him, he smiled again and pretended to tug a forelock like a peasant from the Middle Ages.

There was a knock on the door while Rob was doing that and she went to peep out of her front window and find out who it was before she opened it. She was surprised to see Brett standing there holding a battered-looking umbrella over himself, so let him in quickly and locked up again.

'I heard the cars and saw there was a police car with its lights flashing, so I wanted to check that you were all right, Amanda.'

She was touched. 'Thank you.'

When she explained what had happened, he stared at her in bafflement. 'I thought life was supposed to be more peaceful in the country.'

'It usually is, but last year a builder from a nearby town tried to push me into selling this piece of land to him and played a few dirty tricks then to persuade me. He wrote to me again this week, so I can only think that he must be making another serious attempt to gain a foothold in the valley. Who else can it be?'

Rob rejoined them just then and asked her to say that again, so she explained in more detail about Hotchkin's previous attempt to buy this block of land.

'My uncle says he doesn't trust that chap, not just in business but in anything, Amanda.'

'I thought Hotchkin had given up on getting hold of the trust's land. Why would he suddenly start causing trouble again?'

'Maybe something has changed that makes your land more valuable. Only, it seems strange for him to have waited until after you'd built your units and put in tenants before trying again.'

'Very strange.'

'If he's made you another offer, this probably could

have been caused by him. He's . . . not a nice man.' He frowned and added quietly, 'But why do that now?'

'Who knows how villains like him think?'

Rob stared round, then asked, 'Do you have a spare bedroom, Amanda?'

'Yes. The one with the leak and a third, much smaller one.'

'As I said, I'm looking for somewhere to live temporarily while I find out whether I want to settle permanently in the valley and work with my uncle. My aunt is smothering me with kindness and unhealthy, fattening food. I not only like my independence but I normally eat very healthily. If I moved in here for a while, I could keep an eye on you and the cottage and take my time finding somewhere more permanent to live.' He grinned down at himself and added, 'Keep an eye on my own waistline, too. No wonder my uncle is so plump.'

'I'd be happy to have you move in but if you do, the room will be yours free of charge because you'll be putting yourself at risk as well as helping me.'

'I'll contribute to the power bills and provide my own food.'

'Fine by me.'

He stuck his hand out and she had no hesitation in shaking on the bargain, but she added with a smile, 'I'm not offering to cook for you. I'm not at all fond of cooking and I have to eat sparingly or I crack weight on, so I mainly stick to salads, lean protein and vegetables.'

'I'm lucky. I'm a hearty eater but never put on weight.

Don't worry, though. I can cook for myself or get takeaways. My mum trained me well. She said I wasn't a helpless baby and should be able to look after myself once I left home.'

'Good for her.'

Brett was still standing there. She was starting to think that he was hungry for interactions with other people, so she gave him the occasional smile or nod as they chatted.

Rob was now staring round the garden and studying the front of the house. 'I think you should also get some CCTV points set up here, Amanda, so that if anything else happens we can see who's prowling round and vandalising your cottage. I'd recommend a couple of obvious cameras which are easy to avoid, and some concealed ones.'

'I'd already thought about putting a surveillance system in, here and at the units, but having concealed cameras as well as obvious ones sounds a great idea. I'll need to find someone to install them.'

'I can do that for you, will just need to get the final effort approved by a qualified electrician.'

'Really? Then please do it ASAP. And I'll insist on paying you for your time.'

'OK.'

She turned back to Brett. 'Thanks for thinking about my safety and coming to check that I was all right. I appreciate that. You should get back to bed now. We'll be having a busy morning tomorrow sorting out some new furniture for you from the warehouse.'

As he started to leave, she called after him, 'You did lock your own door behind you when you came across, didn't you?'

'Oh, yes. I'm always very careful about anything like that. I used to get bullied at school, you see. Some kids would try to pinch my school things if I left my bag unlocked or even my personal possessions at home if I was with foster parents who had several children and didn't keep an eye on the situation. Kids who're newcomers often are targeted like that, especially those without any families at all.'

Brett glanced across towards the group of units. Only his had lights on. 'I wonder if Carla was woken by the noise. She's still very nervous and I doubt she'd come out to investigate.'

'She may have slept through it. I'll be round to pick you two up at about nine o'clock tomorrow – no, it's today now, isn't it? We're past midnight. Could you remind her of that if you see her in the morning, please?'

'Yes, of course. And if you need help with anything, don't hesitate to ask me. The gardens will need doing, won't they? I'd love to help with those.'

When he'd gone, Rob said, 'What a nice lad!'

'Isn't he? He's going to be a good man when he grows up.'

'And a big strong one, too, from the looks of him. I really admire what this trust of yours is doing for people trapped in bad situations, as he has been.'

Rob's frown came back. 'The problem is, there may be

a bad situation brewing round here. If Hotchkin has his sights set on starting one of his shonky building projects here, he'll be going after my uncle as well as the trust.'

'Keep it to yourself,' she said, 'but some rather savvy people in the valley have hinted to me that there's a Mr Big behind the scenes and that Hotchkin is a front person for him. No one is quite sure where Singleton, our local MP, stands on such issues. He smiles a lot and seems helpful but when push comes to shove, he does very little for his constituents.'

'My uncle did hint at something like that. Do they have any hint as to who this Mr Big chap might be?'

'No. When Belkin was killed everyone thought the violence would end.'

Rob frowned and said slowly, 'Between you and me, my uncle doesn't think Hotchkin is nearly as dangerous as Belkin was. He says there has to be somebody more powerful behind him.'

When a yawn cut off what she had been going to say in reply, she rubbed her eyes. 'I'd better not go back to bed. I'll doze on the sofa in case they come back.'

'No need. You get some sleep. I'll be able to keep an eye on things for you. I think I'll stay downstairs tonight, though. Can you lend me a blanket or two and allow me to use your sofa?'

'Yes, of course. Are you sure you don't mind?'

'Certain. If I'm going to stay here, I'll want to protect the cottage for myself as well as for you. I'm a very light sleeper and before I allow myself to doze off, I intend to set a booby trap or two outside in case they return, ones that make a lot of noise. Are my clothes dry yet?'

'They should be. It's an excellent tumble dryer.'

'Great.'

'Are you good at setting booby traps?'

He grinned. 'I am, actually, thanks to a misspent childhood. And even the weather is on our side tonight because it looks like it's stopped raining. I'll sneak out of your back door to set the traps now. Switch the lights off and keep watch on the front till I come back. Flick the lights on and off if you see anyone creeping around. I shan't be long.'

About an hour later there was a big clatter outside the back and Rob went running out to see who'd tripped the booby trap. She heard him yelling something.

He came back looking angry. 'They'd brought a ladder and I reckon they were about to damage your roof again. They must think we're fools. Good thing I'm here. I've locked their ladder in your shed and I'll hand it over to the police in the morning. Go back to bed again. That incident has proved that my booby traps are serving their purpose and protecting your house.'

But she still didn't sleep very well. Couldn't.

Nor did he. He was wondering what was going on round here – more than he'd expected when he was posted here, obviously. Though why had it all started up again? He came to the conclusion that they had to have someone newly planted in the town hall and were hoping to change the building by-laws.

His uncle had talked about a new manager of buildings in the valley and said he didn't like the looks of the chap. He'd have to keep an eye on him.

He sighed. He wished Barney really was his uncle. He was a great guy and good at what he did. Roofs he'd installed would never leak.

Frank was in a very bad mood, and with good reason. He'd tried all his usual avenues online and off, and got nowhere in his attempts to trace his ex.

Where the hell could Carla have gone?

And who was helping her? She hadn't the skills or the wits to elude him on her own.

He got online and posted to a small and exclusive group he belonged to, one for 'real men', guys who'd not been fooled by the current ridiculous passion for equal opportunity and diversity.

He asked the other members to keep a watch for his ex and included a photo of her for reference.

But the days ticked past and there was no response.

Damn it, where was she? Surely no one could manage without using the Internet?

Chapter Fifteen

Carla had heard the noise from Amanda's cottage and seen the lights of the police car, but she hadn't dared go across the garden at night on her own to find out what had happened, because then she'd have to come back on her own as well.

When she saw Brett let himself out of his unit and run across to the cottage she nearly called after him to wait for her, but then didn't dare draw attention to her presence, since she didn't know who was with Amanda.

She saw the police car leave and after a while Brett come strolling back, so she braced herself to open her front door and call out to him.

Anger at herself was mounting. She was being cowardly again. She had to get over her fears. Had to. What sort of life would she have if she continued to be too afraid to go out freely, even in the daytime or when other people were around?

What's more, if she never recovered from this situation, she'd always know that her ex would have laughed at what he'd see as his success in controlling her.

And besides, she needed to move about freely in order to find a job as well as wanting to live like a normal human being. For all her reasoning, she had to force herself to open the door.

As Brett came across to join her, she asked, 'Is Amanda OK? I saw the police car and then you went running across to her cottage.'

'Yes, she's fine now, but she's had vandals targeting her cottage and they've done some damage to the roof. She's brought in a guy to fix it. He's called Rob and he's new to the valley. I really liked him and I think you will too. He was looking for somewhere to live, so he's going to lodge with her to help her keep an eye on things round here.'

'Oh, dear. Is the situation that bad? Who's doing this and why?'

'She thinks it might be some builder who wants her to sell him this land.'

Carla looked at him in puzzlement. 'This land? How can he think she'd sell it? The units have only just been built. Two of them haven't even got tenants yet, they're so new.'

'Yes, that's what she said. I'd hate her to get hurt, though, so it's a good thing she'll have Rob to protect her and the cottage from now on, especially after dark. You and I can keep an eye on her house in the daytime whenever we're at home, as well.'

When she didn't immediately respond, he looked at her and added, 'Are you all right?'

'I'm going to be. You must have noticed that I've stayed inside the house mostly, but I decided while I was watching you walk across to the cottage that I was going to stop being so timid. I wonder if I should go to self-defence classes, though, so that if my horrible ex comes after me again, I might be able to hold him at bay while I scream for help.'

It suddenly occurred to her that she could probably read about self-defence online in the meantime. *Do it!* she told herself. *Don't just think about it, do it!*

'Good thinking.' He yawned. 'I'm going back to bed now. Amanda says to be ready to go out looking at the furniture the trust has stored in a warehouse first thing tomorrow. It'll be nice to choose some things of our own, won't it? The units are so sparsely furnished they echo when you walk round them and that doesn't feel as friendly, somehow.'

'What sort of things will you be looking for? Do you like modern or older styles of furniture?'

He looked down at himself with a grimace. 'I need a roomier armchair or sofa for a start, and I don't care whether it's older or newer in style. I'm too big to be comfortable in smaller chairs. And I'd like a rug or two. That'd really help cut down the echoing.'

She nodded. 'I'd like some rugs too. And bedside chests of drawers. But most of all I need a proper desk for my computer and a filing cabinet and cupboard for stationery if they have any. I want to go back to work again, you see, and I need to be online to take orders.'

'What sort of work did you do?'

'I had my own little business, baking fancy cakes for special occasions and selling cakes and scones and whatever took my fancy at the local markets. I can use a different business name for it and carry on doing that.'

A sigh escaped him. 'It sounds more interesting than any job I'm likely to get.'

'Not if the new spectacles make a big difference. In the meantime, I can help you learn to use computers and you've already got one to practise on.'

'Do you really think I could learn all that stuff? It looks so complicated.'

'I'm certain of it. It's fiddly more than difficult. Besides, you don't talk like a stupid person, so it can't be your brain that's the barrier; it has to be something else, like your eyesight.'

That remark sent him back to bed with a sense of wonderment. He was so used to considering himself stupid and she'd just tossed another positive remark at him, one she'd clearly meant.

Maybe, just maybe, his new adult life would turn out better than he'd hoped.

The next morning Brett put on the magnifying glasses and tried to read a page in a book. It was a bit easier but he still couldn't read nearly as quickly as his classmates had. Even the younger pupils had been better than this at it.

He pushed the book aside. He'd have to wait to do this till he got the proper glasses, tailored to his own needs. The optometrist had said they'd help a lot, so perhaps they would.

Brett couldn't resist getting up and looking at himself in the mirror in his bathroom. The new clothes made a big difference and he really liked how adult his face looked when he wore spectacles.

He hadn't allowed himself to hope for the impossible during the past few years, especially during the past year as he'd been called stupid so many times he'd begun to worry about what he could do after he left school. Labouring, gardening, that sort of thing had been all he could think of.

He looked across at the TV news while he was finishing his breakfast and froze. Even with only these glasses, he could read the captions at the bottom more easily and if they were a bit fuzzy that didn't matter. Why had he not tried strong magnifying glasses before?

Because his teachers or foster parents had convinced him he was too stupid to learn anything, that's why.

Only, what if he wasn't stupid? What would life be like then?

When Amanda drew up outside the units the next morning both tenants came out straight away, locked up carefully and joined her in the car.

'No more trouble last night?' Brett asked her as he got in.

'They had the barefaced cheek to try again but Rob was with me and he chased them away. He'd set some booby traps, you see. And he'll be working there today, so I needn't be afraid of trouble while we're away or of going home after our outing. Anyway, enough of my problems. Let's go and find you some more furniture.'

She drove them to an industrial area and stopped at a row of large, corrugated metal buildings.

A man came to peer at them, saw who was getting out of the car and waved, calling a cheerful hello.

Amanda went across to him. 'Hi, Pete. We'll be selecting too much stuff to put in my car today, furniture and so on. Can you deliver it to our units afterwards? You've already got the address, haven't you, from the first things delivered?'

'Yes. Happy to do that. Just give me a knock before you leave. I've still got a key to your furniture warehouse as well, so I'll make sure it's securely locked when I've finished.' He smiled vaguely at her companions and ambled back inside.

Amanda led the way to Number 3 and unlocked the door, sliding the two big panels right open. 'I like to air the place out whenever I come here and I don't need to feel nervous because there are usually one or two people working nearby at this time of day. I've made it my business to introduce myself to all of them.'

She stopped inside to wave one hand in a permissive gesture. 'Just go and explore. If you see anything you like, put it near the entrance. You can help one another carry the heavier items, I'm sure. I'll put a chair outside in the sun and read.'

'Do you have to leave by any time?' Carla asked.

'No hurry at all. You're making homes for yourselves and that's important, so take as much time as you want and get everything you need to feel truly comfortable. I'm in the middle of a very exciting story.' She grinned. 'The only condition is that the pieces you choose should fit into your units. If you want to cram your homes absolutely full of furniture, go for it. That's up to you. Pete will collect the stuff you put in this open area near the door and deliver them to us later today.'

They set off and soon separated. Brett's interest was caught by some Victorian pieces with beautiful woodwork and carvings underneath the dust, while Carla seemed taken by sleeker, more modern styles.

'They're mainly oddments of furniture, not matched sets,' she said, 'but I don't care about that. Do you?'

'Not at all.' He stroked the carved edge of a bedhead. 'I'd love to wake up to this. Look at the beautiful carvings on it.'

She grimaced but didn't say anything.

He grinned. Clearly not to her taste.

They met again in an area where rugs and carpets were hanging from a long high rack, like clothes in a giant's wardrobe.

'How about we work together on sorting through these and getting them down and rolled up,' Brett said. 'We'll need to help one another carry them to the entrance.'

Once again, their tastes were very different, with Carla going for paler colours and blurry, minimal patterns, and Brett for rugs which were, Carla told him, copies of Indian and Persian designs. He chose rugs that were all similar, a mixture of busy patterns in dark reds and blacks on a beige background. 'I want them all to match, if possible,' he said.

By the time they'd finished nearly two hours had passed and they were shocked when they realised that.

'We should have done it more quickly,' Carla said quietly to him. 'She's been hanging around waiting all this time.'

But they found Amanda making up for her disturbed night by sleeping peacefully on a sofa near the entrance with her feet up. Then they had the dilemma of wondering whether to wake her or not.

She solved the problem by moving about, making faint murmuring noises, then opening her eyes when Brett gave a gentle cough.

'Oh! Did I keep you waiting? That was a lovely little nap.' She stood up and stretched.

'Good timing on the nap. We've only just finished. Do you want to see what we've chosen?'

'No. I'll look at it more carefully tomorrow once you've got it in place in the units. It's absolutely your own choice and I don't want to influence that at all. I'll just go and tell Pete that we've chosen what we want and he can come and check out what there is to deliver.'

She went along to the other workshop and brought

Pete back to confirm which furniture to bring. 'Can you bring it this afternoon?'

He looked at her with a pleading expression. 'Would you mind if I do that tomorrow morning early instead? Only, I've just got an offer of a lucrative job that'll take me the rest of the day.'

'I wouldn't like to get between a man and a nice sum of money.'

'Thanks, Amanda. I'll load your stuff up when I get back tonight and bring it round early in the morning because I have another job to do tomorrow as well. Would you mind me coming at around seven o'clock?'

She looked at her two companions. 'Seven o'clock tomorrow morning OK?'

'I'd get up at midnight, if necessary,' Brett said cheerfully.

Carla nodded. 'OK by me. I'm an early-morning person anyway.'

Amanda turned back to Pete. 'Fine. We'll get up early and greet you with a cup of tea.'

As she explained on the way back, he'd said he wouldn't charge the trust for doing these little jobs. His contribution to a worthwhile cause.

'What a nice thing to do!' Carla exclaimed. 'There are some lovely people here in the valley.'

The following morning, Pete arrived just before seven. Amanda's phone rang as they were about to start unloading their things.

'Sorry. I have to take that – it's my emergency calls ringtone. I'll be with you in a minute.'

She moved away to answer it and the smile quickly vanished from her face. She was in brisk mode when she returned. 'There's another person needing a home, and it's urgent. Can you two help Pete carry in the furniture without me?'

'Yes, of course,' Carla said at once.

Amanda paused for a moment to study her tenant's expression. Was it her imagination or was Carla starting to offer the world more than an almost-frozen stare? She hoped she wasn't imagining the livelier look.

Then her mind flipped back to her new tenant and she went back to her cottage to get ready to leave.

'I wonder who our new neighbour is,' Carla said.

They looked across and saw Amanda talking to Rob, who was working on the roof. He nodded and she hurried inside.

A few minutes later she came out again, looking brisk and determined as she got into her car and drove off.

As Pete opened up the back of his small pantechnicon, Brett said, 'I'll help him carry in the bigger things.'

'I can help with the smaller stuff but I still have to be careful with this arm.'

She swung round without looking and jumped in shock as she bumped into someone, letting out an involuntary squeak of fear.

A pair of strong hands on her shoulders stopped her

from staggering backwards and she realised it was the guy who'd been working on Amanda's roof.

'Sorry. I thought you'd seen me coming across. I'm Rob and you must be Carla. Amanda asked me to help you guys with the furniture. I'll be staying with her for a while so I'll no doubt see you around.'

The minute she looked at his face properly, Carla could see why Brett had taken a liking to him. He had one of the most engaging smiles she'd ever seen and he'd only grabbed her for a moment to stop her falling, hadn't dug his fingers in deeply and had let go as soon as she was steady.

'Sorry. I didn't see you, Rob. I was excited about my other furniture arriving.'

'Who wouldn't be? I thought I could help you with the heavier pieces.'

'That'd be great.'

Pete called across, 'Can we get on with it quickly? I've just been given another job and they're in a hurry. It's feast or famine, this week being a feast of jobs.'

Carla returned Rob's smile as she stepped away. For some strange reason, she wasn't at all nervous of this man. Her ex's smile didn't reach his eyes, was just a brief twitch of the lips. This man's smile filled his whole face with friendly warmth.

It was a bit the same with Brett.

They set to work taking the furniture into the two units and as soon as all the pieces had been dumped inside the units, Pete said apologetically, 'Sorry not to be able to stay and help you arrange them.'

'I can stay and help with the inside arranging,' Rob offered.

Brett let out a sigh of relief. 'It'd be great if you could. I chose mainly old-fashioned pieces and some of them are rather heavy.'

'I noticed!'

Brett looked at the rolled-up rugs, standing outside propped against the wall. 'We should lay the rugs first.'

'Definitely. Just tell me which ones to grab and treat me as Mr Muscles for Hire.' He turned to smile at Carla. 'I don't mean to sound sexist but Brett and I are clearly far stronger than you because we're bigger and I gather you have an injured arm, so we should do the lifting and carrying. But I could murder a cup of tea or coffee if you've got any going.'

'It's not really sexist to say that because I'm not very strong physically, as anyone can see by looking at me. I have a friend – used to have – who was stronger than most men and I envied her because she wasn't as dependent on other people's help physically.'

'Used to have a friend? Did you fall out?'

She told him the simple truth. 'My ex has been stalking me and he can be violent, so I've had to disappear, even from my friends.'

His smile changed into a warmly sympathetic look. 'That's rotten for you.'

'Yes.' She changed the subject, not wanting even to think about Frank. 'Tea or coffee?'

'Coffee, if that's OK.'

'Of course it is. How do you like it?'

'White, no sugar.'

'Brett?'

'I'd rather have a glass of water, thanks. I never got the tea or coffee habit and I'm really thirsty.'

She put the kettle on, told them where to lay her rugs, and watched in increasing excitement as her new pieces of furniture were brought in one by one and placed where she suggested. She decided to put the desk near the big window overlooking the park rather than in the smaller bedroom looking out onto the car park. It was also good that no one could see through the special glass coating in the daytime yet she would be able to look out at the beautiful magnolia trees.

The other two went next door to put down Brett's rugs and she made coffee, got some chilled water out of her fridge, then went out to tell them their drinks were ready.

As she approached the door, Rob must have said something that made Brett chuckle. It was good to hear that. Her young neighbour was looking more and more relaxed. She was settling down as well. This was such a nice place to live. She couldn't have hoped for somewhere so beautiful, not even in her wildest dreams.

Oh please, don't let Frank spoil for me this time! How can he possibly find where I am if I'm careful? Only, he had found her last time and she'd thought she was safely hidden then.

How come she had to keep hiding? Why couldn't he let her go?

She felt her determination not to be bullied and terrorised firm up a little more as that thought sank in. Perhaps her primary aim in life should be finding the courage to face him if she had to.

Or, more likely, *when* she had to.

Chapter Sixteen

Matthew Woodley was grateful for the local social worker's offer to pick him up from the rehab place and take him to the remains of his former home to look at the contents of the part not fully destroyed. He could decide what he wanted to keep and Ella, the social worker, would help him arrange to have it stored and, sadly, what should be thrown away.

He suspected this would be a highly traumatic task, but it had to be done so he tried to steel himself to face it.

They arrived just as the partly damaged side of the house had been made safe to be accessed by two men the insurance company had found for him. They looked as if they were about to undertake a space walk, they were wearing so much protective clothing.

Ella was a big help with this very painful task but even so, by the time they'd finished Matthew was feeling physically exhausted as well as emotionally drained. When the foreman said they would pack everything and take it away to be stored, he simply nodded, paid their fees online and left them to sort out the details.

It had been a sad few days since the house fire, but he'd been lucky, he supposed. In the end there had been enough retrieved to fill several sturdy cardboard boxes and there had also been a few smaller pieces of furniture. They reeked horribly of smoke but most of them only needed cleaning properly and airing to be made good again.

What had really upset him most was that he'd lost all his family photographs, which included ones over a hundred years old. Less important to him were his clothes. He wouldn't want to wear those in the wardrobe that had survived till they were rid of that ghastly acrid smell, so he'd have to buy a few more.

He was one of the lucky ones to have anything left, the men told him several times, but he'd still lost many of his favourite books and about half of his old vinyl records, as well as some of his late wife's treasured ornaments.

So now he felt he had nothing left from his long and happy marriage, which hurt so much.

Before they drove away from the ruins of his former home, Ella held out a small notebook and pencil. 'Write down your nephew's details, in case he turns up and I'll give a copy to the people next door. They've already said they'd pass your new address on to him if he came looking for you.'

'I don't hold out much hope of that. He seems to have vanished completely.'

When he didn't take it from her, she thrust the

notebook into his hand. 'Do it anyway. Write down your nephew's name and contact information, then your new dwelling.'

'What's the point? I doubt I'll ever see him or my money again.' He couldn't help the bitterness creeping into his voice.

'You never know. He might have been unavoidably delayed, as out of touch as you were during your time in hospital.'

He did it mainly to shut her up, not because he hoped for anything.

The only items they took with them were a few of his clothes, the ones which would be easy to wash, and a couple of smaller boxes of sentimental oddments that had been stored in the walk-in wardrobe. Once he had found somewhere to live, he could arrange for the furniture that had been retrieved to be sent to him, together with the bigger boxes of miscellaneous 'stuff'.

Actually, he didn't tell Ella, who kept talking about 'finding somewhere nice to live', but he no longer cared much where he went or what he did with the remainder of his life. He just needed a roof over his head and the basic amenities, then he'd quietly endure the remaining years of a lonely life.

She insisted he not make any final decisions till he found a new place and tried living there, and he didn't bother to argue. When the insurance company paid out for the house, he'd buy something small. He'd work out where later on.

She seemed determined to cheer him up, which he found irritating. As if anything could do that now!

He had to confess to her that he didn't know how to start finding somewhere to live but did want it to be at least a couple of hours' drive away from the home he'd moved to, which he felt to be unlucky. He never wanted to see the sad remains again, let alone see a brand new house built there when the plot of land sold.

She said she might know somewhere he could live temporarily and then the next day she asked him if he'd mind moving to Wiltshire for a few months or however long it took for him to get his insurance money and decide where to live.

He repeated what he'd already told her. 'I don't care where I live from now on.'

'Yes, but—'

His patience ran out. 'I've lost just about everything and everyone I cared about, so what does a place matter? Bricks and mortar in Wiltshire would be as good as anywhere else. I'll buy a little house when I'm able, somewhere near to the countryside where I can go for long walks.'

At least he'd regained his old ability to speak bluntly about his feelings and opinions. That was a start, wasn't it?

She gave him a sympathetic look followed by another of her uber-bright smiles. 'Then I'll find out if the people who run this trust have room for you in their temporary accommodation.'

'OK. I'd be grateful. They want me out of this rehab place now. If I can't find somewhere to rent, I'll have to move into a motel and buy a cheap car to get around in.'

She got back to him the following morning and told him there was a unit belonging to the Louise Callier Trust which he could have till he could buy a new home. 'Would you consider that?'

He said it again. 'I'd consider anywhere which put a roof over my head and gave me some privacy, and be extremely grateful for it.'

Actually, he'd prefer to live in a unit, he decided, because he couldn't get the memory of the ruins of his former garden and the spacious house he'd shared with his wife out of his thoughts.

The following day Matthew received a phone call from Ella to say that the warden of the units would pick him up in about three hours' time.

He hadn't enough clothes to make packing an onerous task and he'd not unpacked the things he'd retrieved from his old home, so though he couldn't vacate his room by 10 a.m., as was usually required, he wasn't long after that in moving out, and good riddance to the cramped little space.

He went to wait in the equally small sitting room provided for people who had late pick-ups from the rehab centre. He didn't know quite what to expect from the woman coming to collect him, but he did hope she wouldn't be as unremittingly cheerful as most of the staff were here.

Apparently the units he was going to were there to provide emergency accommodation for people who had nowhere to go and no family to help them. He guessed they'd be shabby places but he didn't care what they were like. Anything would be better than a hotel room.

Time seemed to drag as he waited for this warden person to arrive and sweep him off to Wiltshire. He couldn't help feeling guilty at how relieved he was to have seen the last of Ella when she'd been so kind to him.

He would be relieved to move away from the area, too. He was never again going anywhere near the stuffy little house he'd bought after his wife died. Never.

And it'd be quite interesting to get to know Wiltshire, a county he hadn't ever spent much time in, surely.

It took three hours for Amanda to get to her destination, longer than she'd expected but the roads were extremely busy. Ella had explained the situation to her and Matthew Woodley did indeed sound like a prime candidate for the trust's help.

The social worker said he seemed a nice person but was deeply depressed and she didn't want him to go somewhere he'd be alone, like a motel.

Well, who wouldn't be depressed in his situation? As far as Amanda was concerned, feeling downhearted was a sane initial reaction to some of the things life could dish out to people. It was staying depressed that could be the problem. In her experience, after you'd got over your initial shock, you had to find a way of getting through a bad patch and into a better position *vis-à-vis* the rest of the world.

She made a short detour to look at his former home simply because it seemed the right thing to do if she was to understand his needs. She drew up outside the ruined, fire-scarred remains of what must have been a pleasant home. A group of workers seemed to have just started the final demolition, and the place looked worse than she'd expected. Someone had really cared for the garden they were trampling all over.

She felt sick at the thought of how Matthew must feel if this was all he had left. The poor man had lost his wife, been ripped off financially by his nephew and then become seriously ill – and now this final destruction had taken away his home!

She saw that a rose bush was about to be destroyed and on an impulse got out of the car and went to ask if she could take it to the former owner.

'Sure, lady. I'll dig it up for you.'

She found a carrier bag in her boot and put the bush into it. If he didn't want it she'd put it in her own garden. After she set off again, it took her only ten minutes to find the rehab place.

They showed her into a sitting room, where a thin man with a head of sparse silver hair was standing staring blindly out of a window and didn't seem to have noticed them come in.

The clerk went across to him and touched his shoulder, which made him jump. 'Mr Woodley, your new carer has arrived.'

He turned and saw her. 'Sorry.'

She was surprised at how tall he was. He must have been good looking when he was younger, too. 'I'm Amanda.'

'Matthew.'

'We just have to complete the paperwork,' the clerk said.

He nodded to Amanda and followed her, going through the sign-off with what looked like grim resignation.

'I'll send the porter out with your cases and there are a few boxes too. Will there be room for them in your car, Ms Denby?' She indicated a pile in one corner of the reception area.

'Oh yes. Plenty of room. I have an SUV.'

When they got outside Amanda stopped and turned to him. 'Look, let's get one thing straight from the start, Matthew. I don't consider myself your *carer*, or anybody's carer come to that. Besides, you don't look as if you need one.' She saw him relax a little.

'You're right. I don't. Especially one who never, ever stops being cheerful.'

She couldn't help smiling. 'Sounds dreadful to me. How about I promise not to smile more than once an hour.'

He stared at her and a genuine half smile replaced the grim expression. 'Done. What I need is somewhere to live for the time being, while I come to terms with . . . with the recent changes, and then I need to find something to do with the rest of my life.'

'Sounds sensible to me.'

'Thank you for coming to pick me up.'

'Yes. All part of the service and I, um, happened to be going near to where you used to live, so I did a quick detour to see your former home. Dreadful thing to happen.'

He nodded, his face expressionless again.

'They were about to flatten your front garden so I asked if I could have a rose bush that had been near the gate and they dug it up for me. It's in my car boot now.'

He stared at her, mouth slightly open, then said in a whisper, 'My wife Gillian's rose. I should have thought of that. Thank you so much. I shall have to get a pot for it till I find a new home of my own.'

'It looks very healthy so with a bit of luck it'll survive. Now, you don't need to chat or pretend to be cheerful as we drive along if you don't want to. In fact, I think there would be something wrong with you if you were genuinely cheerful at the moment.'

That made him stare at her, then relax a bit more. 'Thanks. I agree. I'm still – well, trying to adjust to the situation and find my way to the future.'

A porter brought out the boxes and a couple of suitcases just then, which was good timing, so she opened the boot. He hefted them in, stacking them neatly without needing directions. Well, how many times must he have carried luggage in and out for patients there? she wondered.

Matthew was still standing beside the passenger door so Amanda called out, 'It's open. Just get in if you're ready to leave.'

When she joined him, she asked, 'Do you want or need, to do anything else round here? Or do you want to go straight to Wiltshire? I'll be guided by your wishes.'

His voice came out harshly. 'My main wish is to get the hell away from where I used to live and the ruins of my home.'

'Right. Away we go, then.' She glanced sideways to check that he'd fastened his seatbelt, then set off. She didn't chat to him. It'd only be empty words.

An hour later she said, 'I need to fill up with petrol and use the conveniences. How about you?'

He'd been lost in thought and it took him a few seconds to process that. 'I'd better use the conveniences too. And thank you.'

'Oh? What for?'

'Not bombarding me with words and sympathy.'

'I used to be a lawyer, learnt how to fit in with clients – well, most of the time. If you want to chat, I'm happy to do that. If not, I enjoy silence too. Just before we get there, I'll tell you a little more about your new home and neighbours.'

'All right. Thanks.'

After she'd filled up with petrol, she simply carried on driving till they were nearly there. He didn't say a thing till she pulled into a layby on the outskirts of Essington.

'Is something wrong?'

'No. Just wanted to give you a quick summary of what the other two tenants are like, Matthew, and why they're living in trust units so that you don't put your foot in it when you're chatting to them.'

That information shook him out of his own miseries and made him stare at her with a shocked expression. 'You mean people told that lad he was stupid and didn't even try to help him to get fitted with suitable spectacles?'

'Yes. That's exactly what happened. It was suggested that Brett might need them at one stage but the woman in charge of him at the next place told him he was a borderline case, so it wasn't worth the bother of getting them. She should be forbidden ever to foster a child again!'

'You think you've seen it all, that you've had a bad deal in life, then you hear about something like this!' he exclaimed. 'It's fairly normal for things to go badly at times as you get older, but blighting a young life like that is absolutely shameful.'

She was pleased to hear him say that and to see him shaken out of his lethargy. It showed his basic character was caring.

'It turns out that Brett has a serious eye problem, not a borderline one, and he needed very specific, strong glasses. His prescription spectacles will be arriving soon, maybe even tomorrow, and I'm so hoping they'll make as big a difference as the optometrist expects. If so, Brett and I might have an impromptu dance round the patio. If you see us doing it, do join in.'

That actually drew a half-smile from him.

'As for Carla, just be aware that if her ex finds out where she is, she'll be in danger of being attacked, so if you see any suspicious strangers loitering nearby, that should be reported to me immediately.' She waited a moment then added, 'Any questions?'

'No. It all seems very clear. Thank you for telling me about my new neighbours.'

'I'll be giving them a rough outline of your situation too.'

'That's all right.'

She guessed that hearing about other people in difficulties had shaken him up and made him start to realise he wasn't the only person to be going through a hard time in life. It was a lesson she'd learnt too during her bout with cancer.

She very much hoped Matthew would settle nearby when he got his insurance money and find his way into a new life in the valley. She'd done just that herself, and very happily too. Essington was such a friendly place – well, mostly. Nowhere was perfect.

'We're here.' She turned the last corner and pulled up outside the group of units, then gestured. 'Voilà.'

Chapter Seventeen

Amanda got out of the car and waited for Matthew to join her.

He gaped at the row of four units. 'Are they new?'

'Yes, they are. Brand new, actually. You'll be the first occupant of yours. The two units on the right as you look at them have never been lived in. I thought you might like Number 3.'

He stood beside her and studied them, head on one side. 'Yes please. I'd prefer not to be in the end one, I don't know why.'

'It doesn't matter why. If you're happy with Number 3, it's yours. There's a two-step security system, so you'll need to choose a numerical password as well as using this key.' She gave it to him and showed him how to enter his numbers, then turned away while he did that until she heard him open the door.

'Great. Now, come inside and have a quick look round before we unload your things.'

She explained the facilities, then said, 'I'll wait for

you at the car. Have another walk round on your own to get the feel of the place then we'll unload. I can deal with my phone calls while I'm waiting so take as long as you like.'

'Thanks. I'd like to do that.'

Matthew was grateful to be left alone in the unit, which couldn't have been finished for long because it still smelt faintly of paint. He hadn't expected that, had supposed it'd be a run-down cheapie of a place where they dumped homeless people who had nowhere better to go.

No one had come out of the other units to meet him, thank goodness. He'd never lived in a row house before and didn't fancy living in anyone's pocket.

Not wanting to keep such a nice woman waiting, he made a quick second tour and ended up at the big window in the living area, staring out at the park. It'd be great to stroll round it occasionally, and those big trees were indeed magnolias, which had presumably given the park its name. Among his favourite trees, those.

Another thing he hadn't expected was to *like* the new place. It felt . . . friendly, even with nothing happening and no one around.

He went back to the car and found Amanda chatting animatedly to a tall lad wearing glasses, so assumed this was his new next-door neighbour. He forced himself to go across and join them, trying to smile as he was introduced but not, he felt, succeeding very well. Perhaps he'd lost the ability to smile naturally along with everything else.

'I'll help you carry your things in,' Brett offered, 'then I'll leave you in peace.'

And he did just that, which was an immediate point in the lad's favour, because Matthew was longing for some time on his own in an area that could be as private as he wanted – and needed it to be.

This felt especially important to him after his stay in the busy rehab centre, where people were coming and going all the time to the gym and swimming pool, as well as to various other places of torture.

He realised Amanda was speaking to him again and tried to pay better attention.

'There are emergency food supplies which should last you till tomorrow, but then you'll need to go shopping for a range of fresh foods and basic stores. I can't know what newcomers will want to eat, or whether they have food allergies, so I decided not to assume anything or make anything but a minimal effort to fill their fridges and cupboards in advance. I'll pick you up about nine o'clock in the morning to go to the local supermarket if that's all right?'

'Fine by me. I'm an early riser anyway, so I'll be up at whatever time you come. I'll need to buy a car too, if you have time to take me to do that. Mine was stolen and crashed while I was unconscious. The police said it was a complete write-off, but managed to retrieve a few personal possessions from the wreckage.'

'Presumably it was insured.'

'Yes, but it'll take a while to get the insurance money

for that, and even longer to be paid the insurance money for the house, apparently. Anyway, I'll only need a small, second-hand car and I can afford that from what's left of my savings. Is there a car dealer in the valley?'

'Yes. And I've never heard anyone complain about what Parmi has sold them. Her family are from India originally and she's a lovely person, noted round here for being able to guess what sort of vehicle will suit a potential customer. How she does that, I can't figure out. We can go and see her tomorrow as well as do the food shopping.'

She was about to turn away when she raised one finger as if something else had just occurred to her. 'What about banking facilities?'

'Oh yes. I'll need to transfer my account. How much is the rent?'

'You won't be charged anything for the first six weeks, then it will depend on whether you have money coming in. It can be rent-free for as long as you need.'

'That's extremely generous!'

'Our trust also provides a sum for settling-in costs for new tenants too, so the food we buy tomorrow will be paid for up to a certain amount. I don't know how much money you have left or whether you'll need help from social services till your fire insurance kicks in.'

'I have a superannuation fund which pays enough for me to get by on as long as I watch the pennies and don't buy an expensive car.' Sadly, he'd expected to supplement his superannuation with the interest on his savings, but no use dwelling on that. Done was done and Grant had whisked those away. 'I'd like to pop into the local branch of my bank, though, at some stage.'

'Right then. We can do that today if we have time, or you can leave it till after you get your car.'

'The car is more important to me at the moment, I must admit, so if we don't have time for the banking stuff tomorrow, I'll sort that out later.'

He watched her drive away then went back inside, locking the outside door carefully behind him. He liked her. She hadn't wasted time gossiping about nothing and had left him to start pulling himself together. And the lad hadn't pestered him, either, just been helpful then left him to it.

He frowned, wondering about the youngster, who had seemed to understand his new neighbour's need to be alone. How had he learnt about that sort of need at his age? Perhaps Brett had felt the same when he first came here. It must be difficult to adjust to being turned loose as an adult by the care system at only eighteen without having a family support network.

He began putting clothes and other things away, taking his time and thinking about how he would need to access them in the future. This place would actually do very well for the time being and was far better than he'd expected.

Thank goodness he hadn't lent all his savings to his damned nephew. He'd handed over more money than he should have done, given that you couldn't easily replace money after you'd retired. Oh well, done was done.

No one disturbed Matthew so he carried on 'pottering and tottering', as his wife used to call it, not just putting things away but thinking hard.

Later, he made himself some cheese on toast for tea, one of his favourite comfort foods. Then he spent a quiet evening watching the small, old-fashioned TV – well, half-watching it, because he was tired, deep down tired. He didn't know whether it was still the effects of the virus or the deep sadness that had been added to his life since he'd found out that he'd lost his home and most of his possessions.

He flapped one hand dismissively at the universe. Whatever it had done to him, he was coping, wasn't he?

But he did admit to himself again as he got ready for bed in the gleaming new bathroom that he'd been extremely lucky to be offered this place. Perhaps his fortunes had taken a turn for the better.

Now, there was a strange thought. He'd certainly not have believed life could improve so quickly when he got up this morning. Only, it'd gone bad quickly with the pneumonia and the fire, hadn't it? So why shouldn't the opposite be possible?

After he got back from shopping tomorrow, he'd walk across to those beautiful trees and sit on one of the benches in the dappled shade beneath them. It looked so peaceful there. Even the small children he'd watched playing in the park seemed to calm down when they were near them. They drew your attention, made you want to touch them, trees as beautiful as that did.

Then the world faded and for the first time since his illness, he fell into a normal sleep and stayed asleep until past dawn, except for the middle of the night bathroom break his old body insisted on nowadays.

Amanda arrived to pick him up just before nine the next morning and drove him into the town centre. Once again, she didn't pester him with small talk, but as she took him down Larch Tree Lane, she explained its importance as the main artery for the whole valley. Then they went round the approximate circle of the main street so that he could get the feel of the place, once more with occasional comments about the various businesses they passed, useful information not chit-chat.

When she slowed down near their starting point, she asked, 'Supermarket or car first?'

'I think I'd like to go to the supermarket first, if that's all right? It seems such a nice, normal thing to do.'

'That's fine by me. Shall I come inside with you?'

'Yes, please.'

He was glad of her help because apart from knowing her way round this particular supermarket, she'd stocked homes from scratch recently and knew what was likely to be essential and what wasn't. Her suggestions made him realise that he hadn't been eating healthily for a while and it suddenly came to him that it would be worth choosing what he ate more carefully from now on. He didn't want to fall ill again. He'd hated being so helpless.

As they loaded his shopping into her car boot, he said, 'I can't thank you enough for your guidance in there. It'd have taken me much longer on my own to work out what to get, and I'd probably have missed several crucial items.'

'My pleasure.'

'And thank you for paying for this first load of food.'

'It's how the trust was set up. The Calliers are very caring people. Fancy buying a car now?'

'Definitely.'

The car dealer's premises were quite small, selling only second-hand vehicles with about a dozen available to choose from. Parmi was younger than he'd expected with a lovely sing-song accent. It was quickly obvious that she knew what she was doing.

She didn't push anything at him, but listened intently to his wishes and how much he could afford to spend, then pointed out three cars which she thought might suit.

They were all so similar he chose one mainly by colour. He'd always preferred a white car and the seats of this one were the most comfortable of the three as well, which clinched the idea of owning it.

'How soon can you have it ready? I'm paying cash and can transfer the money into your bank account straight away.'

'How about this afternoon? As long as my mechanic is free, that is. Although it has already been checked by him, I always get him to recheck that everything is all right before I hand over a car. I can deliver it to you as soon as he's okayed it if you like. Well, I can as long as you'll drive me back here afterwards.'

'Really? That'd be wonderful.'

'Is everyone in the valley kind and helpful?' he whispered to Amanda as they were waiting for Parmi to phone her mechanic.

She whispered back, 'Most of them are, which is why Parmi's family fitted in so well when they came to settle in England.'

He used Parmi's phone to make a transfer from his previous bank, since he'd lost his own phone in the house fire, and they got through the paperwork quickly and painlessly.

He looked at Amanda afterwards. 'Is there somewhere I can buy a phone? I don't need anything fancy. Then I'd like to go to the local bank and move my account here. Would that be all right? I'm not taking up too much of your time, am I? If so, I'll wait till tomorrow.'

'It's fine by me but you're looking tired. Are you sure you want to cram all this into one day, Matthew?'

'I'd rather get these basic, necessary tasks over and done with, if you don't mind.'

'Well, they won't deal with your bank account transfer in five minutes, so how about I give you half an hour in the bank and do my own supermarket shopping in the meantime?'

'Perfect.'

The bank manager was very obliging, the transfer of Matthew's account was easily accomplished and by the time he went outside Amanda was standing there chatting to another woman. She didn't introduce him but ended the conversation and came across to join him.

'Is there anything else you need to do, Matthew? You're looking rather weary.'

He hesitated, then said, 'I'd like to join the library and borrow some books, if you don't mind. I lost most of mine in the fire and I'm an avid reader. I think I can summon up enough energy to do that, if you don't mind. I can be quick about choosing books, I promise you, because I enjoy most genres. If they have a "new books" display like most libraries do, I'll probably pick up a few from there.'

The librarian took Amanda's word about him being a bona fide resident of the town and he was as quick as he'd promised about finding books to read. 'It won't matter much who they're by. I just need something to take my mind off my own problems for a while.'

By the time they reached his unit, she could see that he was utterly exhausted and would need to rest before his car was delivered.

'Thank you, Amanda. You've been incredibly helpful.'

'You were easy to deal with, so the shopping and buying cars didn't take nearly as long as I'd expected.' She gave him a concerned look. 'But you look too tired to go out again. I could phone Parmi and suggest she brings your car tomorrow morning instead.'

'I am tired, but I'd rather have my own transport. It'll seem such a big step towards normality. Anyway, I'll only have to drive that nice woman back to her premises once she's delivered my car, then I'll be done for the day.' He hesitated, then added, 'I couldn't have hoped for better help in my time of need, Amanda. I'm truly grateful – to you and to the trust which made it all possible. Will you pass on my thanks to the Calliers?'

'Yes. They'll be pleased to hear that it's helped you. Now, only unpack the perishable foods then ignore the others and have a rest, though if you lie down, I think you'd better set your alarm clock and put it close to you or use the oven timer if you don't have one. Otherwise I doubt you'll be awake for three o'clock.'

She was right. He put the food that needed it into the fridge and freezer, stacking them any old how, had a quick drink of milk and a couple of biscuits, then set his battered old alarm clock and went to lie down on the bed.

He was asleep almost instantly and only the shrilling of the clock next to his ear woke him in time to be ready for Parmi.

Chapter Eighteen

The next morning, Brett woke up feeling both excited and apprehensive. Today was the day he'd be getting his special spectacles. He wished he didn't have to wait till late morning for that. It was only seven o'clock and he was wide awake already, eager to get the suspense over and done with.

How much would these glasses help him? He had no idea, but even a slight improvement would be welcome.

He got up, ate his breakfast slowly then cleared up, taking pride in the gleaming surfaces and draining board. Only when he couldn't see another thing to wipe or straighten did he stand smiling round at his immaculate new home. He might not have family to share it with but at least he had his *own* home now. That made him feel so much better.

And after he'd sorted out the spectacles, he'd try very hard to find a job, however lowly, and perhaps even make a friend or two.

When he looked at the clock, he sighed because

it was still only ten past eight. He glanced out of the big window at the park with its occasional clumps of shrubs in strategic places near the path, clumps that mostly looked like patches of green froth to him from here. He decided to go for a walk right round the park. Someone had designed it to give users beauty wherever they walked and he'd wanted to explore the perimeter from the first moment he saw it.

Well, why not do that now?

He went outside, smiling as he used the electronic remote to lock the big window then slipped the little gadget into his pocket. It was so useful being able to lock the door that overlooked the park, so he could go out and be sure his home would still be safe. The designer of these units must have thought really carefully about what the tenants might need, and security would probably be high on most people's list.

After a brisk circuit of the whole park, he sat down on one of the benches set temptingly round the magnolia trees. His surroundings appeared slightly blurred as usual. He wondered what it would be like to see the world clearly at all times, whether it was objects close to you or far away.

No, don't go there, he told himself. *If you expect too much, the disappointment will be greater.*

He might be able to read novels in book form if the glasses worked well, though. That was something he'd often wished he could do because audiobooks, good as they were, didn't always move along at the faster speed he'd have preferred. Nearly all of them seemed to be read too slowly for him. And there wasn't as wide a choice of titles in that format, either. He'd listened to some of them more than once when nothing else had been available.

As he glanced back at the units, he saw his new next-door neighbour come out. He knew it was Mr Woodley because no one else had silver hair that gleamed in the sunlight. He was tilting his head as if to enjoy the sun on his face, though Brett couldn't make out the details of his features.

Then he began strolling towards the trees, not seeming to notice Brett till he was nearly at the benches. He stopped, hesitated and nodded a greeting.

Brett nodded back, not attempting to begin chatting because unless he'd guessed wrongly, Mr Woodley wasn't the sort of person to want casual talk.

But this morning his neighbour seemed a little different. Brett screwed up his eyes, trying to see his companion's expression better. Now that he was closer, it was clear that Mr Woodley was more relaxed today. To the lad's delight, the other spoke first.

'I couldn't stay indoors any longer. I slept better than I have for months and wanted to get a little sun on my face, even though it isn't particularly warm at this time of day. Is there some magic about this valley that makes people relax here?'

Brett smiled because he'd felt the same thing when he first got here. 'I think there must be. It's the nicest place

I've lived in since my mother died when I was little.'

'How old were you exactly?'

'Eight.'

'That's sad.' Mr Woodley sat down on the next bench and gestured towards the units. 'They look great, don't they? I was expecting somewhere run-down when I was offered a place to stay.'

'I didn't know what to expect but I love it here.'

A short silence, then, 'You must have got up early.'

'I was too excited to stay in bed.'

'Oh yes! Today is the day you get your new spectacles, isn't it? Amanda told me about that. I hope you don't mind her sharing information about us tenants. She only gives a broad outline. She seemed nearly as excited as you about the spectacles.'

'I don't mind her telling you at all. I don't know how much difference the glasses will make, but I'm hoping I'll be able to read printed books and papers more easily.'

'I'm needing help to do that for another reason: old age. I can't read without my glasses these days, though I didn't need to wear them at all when I was young. Older eyes change, you see.'

'I've never been able to read easily. The words seem to jiggle about.'

'What a pity. Reading novels is my favourite way of passing the time in the evenings. I only watch TV when I really want to see a programme, or to hear the latest news.'

Brett was surprised that Mr Woodley was continuing

to make conversation but was happy to get to know his new neighbour a little better.

'Do you see much of Ms Hewitt, Brett? I haven't even caught even a glimpse of her yet.'

'I sometimes chat to Carla. She's rather nervous of going out because of her ex stalking her. I've seen her come out into the park when other people are around – but she stays near her unit – and she walked across to Larch Tree Lane with me when we both needed something yesterday. There's a small, old-fashioned corner shop not far down the hill. It sells all sorts of things, nothing fancy, just basic everyday items like tins of baked beans or cartons of milk. It's going to be very useful to have it there, I think, because I haven't got a car to bring a load of shopping home at once.'

It came out before he even thought about it. 'You can come to the supermarket to do your big weekly shopping in my car sometimes if you like.'

'Really? That's very kind of you. I'd be grateful. Oh, look! That's Carla.'

Matthew turned round to see a woman standing in the doorway of Number 1. She was slender and didn't look very tall, with short brown hair held back by something. It was clear that she was nervous from the way she kept staring round. Was she so worried about being attacked? How dreadful!

Brett echoed his thoughts. 'It must be awful to feel threatened all the time,' he said softly. 'I do hope the ex doesn't find her.'

'He must have treated her very badly to leave her so worried about her safety, even when she's standing near her own home.'

'Well, if I see her being attacked by anyone I shall go to her help. Stalking is a disgusting and cowardly thing to do.'

Matthew surprised himself by saying, 'Yes, I'd help her too if there were any trouble. Yell for me if you notice any problems. I've never liked to see anyone hurting someone weaker than themselves, even on TV.'

Strange that he'd made that offer, Matthew thought. He was about the same height as Brett but he didn't have the physical strength of a younger person. Actually, he'd never got into a fight in his whole life, even when he was a young chap. He'd always preferred to defuse a difficult situation with words or back away from a quarrel.

Only, he wasn't going to stand by and watch someone hurt that woman or anyone else.

He suddenly remembered to his surprise that even his cheating nephew had helped a young woman he worked with who'd been getting bullied by her partner.

This probably showed that Grant wasn't all bad, but Matthew still wished he hadn't lent him the money. It was a rotten thing to do, taking an elderly relative's retirement savings. And he must have taken them because after the first few weeks, Grant hadn't replied to Matthew's emails asking how his investment was going, not once.

In the end he'd given up expecting to get the money back, let alone any profits from investing it, and had changed his email address to stop Grant getting in touch again.

He pushed the thought of his nephew away and smiled at Brett, not finding that hard to do; the lad had such an open, honest face. 'I'll continue strolling round the park now. Since my stay in hospital, I've vowed get a bit fitter and to eat more healthily.'

He'd surprised himself by stopping to chat, he thought as he carried on walking, and by offering to take Brett to the supermarket. But there was something very wholesome and likeable about that lad, who'd been shamefully neglected and yet was still willing to put himself at risk to help someone else.

Brett murmured a farewell and watched the old man stroll off across the grass, then wandered back home.

He fiddled around with his computer but didn't know enough to do much yet. Didn't dare, in case he damaged it. And all the time, inside his head, the words *Oh, please let it work out well today!* kept repeating themselves at regular intervals, though he had no clear idea of what sort of 'well' might be possible for him.

The optometrist had talked about 'seeing properly' and Brett hadn't liked to ask what exactly that meant. Any improvement would be wonderful.

* * *

He was ready and waiting long before Amanda arrived to pick him up and groaned in sheer relief when he saw her car leave the cottage and come round to the units. He hurried out to join her.

'Excited?' she asked.

'Very.' He was grateful when she didn't try to chat after that.

The optometrist's shop was on a small side street just off the main shopping area. Brett could have walked there in fifteen minutes or less, yet today it seemed to take ages to get there by car.

Gordon greeted him with a beaming smile and introduced him to Riley, a university lecturer who'd helped get the lenses made more quickly than usual, apparently.

'He's come here specially to be present when you're fitted with your new glasses.'

Brett looked at him in puzzlement. Why would anyone care about seeing that? But if there was one thing he was good at, it was keeping quiet when he wasn't sure what to say.

Riley took over. 'Let me explain: I'm a university lecturer in the department of optometry and if you'd allow me to film the first fitting and your reactions to the improvement in how well you see, for future use with my students, I'd be truly grateful. If things go as we expect, it'll help show them how very important what we do is to people. Our skills can help them improve their whole lives.'

Brett looked at Amanda and she gave a slight nod, so he said yes, because Riley was right: it was extremely important. He just hoped he'd not prove to be the exception to the rule in this. What if nothing ever worked to make him see or read better? How would he ever face a lifetime of blurry vision after this opportunity had made him hope for more?

Gordon picked up a pair of glasses and Brett felt himself tense as he recognised the frames Mrs Wolton had helped him choose.

'These are your multifocals, the ones you'll wear most of the time, especially when you're moving around.'

That seemed to be stating the obvious, but Brett nodded to show he was listening carefully.

Gordon explained next exactly how they worked because of the way they were positioned on your nose, and you didn't have to think how to move your eyes around as he'd expected, just move your head and eyes normally and you'd automatically be looking through a different part of the lens, one right for that distance.

He listened intently, wanting to understand and remember every tiny detail, feeling desperate to be good enough for once in his life.

'Close your eyes now till I tell you to open them.'

He did as he was told and felt himself become even more tense as the glasses were placed gently on his face.

'You can open your eyes now.'

Everyone in the room fell silent but he instantly forgot about his audience as he looked out of the right sort of glasses for the first time in his life. He couldn't hold back a gasp of sheer joy as everything around him suddenly became sharp and clearly visible, whatever its distance away, even the charts on the walls.

He couldn't put his joy into words, was too busy turning his head from side to side and marvelling at how differently he was seeing everything. It was all so clear, so wonderfully, fabulously clear.

'How is it, Brett?' Amanda prompted gently. 'Tell us.'

He couldn't help his voice coming out sounding choky. 'It's brilliant. Everything I see is – it's so clear and sharp. I – didn't expect that.'

'Try reading this.' Gordon gave him a page of laminated card and he looked down at it, froze and gulped as he ran his eyes down the lines of print, which got smaller and smaller, then looked up and stared from one person to another. He could feel that his mouth was open in shock, but couldn't seem to close it.

When he looked down again a tear plopped onto the card, then another. It was an effort to speak at all, a bigger effort not to sob aloud for utter joy.

His voice came out slowly and hoarsely. 'I can read the words – even the tiny ones at the bottom of this page. I can see them *easily*.'

He looked at Amanda and gulped. 'I can probably read *anything* with these glasses on. That means I'm not . . . s-stupid. It really is my eyes that are faulty.'

'I never thought you were at all stupid.' Smiling, she reached out to give his hand a quick squeeze. 'Just as I never doubted you'd be able to see clearly with these glasses.'

Gordon and Riley took it in turns to ask him to read the words on various pieces of paper aloud and film what he was doing. Some of the pages were of different colours and the words on one page were handwritten, but it made no difference. He could read them all easily.

Then he was asked to sit at the big machine at one side of the room, which looked as if it were keeping guard there. He had to stare into the eyepieces and answer questions about what he could see. He was happy to do this, happy to do anything they wanted because today, thanks to them, he could see clearly.

After a while they stopped asking him to do things and exchanged glances and slight frowns.

'There's nothing wrong, is there?' he asked anxiously when they didn't say anything.

'Nothing whatsoever. Indeed, you're seeing even more clearly than we'd hoped. You'll always need to wear glasses to see this well, mind,' Gordon warned him.

Riley chimed in. 'We can't change your eyes, you see. Only time can do that. One day, if you develop cataracts when you grow old, which many people do, you'll need an operation to replace the cloudy lenses in your eyes with artificial ones. When that's done, you may have normal or near-normal vision without spectacles. It often happens. Until then, stick with wearing glasses and preserve your own eyes for as long as possible.'

Brett could only nod. He couldn't stop more tears

welling up again. He had to keep smearing them away as he asked a very important question. 'Does this mean I could always have seen things clearly if I'd worn the right glasses all my life?'

Gordon looked sad. 'I'm afraid so. With glasses you could not only have seen the world around you quite easily but read printed words easily too.'

Brett heard Gordon's voice become harsh and angry as he spoke, though not as furiously boiling with anger as he felt inside. 'Then I've been cheated by the care system, haven't I, cheated for years because no one really cared about my welfare? All they wanted to do was shut me up, and leave me alone in a corner.'

They nodded.

Amanda's voice had a tight, angry sound to it, too. 'You have indeed been cheated. With your agreement, Brett, I'm going to make a serious formal complaint about that to the authorities. I shall be doing it for you but also in the hope of preventing shameful neglect like this from ever happening to anyone else. And I'd like to claim damages on your behalf, too, if you'll let me. The money can go to pay any fees necessary to help you catch up with the education that's been stolen from you so far.'

The two men said the same thing, each offering to bear witness to that any time she needed expert technical support.

Gordon pulled out two more pairs of glasses. 'Let's try these now. You'll be better using different reading and computer glasses if you're doing more than just glance at something on a screen or you intend to read a book for a while.'

Brett found it hard not to sob with joy at the thought of being able to read *for a while*.

Gordon went on, 'These reddish frames have lenses for reading print material such as books and newspapers. Their focus is at the distance most people hold a book or sit at a desk and write something. The blue frames are for when you're using the computer, with a focus for mainly looking straight ahead, though they're bifocals with a print-reading pane at the bottom of the lens for looking downwards, because people sometimes need to refer to printed material which they place next to their computer.'

Brett could only nod then follow their instructions and try using each of the other pairs in turn. 'Wonderful,' he whispered as he read the page of a book with ease, and then moved to try using their desktop computer and referring to the words on the piece of card lying on the desk next to it.

When it was all over and they were getting ready to leave, the receptionist began doing the paperwork and putting the two pairs of specialist glasses that he wasn't wearing into a small carrier bag.

Amanda turned to Gordon. 'How much do we owe you?'

'I'm providing the reading glasses free of charge,' he said.

'But it—'

'It'll be my pleasure to do that, believe me. He's more than owed some help.'

Riley joined in. 'And the university will be paying for the computer glasses. There's something else, too. We won't insist but we'd really appreciate a follow-up of a filmed interview with you explaining how you feel after a month of seeing properly. Would that be all right, Brett?' Head on one side, he looked at the lad and smiled encouragingly.

Brett nodded agreement immediately, smiling at him happily. When he wasn't feeling like sobbing, he was feeling like shouting for joy.

'Good luck with your life, Brett. I'm sure you'll go far. You're an amazing young fellow to have coped with what they've done to you without getting into trouble.'

When they'd left the shop, Brett stopped moving to say, 'I'd really appreciate it if you gave me some time on my own to take all this in after we get back, Amanda. I need to walk round using my new glasses and – well, just get used to seeing the everyday world clearly, indoors and out.'

And he'd weep for joy, would allow himself to do that in private, needed to let some of his pain out.

'Of course I will. But though it's your call how and when we deal with the follow-up stuff, I do hope you won't change your mind about letting me make a legal complaint about this.'

'I definitely won't. It's our duty to do that. I'd be the last person in the world to want any other children being dealt with as I have by a system that's supposed to look after them. Those people have ruined my life!'

She gave him another of her lovely hugs and held him at arm's length by the shoulders, looking very seriously up into his eyes. 'Your life isn't ruined, I promise you. You've only just turned 18 and your life is still very near its beginning. Yes, you've lost some useful time, about nine or ten years of it, sadly, but you'll probably live to be eighty or more. For you, the better part of your life is about to begin and it will go on for far longer than this difficult part has done.'

'I suppose so.'

'I know so. The rest of your days will be spent seeing the world and your place in it clearly. You could even become an optometrist yourself and help other people with visual problems.'

His voice was a mere thread of sound but his face had grown thoughtful. 'I could, couldn't I?'

'Yes, you could.' She started walking again. 'Come on. Let's get you home.'

He was grateful that she didn't try to chat on the way back because he was busy looking out at the town and people, seeing them as he'd never seen them before.

When he got out of the car, she offered him yesterday's newspaper, which had been lying on the back seat. 'Do you want to take this? You can practise some of your reading on it. But don't over-tire your eyes. Take regular rests and remember Gordon said to look into the distance as well as close by. Eyes need exercising too, you know.'

'I'll remember.' He thought he'd remember every word uttered this morning.

'I'll see you tomorrow, then.'

'Yes. But before you go I'd like to thank you for all you've done for me. I'll never stop being grateful to you for bringing me to live here and helping me see properly.'

'My pleasure.' She gave his cheek a gentle, motherly pat, then hugged him suddenly again. 'I think you're right, though. You've had enough traumatic stuff for one day. You need peace and quiet now to take it all in properly.'

Yes, he did need that. But it was wonderful as well as traumatic.

Brett locked the world out, then went to sit on his big armchair looking out across the park. He leant his head back and let silence wash around him like a gentle caress, then he stared out of the window.

This big change seemed to help hope settle more firmly into his heart, hope of an infinitely better life to come.

After a while he got up and walked round his unit, picking up cans of food just to read the labels aloud rapidly (even the small print parts) instead of having to squint at them. He stared out of the window at some little children playing with a ball while their mothers gossiped, marvelling at how clear the whole scene was.

When the family group moved on, he sat down again and picked up the newspaper Amanda had given him. He found an interesting article to read, remembering to change to his reading glasses to do this.

He couldn't help shedding a few more happy tears as he finished the article and looked at all the lovely clear words spread out across the sheet of paper on his lap, reaching out to give them a stroke. Such small things, printed words, but they brought the world to him, even the faraway countries, and he could read about it all so easily from now on, read whenever and whatever he wanted.

Then he sat thinking about it all over again.

It took a while before he could start to accept what Amanda had said: that his life wasn't ruined, had just been put on hold. But oh, the hours of anguish he'd suffered over the years, thinking he was stupid and trying to cope with that and not show himself up for more of a fool than he could help.

And whatever she said, the lost years could never come back, though, could they?

The woman who'd first done this to him should definitely be brought to account. She should never be allowed to look after another child so carelessly again. And the others who should have been caring for him but had never checked out the eye situation properly should be reprimanded too.

Amanda was right. However humiliating it might be to reveal what his life had been like, he'd do and say whatever was necessary to prevent such a thing happening to any other children; even one child was too many.

In the end he went out into the park and walked slowly across to the two big trees, which seemed to be waiting for him to join them. It was wonderful to sit in their shade as the afternoon started to wane, and he enjoyed watching the people walking around the park.

And all the time it felt as if the trees were holding him in a gentle embrace.

His real life had begun now and he'd do something worthwhile with it to make up for the lost years, he promised himself.

Chapter Nineteen

Matthew saw Brett come home, looking rather emotional and wiping away a tear as he went into his unit.

Since he couldn't tell whether the news was good or bad, he hurried across the garden to Amanda's cottage and caught her as she got out of the car and started to unlock her front door.

He didn't waste his time on greetings. 'Did everything go well for Brett? I could see he looked tearful and I don't want to put my foot in it when I talk to him.'

'It went brilliantly well. He can see clearly for the first time in his life.'

He sagged against the door frame for a moment. 'Oh, thank goodness!'

She glanced sideways at him and said, 'Tell me to shut up if I'm poking my nose too far into your affairs, but he would really benefit from having an older man in his life as a role model and mentor, while you don't seem to have anyone close to you left in your own life, Matthew. So you might benefit from a new acquaintance too. You and Brett seem to get on well, so maybe you could help one another.'

She paused to let that sink in and added, 'Only, don't get close to him unless you intend to stay around in his life. We don't want him being let down again.'

'You're quick to make this suggestion.'

She shrugged. 'I'm good at watching and analysing people, always have been. It's a very useful skill for a lawyer.'

'Hmm. Well, for your information, I'd never desert a friend, new or old. And I must say I've really taken to that lad. I hate to think of how he's been treated.' He looked at her with a thoughtful frown, head on one side, clearly wondering about the situation.

'Maybe you can both help each other to sort out where your lives are going from now on, then. Is it worth the effort? Only you can decide that.'

He froze as the implications of this began to sink in.

She waited a minute or two then added, 'Don't rush into anything. Think about it and tread really carefully if you're considering whether to get to know him better and treat him as if he were a member of your family.'

'Yes. You're right. I shall definitely think it over. But I'm not usually afraid to speak the truth about a situation. It upsets some people, but I can't stand pussy-footing around.'

Surprised by the implications of what she'd said and by how positive his own reaction was about the thought of getting closer to Brett, he walked slowly back to his unit, poured himself a glass of cold water and sipped it slowly.

He and Gillian had always wished they had a son or daughter. He hadn't even got a nephew now.

He nodded as he put the half-empty glass down. That lad needed help. He really needed a worthwhile purpose in his own life.

Perhaps this encounter would lead to good outcomes. He'd rather try openly to make friends than sit in a corner nursing his grief as he'd done after losing Gillian. And the thought of her was the final push he needed. She'd tell him to have a go at making a new friend, for heaven's sake.

He smiled. He could hear her voice echoing in his head and, by hell, he would give it a go.

Matthew walked across the park towards the trees, where Brett was now sitting. As he got closer he saw that the lad looked as if he'd been weeping again and all he could think of was comforting him and maybe helping him set his life on a better path.

His own needs came second by a long way because he'd had a good life until his wife died, even if they hadn't managed to have any children. From what he'd gathered, that lad hadn't even started to have a good life since his parents were killed.

'May I join you, Brett?'

The lad looked up and nodded, then looked down again, trying to smear the tears away sneakily.

They sat for a while then Matthew broke the silence. 'I love it here in the shade.'

'So do I.'

'Can I ask how things went this morning? I can see that you're wearing your new glasses.'

'Things went really well but it made me feel sad too.'

'Want to tell me about it? My wife used to say I was a good listener. I miss having her to chat to and you don't seem to have anyone to spend time with either.'

There was silence as Brett seemed to be studying him and considering what he'd said. Matthew almost held his breath as he waited, not wanting to interrupt an important train of thought or press too hard for a decision.

If his young companion rejected his tentative offer of friendship, he'd have to accept that. He hoped it wouldn't happen, though, because he'd suddenly realised how much he wanted a closer relationship with Brett, and with other people too, if he was lucky enough to make more friends.

The lad gave him an earnest look. 'I'd like to tell you about it if you have the time. I really need to talk to someone who – well, someone with more experience of life than I have.'

Matthew gave him a wry smile. 'You can see that I'm old enough to have considerably more experience than you. And yet, I have a rather empty life at the moment, so I've plenty of time to give you. In fact, to tell you the truth, it'd make me happy to help you in any way I can.

I've been feeling rather useless, you see.'

He waited, received a doubtful look and said softly, 'Go on. Tell me.'

He listened in silence to Brett's halting summary of what his life had been like, how he'd felt for all those years. And he thought how brilliantly and maturely the lad had managed to cope with his sadness and the difficulties of changing homes so often, not to mention the lack of real friends his own age because of these moves.

There had even been one foster father who used him as unpaid labour on the farm, causing him to miss a lot of school and get a reputation as a slacker. You shouldn't say someone's death had been fortuitous but in the case of that man, it had.

Actually, he reckoned Brett must have an exceptional brain to have coped with that from such a young age. He didn't say anything to interrupt the flow but he occasionally murmured in what he hoped was an encouraging way, then waited for Brett to continue his tale.

'So that's about it, Matthew. If you have . . . any thoughts . . . on what I should do next, I mean . . . well, I'd welcome them.'

'My first thought is that you've been badly treated. Very badly indeed.'

Then he remembered what Amanda had said to him and the ideas she'd planted had been good ones, well worth listening to, so he waited a few moments, trying to get his own thoughts in order.

Brett also waited patiently, as if he sensed that this conversation was important to them both and shouldn't be rushed.

'Let me tell you something about myself, Brett, before you and I take any decisions. I came here to this unit because over the past year or two I'd lost just about everything I cared about. While I was still feeling disoriented without my wife, a young relative persuaded me to invest in a project he was helping set up which, um, isn't going well.'

He stared into space for a minute or two before continuing. 'Then I found out he'd moved out of his own house and gone off somewhere, not leaving any forwarding address. I don't know where he is now or what's happened to my money. So I'm absolutely alone in the world, have been conned out of a lot of money and am feeling utterly useless.'

'*You* are feeling useless?'

'Yes. So I wonder – would you let me try to help you put your life on a more positive track? Because I think that would make me feel useful again. We should go carefully because I don't want to make any more bad mistakes.'

'Do you think you can help me work out what to do?'

'I don't know. But I can certainly try, make suggestions perhaps for you to consider. And it would make me far happier to have a purpose in life, so you'd be helping me in return. There are downsides to being retired as well as upsides. It can get very lonely.'

Brett looked at him then gave him a lovely smile. 'I'd be grateful for your help, Matthew. This is too much to manage on my own, far too much.'

'Thank you. I can't think of anything I'd like better at the moment than someone needing me. I really miss the companionship I used to share with my wife.'

When he held out his hand, Brett didn't hesitate to shake it to seal their bargain and Matthew didn't let go. He clasped that young hand in both his and said in a voice that faltered slightly, 'You've just given me the greatest gift anyone could at the moment.'

Brett looked puzzled.

'Your trust, as well as a purpose in my life. And . . . an end to loneliness, I hope. As if we were part of the same family.' He saw the lad's face light up at that and knew he had said the right thing.

After that they'd clasped each other's hands in a warm, four-handed promise and offered tentative smiles. Matthew suddenly thought, *To hell with this careful tiptoeing*, and gave the lad a full-on hug, as if he were the son he'd always longed for.

When they pulled apart, Brett said, 'I can't tell you how glad I am to have you to help me. Amanda says she wants to help and she will sometimes, I'm sure, but she's always very busy and she has other people who need her, not just me.'

'While I have been very *unbusy* since my wife died.'

'Your voice goes soft when you speak about her. You

must have loved her very much. What was her name? Tell me about her.'

'Gillian. And I did love her dearly. I loved being married as well.' He choked slightly as he added, 'Most of my family photographs were burnt in the house fire.'

'Oh, that's so sad. But at least you had your years together.'

'Yes. When people spend their lives as a couple, it can make a wonderful basis for just about everything, good or bad. It's not stifling if it's done right; it sets you free somehow. Sadly, not everyone gets it right.'

'I've got vague childish memories of my father and mother smiling and cuddling one another – and me as well sometimes.'

'I'm glad for you.' Matthew waited a moment then gestured to the nearest bench. 'Shall we sit down?'

They sat smiling at one another, not saying anything else for a few more moments. You couldn't rush what they were going to attempt, he thought. Creating a family took time and lots of tiny steps.

After a few minutes, he decided it might be better to move on from the heavy emotion. 'Let's go back and celebrate our friendship with some ice cream.'

Brett looked surprised.

'I confess here and now that it's my weakness. And we can't live our lives in searing emotional crises, can we? Sharing the small things in life can be enjoyable too. What's your favourite ice cream?' He watched Brett slowly relax as he considered this.

'I like all sorts of ice cream. I've only had it as a rare treat, though, so I'm no expert. I never wasted my spending money on it, because it doesn't satisfy real hunger for long.'

And what did that say? Matthew wondered. How often had the lad gone hungry to know that in this wasteful age? Aloud, he continued to try to defuse the tension. 'Well, let's start with my two favourites and then try every flavour of ice cream we can find one by one. I have cartons of my two favourites in my freezer here already: vanilla and chocolate. And I even bought some ice cream cones at the supermarket. All right with you if we test them out?'

And for the first time since they got together Brett's smile was a normal lad's grin. 'That'd be great.'

'Let's go, then.'

This conversation had planted a precious seed! Matthew thought. He hoped desperately that it'd flourish and grow, like the rose Amanda had saved for him seemed to be doing. It'd not be his fault if it didn't.

Chapter Twenty

Carla had promised herself that she'd go out into the park on her own today whether people were walking about there or not. She was pleased with herself for taking a few small steps towards independent behaviour.

Today she wanted to stand beneath the beautiful trees she'd been staring at from her rear window ever since she moved in, and to do that quietly, with no noisy people or children around. She'd not got that far yet on her own, but she would. She had to. She couldn't let Frank still control her life.

The trouble was, she was still afraid to do it. To her surprise she realised that this was partly because Rob wasn't nearby to come to her aid, as he was at the other side of her unit a lot of the time. For some reason, his visible presence working on Amanda's cottage made her feel much safer, almost secure, in fact. No one else had given her that feeling for a very long time.

And she hadn't found a man attractive for a long time, either. But Rob was. Very.

But before she could look at other men, it was important to start regaining confidence in herself; she knew that, but she found even this short walk a very difficult thing to contemplate.

'Just do it, you fool,' she muttered, took a deep breath and set off, walking steadily forward, keeping a careful watch around her but not allowing her fear to make her turn back.

It wasn't until she was part of the way across that she saw her new neighbours sitting on the bench at the other side of the magnolia trees. Relief shuddered through her. It seemed an omen that she was doing the right thing and that fate was on her side for once.

To her disappointment, when she was about halfway there they stood up and moved round the trees as if about to return home. When they saw her, however, they stopped and waited for her instead, standing in the shade and smiling a greeting.

She'd only seen Mr Woodley as he moved from his car to his unit, but he'd looked pleasant so she was happy to meet him properly and chat to them both.

Brett introduced them. 'This is Mr Woodley from Number 3.'

'Pleased to meet you. Isn't it a lovely day?'

'Gorgeous!' he said. 'I've seen you standing outside your unit, Miss Hewitt.'

He looked happier today than he had when he first arrived, she thought. 'Do call me Carla.'

'And I'm Matthew.'

She turned to the tall lad. 'The glasses look great on you, Brett. Was the news good today?'

He beamed at her. 'Yes. I can see perfectly well with these glasses.' His smile faded. 'I should have been wearing them all my life, apparently.'

She was shocked. 'Did no one ever notice that?'

'Early on someone said I might need glasses but the next foster mother said it wasn't important. I think she was too busy to bother. Amanda is going to ask the authorities how they missed that. She's going to be acting as my lawyer and making a fuss about this because neither of us want other children to miss out on things as I did.'

'Good for her.'

Matthew changed the subject. 'Were you about to go out for a walk, Carla? I haven't been right round the park yet, but Brett did a circuit early this morning.'

She took a deep breath and told them the simple truth. 'I was just coming as far as the trees this time. I haven't dared come out here alone before so I promised myself I'd do that today. And since I didn't see you two till I was partway across, I hope that counts as keeping my promise to myself.'

'It definitely does,' Matthew said at once. 'Well done, you.'

His look of warm approval made her feel good. He had a lovely smile, was another man she didn't feel afraid of.

Brett gestured to the nearby benches. 'We'll come

back and sit under the trees with you for a while, if you like. I love the feel of this part of the park.'

That made her feel even better so she gave in to temptation. 'Would you mind? Only, there's no one else at all in sight at the moment and that makes me feel a bit – vulnerable. Stupid, isn't it?'

The two men exchanged quick glances, then Matthew said, 'Not stupid at all, after what you've been through. We don't mind delaying our return. There's nothing pressing except a date with some ice cream cones, at which you're welcome to join us.'

'I'd like that.'

'Um, I hope you don't mind me mentioning it, but Amanda gave us some idea of why you're here so I'm assuming you're trying to get used to moving about more freely without fear of being attacked.'

'Yes. It's taken me a while but I've decided that each day I'll do one of the normal things I've been avoiding since I fled from *him*. Walking across a park on my own might seem simple to you, but it's a big step to me.' Her voice wobbled as she spoke and she was annoyed at herself.

She changed the subject quickly. 'The glasses make you look older, Brett, but in a good way. It's terrible that you weren't helped before, but better late than never, I suppose, eh?'

He looked at her, head on one side. 'That'll be a good motto for me during the next year or two. I intend to make up for the time I've lost as quickly as I can, so I'm going to get help with the subjects I should have studied properly at school.'

'I'm going to work on Brett's reading and maths with him first because they're important basics,' Matthew said.

'I'm wondering whether I should try to read some of the classical books and poems as people did at school.' He grinned and added, 'If only so that Matthew can share which one he dislikes most.'

She smiled at that. 'I'll share mine: *Wuthering Heights*. Such a miserable tale. I prefer happy endings.'

'I do too,' Matthew said. 'I read a lot, so I joined the library straight away, and Brett is going to do the same. But we'll make sure he gets help with science and mathematics.'

'I can't either or I'd offer. I do intend to join the library, though. Where exactly is it situated?'

'On the other side of the town centre.'

'Oh. That's a bit far for me at the moment.'

'Well, I have a car now, as you've no doubt noticed, so I can take you two into town and we can all go to the library to borrow some books. Brett and I can also go to the supermarket every few days, Carla, so you can come too if you like. You won't be able to lug a lot of heavy shopping home, though I suppose you could order it online and get it delivered.'

'I could do that at a pinch but I like to choose my own fresh fruit and vegetables, and look at the specials, so that'd be a big help, if you don't mind. And – I'd rather not have much of a presence online.'

'Ah yes. I can understand that.'

There was silence for a few moments, then Matthew chuckled. 'I'll definitely be going to the supermarket regularly because I'll need to buy ice cream. I was just telling Brett that it's one of my favourite treats.'

'If we go to the library, I could have a quick glance at the latest newspaper adverts too, if you don't mind. I have to try to find a job, you see.'

'What sort of job will you be looking for?'

'Anything. I was working as a cleaner and barmaid cum waitress in a small pub in the country before I came here, but I had to leave suddenly when my ex discovered where I was.'

She hated to see their looks of pity so added hastily, 'Before I met him, I had my own business baking cakes for shops and for children's parties as well, and also selling them at the weekend markets. But he said that was leading nowhere and I should look after him instead so that he could move forward and work for both of us.'

'Rather arrogant of him, not to say old-fashioned.'

'Yes. And I was so besotted at first, I stupidly gave everything up because I thought he was "the one" and we were going to build a life together. How wrong I was! How stupidly credulous!'

'Maybe you could set up a cake-making business in Essington St Mary.'

'Do you think so? I'd like that. I enjoy meeting people. I used to have regular customers for special occasion cakes and I sold all sorts of cakes and smaller items like scones at markets. That doesn't make you rich but I had enough to live off and I loved giving people pleasure.'

Matthew licked his lips and gave in to temptation. 'Do you happen to know a good recipe for chocolate cake?'

'Yes. And my version is a chocolate fudge cake which is absolutely delicious, if I say so myself.'

'Then may I order one from you for whenever is convenient?'

She looked first surprised then delighted. 'I'd be happy to make you one, but I'll need to buy some basic equipment first. I had to leave mine behind and I don't even have a good cake tin now.'

'That'd be marvellous.'

'Perhaps other people might like to buy cakes if you mention yours to them, Matthew. I don't want to be totally dependent on social security. Only – I daren't advertise openly yet. You never know where material you post online ends up.'

The two men exchanged sad glances.

'I'll spread the word as I get to know people,' Matthew said. 'And we'll go shopping as well as to the library tomorrow, eh? In fact if we go early, I could perhaps have some of your chocolate fudge cake with my tea.' He cocked his head to one side and looked at her hopefully.

She smiled. 'You could indeed.'

She looked younger and happier as she spoke of her business, he thought, and Brett was looking a lot happier, too, today. So maybe his own life wouldn't be wasted from now on. He'd heard other people say that helping people could be a very rewarding thing to do in your declining years. He was going to test that theory out from now on.

Your mirror didn't lie to you and even though he was quite fit for his age, he knew he looked the part of a grandfatherly figure these days. And felt it too, in both good and bad ways. His right knee could be quite painful at times. He'd injured it playing football as a lad and he joked that it had never forgiven him.

Oh well, onwards and upwards. That was also a pretty good motto to get you through life.

The following morning the trio set off immediately after breakfast. They spent some time in a shop selling cooking equipment and Matthew could see how much Carla was enjoying choosing her new tools.

She looked at some regretfully and pushed them away. 'I had to leave my equipment behind when I ran away. I had some really great baking tools. I wonder what Frank did with them.'

The proprietor must have overheard them chatting about her favourite cakes, because when they were paying, he asked, 'Are you taking orders yet for making cakes?'

She didn't hesitate because this would be another good step to take. 'Yes, I am.'

'Then how about parkin? My mother was from

Lancashire and she used to make it for us. I've tried various recipes, but mine is never quite right. Is it in your repertoire?'

'Yes. I had a man from Lancashire who used to buy a loaf of parkin from me at the beginning of every month.'

'What a brilliant idea! Can I do the same, do you think? First Monday in every month maybe? My name's Neville, by the way.'

'And I'm Carla. I'd be happy to keep you supplied, only I don't have a car yet, so you'll have to pick it up yourself.'

'No worries. Give me your address.'

'We're in the new units fronting onto Magnolia Gardens. I'm at Number 1.'

'I know where they are. My wife and I are nearby, just off the opposite side of Larch Tree Lane a bit further up. We often go for a walk round that little park in the evenings.'

'Your parkin will be ready by late afternoon so any time after your shop has closed would be suitable.'

'Fine by me. Do you have a business card?'

'Not yet. I've only just moved here and . . . I lost nearly everything I owned.'

He looked at her and said quietly, 'I could print you out a page of cards. I have a special type of paper and app to do that with. No charge. Just goodwill from one business to another.'

'Thank you. I'd be grateful.' She wrote down her particulars.

When they got into the car, Matthew said, 'I bet there's quite a demand for your services. You should start thinking about leaflets, even if you don't want to advertise online yet.'

Her elation seemed to fade visibly and Matthew asked what was the matter.

It was a few moments before she replied. 'I'm already worrying that Frank might find out what I'm doing. What if he came after me again?'

'You've got friends close by this time. What you should do is yell for help at the top of your voice and take refuge with either of us,' Matthew said. 'We're only next door, after all. Not far for you to run to.'

As they walked back to the car, Matthew said, 'You know what? There are a couple of detectives based in the valley as well as the uniformed police. Amanda mentioned them when I was talking about my nephew. They live near us too, in Hawthorn Close. You should contact them and let them know your problem in advance, then if you call for help the police will know it's genuine and urgent.'

'Even though Frank hasn't found me yet?'

'Even so. I'll come with you if you like.'

'I'll think about it.'

'You do that. Now, let's forget about your ex and buy the ingredients for my cake. I think we'll save the library visit till last today.'

Chapter Twenty-One

A youngish woman who was walking along on the other side of the street chatting to an older man stopped dead and stared across the street. 'Surely that's Linda Prosser, who used to live next door to us? Yes, it is!'

'What? The neighbour of yours you told me about who ran away from her partner a few months ago? What would she be doing round here?'

'I don't know, Uncle Ron. She's the last person I'd have expected to see in Wiltshire.'

'Why don't you go across and say hello, find out what she's doing here?'

'No. Definitely not. It was her partner that Dennis and I were friendly with, not her. I didn't think much of her, actually. She was such a meek, nondescript creature. Frank had a lot to put up with from her, poor chap. I'm surprised she managed to run away at all. Someone must have helped her.'

'You *are* hostile to her.'

'Well, she ran away and left him in the lurch just

as his business was taking off. He'd been depending on her support and he's had to give up completely on one project without it because of his broken leg. I can remember how much that upset him.'

Two men joined the woman she'd pointed out and began chatting animatedly as they walked on, stopping once to look in a shop window and point something out to one another.

Marion tugged her uncle into a shop doorway to watch where the woman and her two companions went.

'You won't find out what she's doing this way,' he said.

'No. Could you do something for me? Walk along the street and see if you can overhear what they're talking about.'

He stared at her then shrugged. 'Very well.' His niece had always been nosy and could be spiteful at times too if she took a dislike to someone. He was well aware that Marion came to visit him only because she had expectations of inheriting something after he died since he and his late wife hadn't had children.

He had considered leaving her something because she was his only close relative but he'd changed his mind about that lately because of her spitefulness about the world's other occupants. He wished he could be here to see her face when the will was read. It amused him to keep her hoping.

He stopped near the group and pretended to be considering the goods on display in the same shop window, which were mainly pieces of cooking equipment.

The woman went into the shop and the two men waited for her outside.

'Carla's looking a lot better than when she arrived, isn't she?' the younger bloke said.

Carla? Ron frowned. His niece always referred to this woman as Linda. Had she changed her name? If she was running away from Frank, perhaps she'd felt unsafe. He was beginning to wish he hadn't got involved in this.

'Living in the units has made us all feel better,' the older man said. 'The Calliers did us a great service setting up that trust.'

The lad smiled and it was a lovely smile too, unlike his niece's sneering, superior twists of the mouth. Marion always smiled *at* people, not with them, and definitely not because she was glad for their sake.

The three people moved on and Marion came to hide in the doorway of the next shop. 'Look, Uncle, they've gone into that sweet shop now. How about you follow them inside and buy a bar of chocolate? You might be able to hear something else. I can't do it, because Linda would recognise me.'

He shrugged and left her hiding in the doorway, moving briskly up the hill and into the sweet shop. He'd carry on eavesdropping because the group had caught his interest, but he wasn't sure whether he'd tell his niece everything he overheard, especially the poor woman's new name.

There only seemed to be one shop assistant and she apologised for keeping him waiting, so he smiled and said he wasn't in a hurry.

'Let's buy a box of chocolates for Amanda,' the older man said suddenly. 'I'll pay for it because I know you two are watching every single penny. She's doing a good job as our warden, isn't she?'

They didn't say anything else of great interest, though he found out the older man was called Matthew and the lad was Brett.

After they'd left, it didn't take Ron long to buy a packet of fancy chocolates for his niece and by the time he rejoined her, the trio were further along the street, looking at some toys and laughing together.

'Did you hear anything interesting?' Marion asked.

He hesitated.

'Aw, come on. Tell me.'

Oh, what the hell? She was his niece, after all, and she couldn't do much with the information when she went back home. When he told her what he'd overheard, she gaped at him.

'Linda's changed her name? No wonder Frank has been having trouble finding her this time. Why don't you follow them a bit further? See where these units are.'

'I know where they are: on the edge of Magnolia Park. I used to walk round it to look at progress on the buildings.' He was already regretting sharing the woman's new name. 'You really should leave that poor woman to get on with her life now.'

'If you thought that, why did you follow them into the shop?'

'Because I'm a nosy parker.'

'Oh well, we'll leave it at that.' She changed the subject and asked him if he wanted to go into the garden centre.

He shrugged. 'Not really. I'm getting a bit tired now.'

'I'm sorry if I've tired you out,' she said at once.

As they turned back towards his home, she said, 'I wonder if I should email Frank and tell him where Linda is now and her new name? I've a good mind to do that.'

'Stay out of it, Marion. "Always leave married couples to sort out their own affairs" is a good rule in life, because you never know the whole story of what goes on behind closed doors.'

'Sometimes you can be pretty certain of what's going on. We live next door to Frank, don't forget. Anyway, they weren't married, only living together. I don't know why she even took his name.'

'That's one thing you don't know for a start; even more reason to take my advice and stay out of it. They clearly weren't certain enough to commit to one another.'

'Oh, very well. I won't say anything.' But she crossed her fingers behind her back as she told that lie.

When they got back, Marion went to 'freshen up' and took her time about it. She couldn't help thinking about the situation. She liked Frank and always enjoyed chatting to him. She didn't agree with her uncle and felt quite sure he'd been the injured party in the break-up of that relationship. Pity he wanted that stupid female back, really.

At least, since the two of them had only been living together, he wouldn't have all the legal hassles to unpin. Or would he? She couldn't keep up with the way the law kept changing about that sort of thing. The house had already belonged to him when he and Linda met, or rather, the mortgage had, so surely he wouldn't have to sell it and share the proceeds with *her*.

Marion called down to her uncle that she'd not be long and closed her bedroom door. Her husband would be at work now but she sent an email to him about who they'd seen.

Dennis phoned her at bedtime to say he'd told Frank that she'd seen his ex and he said to tell her thank you. She was glad she'd done it, felt it had been the right thing to do, whatever her uncle said.

'He's well rid of her,' she said.

'I agree. But the poor fellow still seems besotted. He told me it made him feel sad to know she'd gone so far away. He still can't work out why she left him, even.'

She sighed. 'Well, we've done what we could to help him.'

When he put the phone down, Frank brandished a triumphant fist in the air. Of all the pieces of luck for Marion to have spotted his ex in Wiltshire. That information about where she was and her new name would surely be enough for him to find her.

He laughed out loud several times thinking about it. Dennis was a real prat, but a useful prat and had proved that yet again.

He bought himself a bottle of whisky that evening while he was out getting some fish and chips for tea. He felt like celebrating being on track again to find Linda. Only, she was calling herself Carla now according to Marion. Well, it'd make no difference. He'd still be able to find her now.

It was remarkable what a small world this could be. He'd hoped one of his friends would spot her, but had expected it to be online not in the flesh.

He poured out a big glass of whisky and sipped it appreciatively; it was such a rare treat. This meant he could go after her and teach her a lesson she'd never forget. But he intended to plan this carefully. He didn't want some interfering member of the plod brigade coming after him, as they had done in a previous encounter. It had been their fault that things had gone so wrong that time, not his.

The whisky bottle was a third empty by the end of the evening, an unusual indulgence for a man who usually watched what he put into his mouth in order to keep fit.

Frank groaned when he woke in the morning lying on the sofa with the hearth rug over him like a dusty-smelling blanket. He didn't usually drink so much. It could lead you to do stupid things, too much alcohol could, as well as always leaving him with a bad headache if he had more than two small drinks.

One of his first thoughts as he started planning his next move was that he must work out how to give himself an alibi. He had enough friends who'd swear he'd gone to the pub with them, but he needed to get hold of a vehicle as well, one that couldn't be traced to him. He'd use it to get across to Wiltshire and then change to another vehicle part of the way back, leave the last one in London and come back by train.

He didn't intend to risk being traced via a car hire firm or a CCTV camera. Those damned things were everywhere, infringing on people's privacy and civil liberties.

Over the next couple of days he came to the conclusion that he didn't really want Linda back again permanently. But he did need to teach her a lesson or he'd never feel right about the way they'd split up, with *her* leaving him. He prided himself on not letting anyone get the better of him. Never, ever. Especially not a woman.

He shouldn't leave it too long to go after her, either. He knew where she was now but she might move on at any time. What he hoped was that since she'd seen no sign of him for a while, she'd have started thinking she was safe and grown careless. He had to leave checking on that till he got there and found out what exactly she was doing and how best to terrify her. Ah, he'd really enjoy doing that.

He wondered if he'd lost his old skills. Could he still steal a car without being caught? He smiled as he thought about it. Of course he could. It'd add an extra layer of pleasure to do that, take him back to the days of his youth. But he'd better pinch an older car, one whose security systems were easier to manipulate, a much older car, in fact.

It was a good thing he worked his own hours. His head was thumping so badly this morning he didn't think he'd be able to concentrate and when he went to stand in the back garden, even sunlight this weak hurt his eyes. Four aspirins hadn't done more than reduce the headache a little.

He didn't have much tolerance for boozing, never had done. And though he loved the taste of it, he'd have to be more abstemious with the whisky. He'd vowed last time not to have more than two drinks and was annoyed with himself for breaking that vow.

Chapter Twenty-Two

After baking the cakes that had been ordered, Carla nodded happily, pleased with how well they'd turned out. She decided she could now make a pretty good fist of cooking professional-quality cakes even in a small oven like this one. She would put the word out and see what happened, placing cards in shop windows, a little advert in the local paper, that sort of thing.

As Matthew drove his neighbours home two days later after another visit to the shops, Brett asked hesitantly, 'Could I come and watch you do the cooking, Carla? I've never tried to make cakes from scratch but it doesn't sound hard. Is it expensive?'

'Some cakes are very easy to make and can be as cheap as bought cakes, simple ones anyway. Why don't I give you the ingredients and you can try making one under my supervision.'

'I can't ask you to give me the ingredients.'

'You didn't ask me, I volunteered. And I bought larger amounts so they didn't cost me as much as they would

you. I'll keep an eye on you this first time. You can dress
it up with icing and a layer of jam once you've let it cool
down.'

His face lit up with delight. 'Really?'

'If all goes well you can buy a simple cookery book
and make them for yourself whenever you feel like it.'

Matthew winked at her and raised one thumb from
the steering wheel in silent encouragement.

When they got back to the units, Matthew stopped
his car and couldn't hold back a yawn. 'I'm feeling rather
tired now so I'll leave you two cooks to get on with it. I'll
have a little lie-down and perhaps even a nap.'

'You're probably still getting over the last traces of
that virus that laid you out,' Carla said.

'Maybe. I definitely don't feel like my old self, not
completely anyway. But I do feel a little better each day,
so I reckon I'm on my way to good health again for sure.'

Rob waved to them from where he was getting out of
his car outside Amanda's cottage and came across to say
hello. 'I've just been putting up a new gate for a customer
of my uncle's. What have you lot been up to?'

'Shopping,' Brett said. 'Carla's going to make cakes
for people and she's going to teach me how to bake
them.'

'I used to earn my living baking cakes,' she said. 'Till
I had to run away.'

'You don't know a good recipe for rich fruit cake, do
you?' Rob asked.

She smiled as he licked his lips without realising it at

the mere thought of his favourite cake. 'Yes, of course I do.'

'Could you bake me one with lots of fruit in it?'

'Yes.'

'Then I hereby place an order. And the sooner the better. The mere thought of it makes my mouth water.'

'You don't have to support me, you know,' she said. 'And you haven't even asked the price.'

'I'm not *supporting* you. Well, I am in a way because I love cakes but my attempts so far to make a good fruit cake have turned out heavy and they also like to torment me by sinking into a squidgy mess in the middle.'

She chuckled and shook her head. 'It's not that hard. I usually boil up the mixed fruit in some port wine before I start. Gives it a lovely deep flavour. Unfortunately I haven't got any wine here.'

'I'll provide you with a bottle next time.'

He put his hands together in a pleading prayer-like gesture. 'I'd absolutely love a home-made fruit cake to eat with sharp Lancashire cheese like my grandma used to serve it. This is a firm order, whatever it costs.'

She did some mental calculations and hesitantly gave him a price for his cake. Matthew at once said he intended to pay her as well.

'If you don't take a fair amount of money, I'll shove more through your letter box,' he added. 'You need the money and I need regular cakes. Easy peasy. Both our problems solved.'

So she named a higher price and both men immediately

declared that she still wasn't asking enough.

'I've bought cakes from market sellers regularly since my wife died,' Matthew said, 'and none of them charged so little.'

'But you two are friends of mine, at least I hope you are now, so I don't want to charge you a lot, just enough to cover my costs.'

'We're definitely friends, except when we're customers. And your first cake was so delicious I want to order regularly. I won't dare do that at such a low price, though, because I'll feel to be taking advantage of your kindness. Believe me, a cake will not only taste nicer if I pay the right price and I know you're making a fair profit, but I'll not be afraid to order one again.'

'And I'll supply you with a bottle of cheap port to boil the fruit up in as well as paying a proper price,' Rob said.

She gave in. 'Just a cheap sort of port, then.'

'And the price?'

She named a higher sum.

'That's more like it. Add another ten per cent and we have a bargain.'

'Oh, very well. And . . . thank you.'

'You're on. And can I beg a cup of coffee from you to celebrate the prospect, do you think? I won't try to pay for that. Amanda only buys tea bags and cheapie instant coffee, and I haven't sorted out some decent coffee yet. That one you made me the other day was good.'

He was smiling at her very warmly. Carla's own smile faded and she gave him a long, level stare that was full of something akin to irritation.

Matthew took one look at her expression and stepped back, tugging Brett's arm and saying hastily, 'Give Brett a yell when you're ready to start baking, Carla. He can come and help me put my things away till then.'

She didn't try to stop them.

'I think they guessed I wanted to speak to you privately,' Rob said. 'I was wondering if you'd like to come out for a drink with me one evening.'

She took a deep breath. 'I have to say this straight out. If you're trying to chat me up, Rob, don't. I can't even think about that sort of thing without feeling sick. I'm still getting over Frank and the violence. I'm so glad I never married him. He did ask me but I said I'd rather wait to take a step as important as that. So we compromised on me taking his name.'

She paused then repeated, 'I'm definitely not ready for another relationship or even a date, not with anyone, however nice. I don't know whether I ever will be.'

He looked at her and sighed. 'Any time you change your mind, let me know. How about a mere friendship, then? You've started one with Matthew and Brett, after all, and I'm just as nice as they are.'

He pretended to flutter his eyelashes at her and she couldn't help smiling.

'You can't leave me out when we all live so close to one another, Carla.'

She hesitated, then nodded. She would have been attracted to him in other circumstances, but wasn't going to follow up on that now. She'd vowed not to get entangled with any other man romantically for a long time, if ever, and had meant it.

His expression was totally serious now. 'I think what's important for you at the moment is that you need a bodyguard more than a relationship. My mistake was to step in too soon with the latter. So, our friendship will serve the purpose of keeping me around. Just in case you need help.'

She sighed at this recurring need, but nodded agreement.

'You haven't heard anything from him, have you? That isn't what's making you more nervous than usual?'

'No. Things are going well, Rob. I've seen no sign of him. How could he possibly find out where I am? Or do you know something I don't?'

'If you mean, have I heard of a stranger in town answering to your description of your ex, no.'

She let out a relieved sigh.

'The trouble is, things might be going well now, but if this guy is as big and nasty as you've told us, I'm worried about your vulnerability should he find you. Amanda's worried too and, actually, so are the other guys.'

She looked at him in dismay. 'Am I such an object of pity?'

'It's nothing to do with pity. You're a friend and real friends look out for one another when there's trouble.'

She stared down at the ground, trying not to show how touched she was by this, then she said firmly, 'I didn't want to involve anyone else in my troubles, Rob. Friends shouldn't drag one another into dangerous situations and Frank can become very violent indeed when he gets angry. He'll be furiously angry with me at the moment, I'm sure, for daring to escape from him. He called it being masterful and said that was how men should treat women; I called the way he behaved bullying.'

She paused and added, as much for herself as for him, 'I still have to be ready to get away from here at the drop of a hat.'

'That's no way to live.'

'Yes. I've noticed. It definitely takes the edge off everything. But at least I'm still alive.'

'I strongly believe you shouldn't run away this time if he turns up. Just for your information, Carla, you should know that Matthew, Brett and I have already agreed that we'll keep an eye on you. For the time being you should stay near enough to one of us at all times so that we can step in if there's any trouble . . . whether you want us to intervene or not.'

'Didn't you hear what I said about him? He's dangerous. I can't ask you to risk yourselves, maybe even your lives. There have been times when I've thought he might kill me.'

He was startled. 'He's that bad?'

She nodded.

'That makes it even more important that you're not facing him on your own. And I can just about guarantee to come off best in any encounter. I've done self-defence courses and learnt to fight in different ways when I've lived in rough areas.'

'I don't care if you're the world champion of karate, or whatever other style of fighting you know, I still don't want to put you in danger. If there's any hint that he's found me, I shall definitely run away again. And I have to tell you that I feel sure he will find me one day.' She had to keep saying it to remind herself of how dangerous Frank was – and how she didn't want to involve her friends.

'So you're prepared to spend the rest of your life moving on at regular intervals, not having real friends or a family? *The rest of your life!*' Rob paused to let that sink in. 'Are you really going to let him do that to you?'

'What choice do I have?'

'You can stay here and let us help you fight.'

'He's vicious and surely you've noticed that I'm quite a small person.'

'I can be rather vicious too when dealing with bullies and thugs, and in case you haven't noticed, not only am I quite a big, tall guy but so is Brett.'

She stared at him, torn every which way, wanting to accept his help and friendship, but not wanting to put him and these lovely neighbours in danger.

Rob's voice grew soft and pleading, 'Carla, *please* don't give in to his bullying. Let us have a go at protecting you if he finds you. I don't think we'll let you down.'

Tears rose in her eyes. 'I've never met such kindness in my whole life. I could so easily make Essington my home.'

'Yes, it's rather captured me as well. I'm thinking of settling here permanently, which has surprised me, I must admit.'

She stared at him and he stared back at her. Then he smiled gently. 'To get back to our original topic of conversation, please make me a rich fruit cake. I'll buy the port this afternoon and drop it in.'

It was his turn to sigh and add, 'But we'll keep the cup of coffee for another time because I reckon you need to think very hard about your future. My desire to chat you up won't change but it can be kept till another time, a happier and safer time. Or I'll never speak of it again, if you prefer that. Your choice when the time comes. I've never tried to force myself on a woman in my whole life.'

She opened her mouth to protest then snapped it shut again because after giving her a quick nod he'd turned away and started walking back towards Amanda's cottage.

She didn't move, watching him till he'd gone inside it, feeling a deep regret as she admired his lithe body striding along.

Then she followed his example and went inside her own home, locking the door carefully behind her. The question he'd asked might have been written in words of fire on the wall, it was so vivid in her mind and seemed to be leading to other important questions.

Are you really going to let him do that to you?

Are you really going to keep on running for the rest of your life?

She went to stare out of the big window, feeling as if her very soul was aching to stay here near the beauty of the magnolia trees, and the even more wonderful beauty of friends like these.

The next question was inevitably: *Did she dare try to stay here?*

A chill ran through her and the doubts circled round again. Women were killed every week by crazy ex-partners. You heard about it in the news. You thought how sad it was. But you never expected to become one of the victims of such treatment.

What's more, her new friends couldn't be with her every minute of the day and night. No one could.

But oh, she wanted so much to stay here!

In the end, she pushed her worries aside and decided to start making the cakes. She went to summon Brett, who followed her back looking excited. That lifted her spirits.

She explained exactly why she was doing things and he listened intently, earnestly stirring his cake mix and then sneaking a taste on his fingertip as he put it into a greased baking tin.

When it was time to take it out of the oven, she summoned him back to join her.

His smile at the sight of a perfectly risen cake could have lit up a whole house at midnight. And for some weird reason that was what made the decision for her. She wasn't going to leave here. She was going to make a stand. She wanted to be able to smile freely again and have friends like these.

When she handed over the other cakes, she told her neighbours that she intended to stay.

Matthew said quietly, 'I think that's the right decision, my dear.'

Rob didn't smile, simply nodded and said, 'I know something about self-defence. You don't need to go online. I'll teach you a few tricks. You won't be able to beat a man much bigger than yourself, but if you can delay him, at the very least you'll give yourself time to scream for help. I'll teach the other two a few tricks at the same time. It never hurts to know how to protect yourself, even if you're a man and not expecting trouble.'

'Thank you.'

He fumbled in his pocket and paid her for the cake, then picked it up and sniffed it with an expression of sheer ecstasy on his face. 'I can't wait to cut myself a slice.'

'Do you have some cheese to eat with it?'

He rolled his eyes. 'Is there life without cheese? I have some mature Cheddar, which will be perfect, but next time I go to the shops I'll look out for some tangy Lancashire cheese in honour of my grandma.'

'Then I'll leave you to enjoy it. I must admit I'm an absolute cheese addict too.'

She'd made herself a small fruit cake and ate a slice slowly and with great relish to finish off her evening meal. With cheese, of course.

When she went to bed, she expected to lie awake worrying about her decision, but she slept better than she had for ages.

Chapter Twenty-Three

Someone knocked on the door the following morning and Brett opened it to find Amanda standing there with a very old man on crutches on one side of her and a young guy holding three paper carrier bags on the other. They were all smiling at him so he knew immediately that nothing was wrong.

Amanda took the initiative: 'Hi, Brett. This is Arthur Keevil, who was one of the founding members of our local residents' association, but has now stepped back from running it, leaving his daughter in charge.'

'But I'm still poking my nose into residents' affairs from time to time,' he said.

The old man had a lively boyish expression on his wrinkled face, which made Brett feel cheerful just to see it.

Amanda chuckled. 'We can't get rid of him. And this is Norris Thorson, great-grandson of Ben, another of our founding fathers, as I like to think of them. We'll take you to meet Ben another day.'

Arthur took over again. 'I still try to welcome newcomers to our valley whenever I can, Brett lad, and it's particularly good to see more younger people coming to settle here.' He flapped one hand towards the bags the young guy was holding. 'Give him one.'

'Yessir!' Norry held out one of the carrier bags and Brett took it automatically.

'Housewarming present,' Arthur explained. 'Chutney and jam made by my daughter, and mostly from produce grown on our own allotment. The chutney's best served with cheese.'

Brett didn't know what to say to this, felt a bit shy and only managed to stammer, 'Thank you, sir. That's, um, very kind of you. I shall enjoy them, I'm sure.' He'd never even tried home-made chutney. If it was as good as home-made cake, he'd have to get the recipe.

'I've brought young Norry along specially to meet you. Think of him as another welcoming present.'

Norry grinned and rolled his eyes but didn't protest as Arthur clapped him on the shoulder and said, 'This lad knows all the younger folk in this part of Essington, and he'll be able to introduce you to some of the less wrinkled citizens so that you can make a few new friends.'

Norry didn't seem at all upset by this, but chuckled and waved the hand not holding the carrier bags in a sort of salute. 'Nice to meet you, Brett, and feel free to call me Norry. Welcome to the valley.'

Something about the younger guy's face said that he

was a kind, friendly sort of person, not a bully, so Brett began to feel a bit happier. It'd be wonderful to know some younger people as well.

They seemed to be waiting for him to reply, so he said, 'Nice to meet you, too, Mr Keevil, Norry. Would you, um, like to come in and have a cup of tea?'

Amanda was standing by the side of them now and nodded vigorously to show her approval of his invitation. She was good at guiding his behaviour in various subtle ways, Brett was finding.

'I'll keep the offer in mind for another time,' Arthur said. 'I have to attend a meeting soon, and Amanda has kindly offered to drive me there. I'll leave Norry with you, though. He never says no to a cuppa.'

The younger chap grinned and flourished another of his mock bows. He was even taller than Brett and looked to be a few years older.

Arthur took a shuffling step backwards just as Carla came out of the first unit. She hesitated as if wondering whether to go back inside and Amanda quickly beckoned her across to join them.

'Arthur, Norris, this is Carla Hewitt, another of our tenants.'

The old man gave her hand a vigorous shake. 'Great to meet you, Carla. We've brought a housewarming gift for you.'

Norry held out a carrier bag and as she took it Arthur explained its contents for a second time.

'We'd heard that there were three people living in these

units now, so came prepared. Welcome to Essington St Mary.'

'The chutney will be lovely. Thank you.'

Norry turned back to Brett. 'Can one of you take the other bag and give it to the third newcomer? Matthew something or other, isn't it?'

'Matthew Woodley and, yes, I can do that.' Brett accepted the third carrier bag. 'He's having a little nap because he's just getting over a bad bout of pneumonia and gets a bit tired. I'm sure he'll be delighted with your gift.'

Amanda nudged Arthur. 'We have to leave now if we're to get you to your meeting on time. I'll see you later, Brett.'

He watched them get into her car, feeling sorry for the way the old man had to slowly ease his stiff body into the passenger seat, then he turned to Norry and gestured to his unit. 'Do come in. I'll put the kettle on.' He turned to invite Carla to join them but she'd already gone back into her unit.

'Do you mind?' Norry asked.

He looked at his guest in puzzlement. 'Mind what?'

'Me being thrust on you like this.'

'No, of course I don't. It'd be nice to meet some people closer to my own age.'

'I'm a bit older than you, though I'm not quite a wrinklie yet, but I know a lot of people in the valley. There's a café where us younger folk hang out. How about coming there with me now? I'll buy you something to drink, tea, coffee, soda or whatever, and introduce you to a few people.'

'Won't your friends mind having me dumped on them without warning?' he asked bluntly.

'On the contrary. It'll give them a chance to boast that they were among the first in the valley to meet you.'

'I'd love to come, then, but I have to warn you that I'm not very good at chatting to people I don't know.' Brett was already feeling a bit anxious about what could be an ordeal. He wasn't used to being a member of a group.

'Practice makes perfect. We heard about your glasses, by the way. Rotten luck being treated like that.'

Brett was astonished at how quickly that news had got round and it must have shown on his face.

Norry chuckled. 'You'll get used to it. Newcomers are always checked out and information about them passed round in various ways. My great-grandad isn't good at getting out and about in person these days, but he still finds things out nearly as quickly as I do. Now, it's only about a quarter of an hour's walk to the town centre if we cut along Hawthorn Close. How about we go to the café now and I'll come round to your house for a cup of tea with you some other time?'

'I'd really like that.' Brett switched off the kettle and caught sight of himself in the mirror. Thank goodness he had decent clothes to wear these days!

He appreciated the way Norry told him about the places they passed from a lad's point of view. He'd enjoy the display of blossoms on the trees in Hawthorn Close next spring. And he loved the tale of Arthur Keevil standing up to the bullies by chaining his wheelchair to the heritage-listed tree they were intending to cut down to make a parking space.

And then they reached the café, which was a happy, noisy space. He went in feeling nervous but soon found himself able to cope quite easily because all he needed to do most of the time was listen, smile or just nod at other times, then answer questions about himself honestly. To his relief no one asked awkward questions whose answers might have embarrassed him, and they didn't make snide remarks about his answers, either. They were just . . . interested in a newcomer.

When Norry said he had to go home and help his mother, Brett left as well because he'd promised to have lunch with Matthew.

'Do you remember the way home?' Norry asked.

'Yes, thank you. I'm good at remembering places.'

'OK. See you around, then. You've got my phone number.'

'Yes. And you've got mine. Thank you again for taking me to meet people this morning.'

'My pleasure. You did well, by the way. They liked you.'

Brett could feel himself flushing. He wasn't used to compliments and had now received several in the past few days. It was good to know that Norry thought he'd fitted in, too.

As he walked home, he stopped to buy a newspaper from the corner shop. His life was so much more enjoyable these days. He was looking forward to reading the news and some of the articles once he got back. He still marvelled each time he picked up a book or paper and read it easily.

Shortly after he got back to his unit, someone rang the doorbell. He opened it to see his friend and mentor and made Matthew a cup of tea as he told him everything he could remember about going to the café.

'Sounds like you did well, Brett lad. If you come round to my unit in half an hour, I'll have lunch on the table.'

'Are you sure?'

'Yes, of course.'

'Then I'll look forward to it. You're teaching me some good things to make for meals.'

It brought a lump to Matthew's throat to see a normal lad's expression on Brett's face. A big lump!

Chapter Twenty-Four

When Amanda came back from dropping Arthur in town, she watched from her cottage window as the two young men left together, using a pair of binoculars to get a better view. She had recently bought them and was going to keep them handy on the windowsill for keeping an eye on her little world. She was, after all, the official warden here.

Later she chatted to Rob over a cup of tea. 'The two youngsters left together. I hope they've gone to the café Arthur told me about.'

'Bound to have. Even I've heard of the place. I should think Brett will be well received there. I've never met anywhere like this valley for people spreading gossip quickly and they'll already know he's had a difficult life.'

'They've got me trained now to watch the world round here and share news as well,' Amanda said with a smile.

He grinned and indicated the binoculars sitting on the windowsill. 'Are those new? I don't remember seeing them before.'

'I decided that as warden I'm duty-bound to keep an eye on things.' She could feel her smile fade. 'Especially with one of our tenants in danger.'

'Yes. But remember, we three guys have already agreed to keep an eye on her.'

'I'd join in too if I saw her being attacked. Though if her ex does turn up, *you* can always arrest him, can't you?' She grinned at the shock on his face.

He didn't attempt to deny it. 'How did you find out?'

'That you're an undercover detective? Barney Murcott hinted at it when I was worrying to him about Carla being in danger.'

'Well, don't tell anyone else.'

'I won't. I bet Barney's not really your uncle either, is he?'

'No. I wish he were.'

'How long will you be based here, Rob?'

'For some time, I think. There are some investigations being carried out into certain matters which I will *not* tell you about or even hint at details of, and do not say anything if you guess – not if you value your life.'

She was startled. 'Is the situation that serious?'

'Yes. However, I will tell you that I'm also keeping an eye on a certain builder called Hotchkin, so if he keeps pestering you about selling this place to him or some unknown person plays dirty tricks on you, I'd appreciate you letting me know.'

'But he's not your main target?' she guessed.

He looked at her solemnly. 'No. And the main target

is too dangerous for you or your friends to get involved with in any way, so I repeat, back off. You're a small minnow in this pond, and they're huge sharks.'

'All right. Point taken. Barney hinted that there's something come up which I need to know about, though, possibly connected with Carla's stalker. Am I right?'

'Good old Barney. Very useful guy to know. He always keeps a watch for strangers in the valley, people who don't have an obvious reason to be here. Which is one of the reasons he got me dumped on him.' He hesitated then continued. 'I'm also keeping in touch with a team investigating the murder of a young woman in Bristol three years ago. It's not a high-priority case now, as they couldn't find her ex, who was the main suspect, and they've exhausted all avenues for the moment. Normally it'd have faded away quietly and their schedules had been filed with the other cases, but the victim was related to one of the team so they've never quite let it drop. Apart from anything else, he doesn't want anything similar to happen to other young women.'

'Good heavens! For an allegedly peaceful valley there's a lot going on behind the scenes.'

His expression was more solemn than usual. 'Bad things happen everywhere, Amanda, and more often than people living peaceful, honest lives usually realise. Anyway, the Bristol team think the chap whom they suspected but who disappeared, completely, has been sighted again. If so, he's changed his name and appearance so they're not positive of the ID. Unfortunately, they only have a couple of poor CCTV shots of him from back in the day.'

'So you're involved in this case as well now.'

'I was involved for part of the time back then and one of our major problems was that he was very skilful at avoiding being photographed, even by his then girlfriend.'

'How is this connected with us?'

'A guy came to this valley recently in a hire car, a guy who'd told the company he hired it from in London that he was going to Birmingham.'

Amanda shot him a quick surprised glance.

'Luckily for us this hire company puts tracers into all its vehicles, even the older, cheaper ones, and when their customer didn't go anywhere that he'd told them, they reported the incident to the police as a matter of course. The information was then passed on to the Bristol team.' He shrugged. 'News of this visitor has reached Murad and Vicki, so those two will be on the alert too from now on.'

'What does he look like?'

'In his late thirties, sporting a beard now.' He grinned. 'He may think that disguises him but it also makes it easier to doctor the photograph we do have, which gives us a closer resemblance to our suspect.'

She said in a flat, unhappy voice, 'You're talking about Carla's ex, aren't you?'

'Yeah. Could be, anyway. We're not 100 per cent certain but there's enough to make it worth me keeping an eye out for him coming here again. Also, I've been wondering whether perhaps she has a better photo of him? Only she's a bit wary of me.'

'She's wary of all men, for obvious reasons. Just ask her straight out.'

'Maybe I will. And remember, this information is to go no further.'

'Of course not. But if it is the same person then she's in even more danger than we'd thought. If I can be of assistance to you in any other way, don't hesitate to call on me.'

'There is one other thing I've been wondering about, actually. Can you persuade Carla to report the possibility of her stalker following her here to the local police?'

'I might be able to.'

'Or—' he frowned and said slowly, thinking aloud, 'better still, how about persuading her to speak to our two local detectives? They live nearby in Hawthorn Close.'

'I'll definitely try to persuade her to do that.'

'Murad and Vicki are very well thought of in the force. Before I came here I was told to contact them if I needed help or found anything worth reporting, but otherwise stay under cover. And you're right, they are very good at their job. It's my guess they're destined for higher things one day.'

'Have you made yourself known to them?'

'Not yet, no. I'd rather stay under the radar, so please

don't mention me to anyone. It's why I'm asking you to help.'

'I'll speak to Carla for you. And I can be very persuasive when I try.'

'Thank you. Now, I need to go up and work on your roof again.'

'Because it needs it, or because being up there gives you a bird's eye view of the district?'

'Both. I may as well make myself useful while I'm keeping my eye on what's going on in this part of town. We don't want any more leaks of either water or information, do we?' He winked at her and added, 'By the way, because I recognise that look – I have an aunt who also likes to speculate on who will end up with whom as a life partner – I'll tell you now that when all this is over, I'm thinking of retiring and setting up as a private investigator. I fancy settling down in the valley: home, wife, kids, the whole shebang.'

'And you'll welcome any chance to get to know Carla better as well.'

'Yes.'

'That doesn't surprise me in the slightest, Rob.'

He chuckled. 'I knew it. I'd appreciate you putting in a good word for me when the time comes.'

'Happy to do that.'

Amanda's chance to speak to Carla about her ex came the following morning, or rather she made an opportunity. She decided to offer her a lift to the supermarket as an excuse so drove round to the units before she started doing her own shopping.

Carla shook her head. 'I don't need to buy any more supplies at the moment, but thanks for the offer, Amanda. Another time.'

'Then just come out with me for a while and we'll have a chat somewhere peaceful. My car is nice and private and it'll do you good to get out and about a bit. You're spending far too much time inside your unit, you know.'

Carla stiffened. 'Why is it so important to do this? Is something wrong?'

She sounded so anxious that Amanda could have kicked herself for handling this awkwardly.

'The chat is just about your general safety, not about a specific threat. There's something I've thought of. But I really do think you should get out more. In fact, I'm thinking of buying a car for the temporary use of our tenants. Just a cheap little second-hand one. Would you use it if I did buy one?'

'Yes, I would, mostly for when I want to sell cakes at the market. I can't afford to buy myself a car yet but I need something to carry my stocks in.'

'And Matthew could use it to teach Brett to drive.'

'He'd love that.'

'I'll ask Parmi to look for one, then.'

'Good idea.' But Carla still looked wary.

'Let's drive up to the top of the hill. You haven't been up there yet, have you? I know a place with a rather lovely view and I can guarantee we'll not be interrupted there.'

Carla could see how determined their kind warden was, so gave in. 'I'll just lock up.'

There were only three other cars parked at the top of the hill and no sign of their owners, who were presumably off walking along one of the signposted trails that led out of the car park. And the views from one corner were indeed pretty.

Amanda stopped as far away as she could from the other vehicles and said bluntly, 'There. Let's just enjoy a few peaceful moments first.'

After a while she sighed and said, 'Now, I'm concerned about the best way to keep you safe.'

After a long pause, Carla said, 'So am I. I worry about that quite a bit.'

'I'm sure you do. I think you ought to inform the local police about your ex stalking you. That's been suggested before, hasn't it, and you did nothing about it?'

'Because I thought that might draw attention to me.'

'I'm not talking about the uniform branch this time but about our local detectives. They're a highly capable pair. What's more, Murad and Vicki share a house in Hawthorn Close, which is conveniently close to our units if you need to call for help. It'd be good for you to have them on your side.'

She shuddered. 'If you're taking it so seriously, perhaps I'd better get ready to flee again, in case my ex finds out where I am.'

'*No!*' It came out with more force than she'd intended.

'Carla, that's *not* why I told you and I definitely don't think you should do that. If he's so obsessive, he'll only come after you again, and if you move away you'll be somewhere without friends to help you, which could be even more dangerous than staying here.'

There was silence as Carla sat staring down at her lap, her hands twisting in and out of tangles of fingers and the fringed ends of her scarf.

A sudden fear of her companion fleeing again made Amanda say, 'There's something else these detectives want to ask you about, but we're not sure whether you can help them with the details.'

'What?'

'I think they'd rather tell you the details themselves. How about I arrange for them to come and visit you after dark tonight and they can explain the situation?'

'You've spoken to them about me already, haven't you, Amanda?'

'Only to give them the barest summary of your situation. I can guarantee they're not on the side of your ex, and you surely aren't going to complain about them keeping watch for strangers matching his description from now on?'

There was dead silence, so she said it bluntly and very emphatically: 'Carla, fleeing can only ever be a stop-gap measure if he's so determined to find you. I truly believe that getting the help of the people round here gives you the best chance of keeping safe and getting rid of him permanently.'

The sag of Carla's shoulders told her she'd made her point even before the younger woman said in a low voice, 'All right. I know that really. I'll speak to them.'

'And I'll speak to Parmi about finding us a car.'

Amanda dropped her passenger back at the units but continued to worry about her. The shadow of her ex seemed to be looming again, even before he'd found Carla. What sort of man was he to put this sort of fear into a woman? Well, he wasn't a real man, he was a piece of filth, as far as she was concerned.

This had to be settled once and for all or Carla would never have a decent life.

She seemed attracted to Rob and Amanda had seen her stare at him sadly sometimes as if she didn't dare follow up on that attraction. If Amanda could do anything to help the poor lass towards a normal life, she would.

She phoned Vicki and arranged a meeting with Carla, then passed on the information to the younger woman.

Chapter Twenty-Five

At eleven o'clock that night, two figures dressed in black, with hoods pulled down to shadow their faces, slipped around the edge of the park and tapped on Carla's sliding door.

Since Amanda had told her the exact time of their visit and the way they'd approach her unit, Carla was waiting inside, standing motionless in the shadows to the side of the big sliding door with the curtains half-open.

She saw them coming but did nothing till the two police officers had given the required pattern of taps on her window. Only then did she let them in, drawing the curtains fully before switching on one small lamp.

She studied their faces for a moment or two as if memorising their appearance, then said, 'Please sit down. Would you like a cup of coffee or tea?'

It was Murad who spoke. 'No, thank you, Carla. I'm Murad and this is Vicki. We're here primarily to gather information. We'd be grateful if you could tell us more about your former partner.'

'What exactly do you want to know?'

'Every single thing you can remember about him: when and how you met him, how he first approached you, when he started to treat you so badly, how seriously he beat you. And we'd like to record it, if you don't mind.'

'Oh. Well, I suppose it's necessary.' It made feel her sick, though, to think of her own stupidity.

'It is necessary. We need to catch him.'

'All right, then, you can record our conversation.'

Vicki said, 'Thank you. Now, tell us everything you can think of. You never know when a tiny detail will make all the difference, you see.'

Carla hated to relive her time with Frank, especially the later months when he'd grown stranger and quite terrifyingly violent. She felt herself flush with shame as she told them the details. The longer she was away from him, the less she could understand why she'd let him treat her like that, why she hadn't left him sooner.

Since then, however, she'd read about such men online and how they groomed women. Her own so-called relationship followed the same pattern as those others had.

When she'd finished her halting tale, prompted occasionally by questions from the officers, she sagged back on the sofa, wiped her eyes again and stared at them, feeling numb.

'Well?' she prompted as the silence continued. 'Does this show you anything more than you knew before?'

'It fits in with what we've heard. Corroborates certain information, let us say. And that's extremely important.'

Murad exchanged glances with his partner and at her slight nod, he continued, 'There is another case that some of our colleagues have been dealing with and I gather Amanda has already told you that a young woman was murdered in Bristol nearly three years ago. From what you've told us, it sounds as if it's worth checking out this Frank, as he now calls himself. It was a man who called himself Ernest who was involved then.'

Carla stared at him in shock. 'Frank had some books with the name Ernest inside, crossed out. He told me they'd belonged to a cousin of his who'd died.'

'Aah.'

Vicki took over. 'The man we're looking for has been eluding the police for years and has changed his name two or three times. Do you have any photos of your ex? He doesn't usually let anyone photograph him, so all we have are a few fuzzy CCTV images at present, but we live in hope.'

'Well, actually I do. I took one photo secretly when I first met him and he refused to have his photo taken with me. And another photo later. That second one has a clearer view of his face.' She hoped her early obsession with such a good-looking guy would pay off now.

'Could you get the photos for us?'

'Yes.' She went into the bedroom, took the shabby suitcase out of the built-in wardrobe and put it on the bed.

Vicki had come to stand in the doorway and watch her.

She had to fiddle around inside the torn lining at the bottom of the suitcase because the envelope had slipped into a corner.

'Have you kept that suitcase from when you were with him? If so, we'll need to check it for tracers.'

'No. I bought it from a charity shop after I'd left him.'

'Good. It's safe to use it, then.'

Carla looked down at the photos and shuddered. He didn't seem handsome now, more like a soul-less exhibit from Madame Tussaud's waxworks displays. 'I nearly threw them away because I hoped I'd never have to see his face again. Then I realised I'd better keep them, just in case I ever needed to report him to the police.'

'You should have reported him for violence earlier.'

'I didn't dare.' She shuddered as she passed across the images of Frank's face, beard-free in the earlier image and bearded in the second one.

'What was in the letter that was also in the envelope? Was it from him?'

She could feel herself flushing. 'No. I've written an explanation of what he was like towards the end, just in case—' She faltered, hating to say it.

'In case what? I can guess but I don't want to put words into your mouth.'

'In case he killed me. I've also put a copy of this letter on the laptop Amanda gave me.'

'I don't blame you for doing that but the letter will do more good in our hands now than hidden in your suitcase or on your laptop.' Vicki held out her hand in an imperative gesture.

Carla still hesitated for a moment, then sighed and passed the letter to her.

'Is that the man you were looking for?' she asked when Vicki didn't comment after reading the letter and studying the photos again.

'Let's see what my partner thinks.' She turned and went across the living area to show them both to Murad, who was standing near the window keeping an eye on the park by peeping occasionally round the edge of the curtain.

He secured the curtain again and came back to stand closer to the lamp, holding the photos near it and whistling softly. 'Looks like we've hit gold here, Vicki.'

She smiled at Carla. 'So there's your answer. Yes, it is him. Quite clearly him. Only, I didn't want to say anything till Murad had commented.'

He'd been reading the letter and now folded it up again and put it back in the envelope with the two photos, slipping them into an inside pocket of his jacket.

'What next?' Carla asked.

'We can believe what we want but we still have to prove beyond reasonable doubt that he committed the crimes,' Vicki said. 'His friends insisted he was with them the evening the other woman was killed, and they kept repeating the same details all through the investigations, however hard our colleagues pressed them. I'm sure the same friends will help him whenever he asks them, so we need to have some other, better proof of him committing a crime.'

Murad scowled and said in a harsh tone, 'Our colleagues in Bristol couldn't shake them at all.' He looked across at Carla. 'We always feel it's suspicious when everyone says exactly the same thing.'

She had a sick feeling in the pit of her stomach. 'Maybe I should change my name and get on the next plane to Australia!'

'Or maybe you should stay put and help us catch him once and for all, so that he doesn't hurt any other women,' Vicki said. 'You're among friends here, not fighting on your own. And two of those friends live right next door to you.'

That, of course, was the main thing keeping her here. 'What exactly should I do, then? I'm living on charity at the moment, not even paying rent. I'd rather get a job.'

'I don't know yet what to advise, other than to be ultra-careful what you do and where you go. Do nothing on your own. Stay near other people if you go out of the house. We'll get Mr Murcott's nephew to put better CCTV cameras around here and hope we'll catch your ex, snooping around, if it's him.'

Murad spoke more gently. 'You have several friends keeping an eye on you here, Carla. That's so important. How about sleeping in another unit as well, not your own? I'm sure the others wouldn't mind you occupying their spare bedrooms. And there are emergency alarm buttons in all these units, I gather.'

'Yes. One near the front door and one in the main bedroom.'

He waited and when she didn't say anything else, he pointed out quietly, 'You'd be completely on your own in Australia or in another town in England.'

She knew it, really, had also become increasingly sure since she'd come here that she didn't want to spend her life fleeing as if *she* were the criminal, not Frank. It was wonderful to have friends.

After she'd let the two detectives out, Carla locked the sliding door and drew the curtains tightly across it. Then she went round for the third time that evening, checking every single window and door to make sure they were all locked, which of course they still were.

She didn't sleep at all well, kept dozing then jerking suddenly awake to wonder whether she'd heard a human-created noise outside her bedroom window.

The safe feeling had gone even from this place now, but she'd accepted that it'd do no good to run away again . . . and again.

Somehow she must do whatever was necessary to keep herself safe here. She'd accept help, of course she would, but she couldn't rely on other people doing everything.

Rob had said he'd teach her a few self-defence tricks. She'd remind him of that, then practise the moves carefully. She'd not mind if Rob touched her casually as they did that, just as she didn't mind Brett or Matthew touching her. Rob wasn't Frank, was nothing like her ex.

She'd sworn never to trust another man, yet she'd met several here whom she knew she could trust absolutely, Rob included.

Who was she kidding? She wished Rob could do more than touch her casually – but only once things were safe again, when she wasn't always looking over her shoulder, worrying. Surely life could get back to normal again one day?

Why were things always so complicated? This was a terrible time to meet someone she fancied.

She thought about the situation in the units, then invited Matthew and Brett round for a coffee because it seemed only fair that they should be made fully aware of her background and therefore understand how dangerous Frank was likely to become if cornered. She wanted to be sure they could keep themselves safe.

She gave them a quick summary of what she'd been through before she came here, then told them what the two detectives had said. Finally, she showed them the photos of her ex on her computer, emailing copies to them afterwards.

'I'll help Brett print out a copy, in case we have to show the photo to anyone,' Matthew said. 'It'll be good practice for him at using his computer.'

Brett nodded. 'Thanks! And by the way, I never forget a face, Carla. He won't get past me, however carefully he's disguised.'

'Right. That's settled.' It was time to change the

subject so she turned to Brett. 'It's great to see how well you're coping with the glasses, Brett.'

He caressed them with his fingertips, without realising he was doing it, she guessed.

'They make such a huge difference. It's absolutely marvellous.'

But Matthew wasn't as easily distracted from her situation. 'Before we let the topic drop completely, Carla, I have something that might help you if there's ever a problem. This.' He handed her what looked like a fancy, old-fashioned fountain pen. She was surprised to find it much heavier than she'd expected.

'It was given to me for a joke, but actually, it's got a hidden squirter in it and I'll show you how to load it. But you should put neat vinegar into it, not water, once you've practised using it. That will sting the eyes, you see, if it catches anyone in the face. I don't think it'll cause any permanent injury but if you need to defend yourself, it might make an attacker yell in shock and jerk away. It's, um, not police approved.'

She gave him a wry smile. 'That's the last thing I'd care about if I was being attacked by Frank. Thank you.'

'You're welcome. I found it in my box of retrieved oddments from the fire in my house.'

It looked so harmless, just like a large, old-fashioned fountain pen, but she felt sure he was right about using vinegar.

'You'll need to practise using it so that you can pull it out and press the button very quickly every time you try.

Every single time. You can't afford to waste even a few seconds fumbling around when faced with an opponent attacking you with serious intent to harm.'

He showed her again exactly how it worked and how to fill it, watched her use it a few times, then said, 'Practise using it several times today just with water, then carry it with you at all times already loaded with vinegar, just in case.'

'I think it'll fit comfortably in the pocket of my jeans – yes, it does. Look.' She pulled it out as if she were a sheriff in a Western movie faced with a gun-carrying outlaw. 'It's easy to pull out, too.'

'Good. I'd appreciate you returning it to me when you no longer need it, because my cousin, who is now dead, gave it to me when we were lads so it has sentimental value. I take it out sometimes and think about him. It's one of the few things from my youth that were saved from the house fire.'

She was left feeling very unlike herself. She'd never got into fights of any sort, even as a child, let alone carried a weapon as an adult. And though it wasn't a proper weapon, it made her feel better just to have it within easy reach.

She glanced at Brett and the sight of him also gave her courage. If that lad could cope with such a difficult life for years on end, and then deal with huge changes, so could she.

She couldn't afford to be half-hearted about defending herself, though, if she was going to stop running away.

Knowing how determined her ex could be about getting his own back on someone, she had to face him boldly. Could she do that?

She must.

But surely Frank couldn't be a *murderer*?

Chapter Twenty-Six

Grant Woodley arrived in the UK from South America very early in the morning after a long and exhausting journey. He sighed with relief as the plane landed at Heathrow and, once through Customs, set about hiring a small car which would be inexpensive to run.

He tried contacting his uncle while he waited to take possession of the vehicle but got no response even though he was now back in what he thought of as 'digital civilisation' – in other words, places where the Internet was easy to access and other people were used to responding quickly to messages.

It was such a relief to be back and done with that project for good. It hadn't gone well at first, thanks to his associate's carelessness. That had given him a lot of sleepless nights and he'd worried about losing his uncle's money even more than about losing his own. He'd been stupidly optimistic when he went into it, hadn't checked that his associate, a charming but incompetent chap, would be able to do what he'd promised.

When Grant had found out how bad things were, he'd flown to Brazil and taken charge of the whole project himself, sacking the incompetent associate and hiring a local guide to take him to where the trial project was being conducted and help him for a while there.

He'd grown increasingly worried about not being able now to get in touch with his uncle but he hadn't dared leak a word online about the problems. If anyone had found out, the whole thing would probably have failed, and rapidly too. Business confidence was so important.

Hiring Miguel was one of the best decisions he'd ever taken. His guide quickly realised this was his chance to get rich and worked just as hard as Grant. Together they'd managed to turn things right round, at first working twenty-hour days and drinking a great deal of coffee.

Without Miguel he'd have lost everything and he'd made sure he rewarded him suitably and left him in charge with a share of the profits and glowing references for the new owners.

This had been Grant's first and would definitely be his last venture into even slightly risky investments, he'd vowed. Only, he'd desperately wanted to set up in business on his own in the UK, not in an area challenging the big companies but just settling into work that would keep him ticking along steadily in an interesting niche he'd spotted. But this time he'd take care to set things up properly and hope that technology wouldn't change the area too quickly.

He did *not* want partners or investors tugging the strings of power in stupid directions.

The thought of ruining his uncle had upset him more than anything else but thank goodness, he was now the bearer of good news. It looked like there was going to be a decent profit for both himself and his uncle, enough for him to make a modest start and his uncle to enjoy his retirement more fully.

Grant had a reasonable offer for his South American company, had insisted on a non-refundable deposit and now the big final payment was about to go through so he was nearly out of the woods.

When he stopped at a motorway services place for a quick break, he tried yet again to contact his uncle with a similar lack of response. He couldn't understand it. He was certain he had the correct phone number, was good at remembering things like that.

Surely his uncle Matthew hadn't dropped dead? The poor fellow had been very unhappy since his wife died suddenly, but he hadn't seemed ill, just grieving deeply. Indeed, he'd always looked younger than his age and had seemed to enjoy good health most of the time.

When he at last turned the corner into his uncle's street, Grant gasped in shock and braked to a halt so suddenly his car ran up on the verge and barely escaped hitting a nearby street tree.

His uncle's house wasn't there at the end of the circular cul-de-sac any longer. There was only an empty block. How could that have happened?

When he parked next to it, he saw the signs of burning in the battered remains of the garden round the now bare patch of ground. What had happened to his uncle, though?

Grant went to hammer on the door of the house next door but there was no answer, so he tried two more houses, also in vain. Most people would be at work now, he supposed.

To his relief someone further along the street was just backing out of their garage. He ran across and flagged the driver down, explaining who he was and asking if she knew anything about his uncle.

'His house burnt down a few weeks ago,' she said.

'Yes. I can see that. But what happened to my uncle?'

'He was already in hospital when it happened, pneumonia I think someone said. So he wasn't around to get hurt.'

'Do you know where he is now?'

''Fraid not.' She started to put her car window up and Grant stuck out his hand to stop it closing.

'Where are the next-door neighbours? Surely they must know more?'

'I heard they'd gone away for a few days. Sorry. I really don't know any details. We don't live in each other's pockets in this street so I only knew your uncle by sight.' She pushed Grant's arm off the window. 'Please take your hand away. I'm going to be late for work if I don't leave now.'

He stepped back and watched the window slide up.

Then, as the car started to roll down the drive, it stopped and the woman let the window down a little way again.

'You should contact the police. They were going to and fro for a while. Apparently it wasn't an accidental fire. So they may have your uncle's contact details. Oh, and now I come to think of it, his car was stolen while he was in hospital. I heard it was a total write-off. Now, I really must go.'

Grant tried to process this information in his mind as he watched the woman drive away, then he went back to the block of land. He saw something on the ground near the back and walked slowly across to find a sign saying *FOR SALE* which had been knocked down and lay half covered by the battered and singed remains of a bush.

He dragged the sign out, noted which estate agent was dealing with the sale then set the sign carefully upright again.

After that, he wrote a note to the next-door neighbours asking them if they had any contact details for his uncle. If they did, could they kindly tell him that his nephew had returned to England and needed to speak to him urgently. Or else email or text Grant the info about how to get in touch.

He gave them his own UK contact details even though these hadn't changed and his uncle ought to know them, then made his way towards the town centre. Surely someone at the local police station would know where his uncle was? Or someone at the estate agent's?

What he didn't understand was why his uncle had

shut down his former website, a very simple little one that Grant had set up for him. That wouldn't have been affected by the fire, after all.

And even if his uncle's phone had been destroyed, his phone account should surely have still been available on another device?

What the hell was going on?

Chapter Twenty-Seven

At the weekend, Frank decided to go and check out the small town where his ex had been seen by his neighbour's wife. She'd reported it immediately to her husband, who had got in touch with Frank.

Marion was much better trained as a wife than Linda had been – how the hell had a chap as weak as Dennis managed that?

Once Frank found his ex – Linda/Carla, or whatever she was calling herself now – he'd watch her for a time, then perhaps put a tracer on her car or in her handbag, or whatever he could access most easily.

He'd then go straight home again, work out how to deal with her, then return and capture her. He'd make her regret leaving him like that when he was helpless in hospital, by hell he would. It still made him furiously angry to think of her doing that.

He wasn't sure yet how far he would go in chastising her, but not as far as that other time. That had been a big mistake because the police had made a huge fuss about the incident and brought in extra resources. They'd nearly caught up with him, damn them. Good thing he'd had most of his spare money stashed away for emergencies.

No, he'd not allow himself to lose control of his temper to that extent again. He wasn't sure whether he was going to take his ex back. Could he ever trust her again? Well, first thing was to teach her a major lesson. No one treated him like that, especially not a woman.

He smiled at the mere thought of dealing with her. He was going to enjoy making her regret disobeying him.

He decided to tell his friends he was going up to Birmingham and wouldn't be able to meet them for drinks as usual. But he'd be obliged if they would tell anyone who asked that he had been with them at the pub.

John got straight back to him to say he'd not be doing that. Last time had been a special favour and if this was linked to Frank pursuing his ex, he should let her go and get a life.

Frank had a life and a good one, thank you very much. But it was a matter of pride not to let a small female like her get the better of him.

He went to London and hired a car, with the intention of leaving it in the car park in some big town, pinching another vehicle temporarily and going to Wiltshire in that to scout round this little town where she was hiding.

He was good at planning but needed to know the whole set-up first. He looked into the mirror and smirked. He doubted whether she'd recognise him if she passed him in the street these days. He now had greying hair, had gone for the distinguished older man look this time.

And she'd have no photos to show the police anyway. He grinned. He didn't do photos. As he always told people, he didn't need them because he already knew what he looked like.

It'd be better to go there mid-week, he decided in the end. There were usually more people out and about at weekends, getting in your way. He would take a quiet stroll round the town centre and find out exactly where this Magnolia Gardens was situated. If these charity units were brand new they should be easy enough to spot.

How the hell had his ex got away from his surveillance? he wondered for the umpteenth time. He'd had the tracers carefully placed and keyed into his computer so that he could keep watch on her, even when he'd been in hospital. And she wasn't good with digital stuff.

He'd also had a tracker in his own car so that it'd be easy enough to follow what she was doing with it on the rare occasions he allowed her to use it.

Once he came out of hospital, he'd found the exact location of that sleazy pub where she was working hard for peanut wages and kept an eye on things. Unfortunately, when he'd recovered enough to go after her, he'd run up against the owner of the place, who'd stepped in to rescue her.

He could have beaten the fellow to a pulp and taken her away by force there and then, only he hadn't wanted anyone to see him do that and identify him later. That was the trouble with being a big guy. People noticed you and remembered you.

Well, her getting away would only delay the inevitable. He'd make sure this new place would be her last taste ever of feeling free to do what she wanted. She'd be looking over her shoulder for the rest of her life once he'd finished with her because he definitely intended to keep her for a few days to have a bit of fun with her before he let her 'escape' again. He loved the way she screamed.

Once she'd settled elsewhere he'd remind her forcibly every once in a while that he was still in charge of her life. He was so looking forward to setting all that up. It would present a nice little challenge.

He used his satnav to find where this Magnolia Gardens place was situated. Easy to find the park in such a small town. When he got to Essington, he found a rather nice pub and enjoyed a leisurely meal. There was hardly anyone else dining there. Talk about sleepy hollow!

He finished his coffee and left, strolling up the main street. It wasn't hard to follow mentally the map he'd memorised from the Internet.

He turned off Larch Tree Lane at Hawthorn Close and followed a partly overgrown path that had been shown as a right of way. It led between the car park at an old folks' complex and the back gardens of a few scruffy houses.

He laughed when he saw Magnolia Gardens because it was such a small place, a perfect setting for *her*. No fine vistas here or restaurants overlooking manicured gardens, just a couple of untidy groups of shrubs and some lumpy old trees plonked in the middle. Even the path round the edge was only of messy gravel.

Dusk was falling now and the park was empty. He'd walk round the edge to get to the units from one side, so pulled out a beanie he'd brought to ensure anonymity, dragging it down to hide most of his face. He didn't like wearing it, because he hated to look scruffy, but it served its purpose and make him look like dozens of other older guys.

By the time Frank got to the units it was fully dark. A woman walking along the path towards him stared at him nervously and speeded up. When she'd gone, he strolled across to sit under the trees in the centre and study the units, wondering which of them *she* lived in. Unfortunately, all the occupants had drawn their curtains so he couldn't see who was inside each dwelling or even tell whether they were all four occupied.

When it was fully dark and there were no more people walking about the park, he went across to the units. He had to shove his way through some vegetation to get round the side to the parking area at the rear. He found only one vehicle there, outside Number 3.

He resigned himself to a boring stint keeping watch from behind a summer house and was rewarded a quarter of an hour later by an older guy coming out of Number 3 and knocking at the door to Number 1.

Bingo! Linda answered it and the two of them had a little chat before she shut the door. The old fellow got into his car and drove off. The vehicle might not be hers but Frank would bet she cadged lifts in it every now and then.

Was this really where she was living permanently instead of in the beautifully maintained executive residence he'd provided for her? Stupid bitch didn't know when she was well off!

He hung around for a tedious couple of hours and was rewarded by the sight of the old guy coming back. Frank watched carefully as he did a two-part unlocking procedure on his entrance door. Hmm, he'd better be careful not to trigger that in future.

He slipped behind the car and planted a tracer under it on principle, but he wasn't at all sure it'd do much good. That chap was too old for Linda, a real dodderer, so they were likely just neighbours.

She didn't seem to have a vehicle of her own and he doubted she'd be able to afford one for quite a while if she was poor enough to be given charity housing. Well, he'd creamed off most of her money from the bank, hadn't he? He grinned. What a gullible fool she had been to go into a joint account with him! Typical woman. Unable to reason out financial matters.

The tracer would no doubt yield some information during the next few days and in any case, Frank had found out what he needed to start making plans. He'd come back better equipped to grab her. He'd need some sort of van where she'd not be seen if he put her in the back, nicely tied up like a gift-wrapped parcel.

He chuckled at the thought of that. She'd be terrified, and with reason. Oh, he was going to enjoy himself so much when the time came.

He sighed as he got into the car he'd pinched and set off again to pick up his hire car. It seemed to take forever to get back to London and once there he had to spend the rest of the night in a multi-storey car park, dozing and uncomfortable in the hire car. He returned it as soon as the hire place was open, then caught the next train home and went to bed.

He'd done well. Very well. Had found out a lot. And she had no idea what was coming to her.

Pity he was being careful with the whisky or he'd have been planning another little celebration tonight. He couldn't understand why it upset him so much these days. He'd had no bad effects from it when he was younger.

Chapter Twenty-Eight

The following morning when Rob was checking the previous evening's CCTV he saw a recording of a shadowy figure moving around the car park behind the units. It was a man and a big fellow at that.

The intruder hadn't tried to break into a unit but he had spent a couple of hours hanging around. At one stage he'd fiddled around near one of the rear wheels of Matthew's car. What the hell had he been doing?

Rob didn't tell Matthew about the intruder yet. He wanted to find out whether the guy had planted some sort of tracer on it, which seemed the likeliest explanation.

He went across to the car and moved carefully round it, shining his torch under the arch of the wheel where the intruder had fiddled around. He crouched at an uncomfortable angle trying to see whether anything had been put there. And yes! There was a small bump under the wheel arch. It was new and shiny, not covered with mud like the nearby surfaces.

He used a torch and a small mirror to study it, not touching it, and yes, it was a tracer, the sort of two-way cheapie you could buy anywhere and link electronically to your computer before using it. It was probably being monitored so he didn't touch it let alone try to remove it.

Pity the intruder hadn't shown up more clearly on the CCTV shots. He'd covered his face and been wearing anonymous clothes: jeans and a hoodie. It could have been Carla's ex, though, probably was. She'd said he was a big man. This one had a beard.

How the hell had this Frank managed to find her again so quickly? No wonder she was scared of him. They'd better not underestimate his skills.

Rob decided to warn the others but he hoped they'd let him leave the tracer where it was, then the fellow wouldn't realise he'd been discovered. With a bit of luck, they'd catch him coming back.

He pored over the CCTV images, using magnifying techniques. The guy was tall and burly, with a greyish beard, one of those long fuzzy ones that dominated the face. Ugh. Rob had heard kids yell out 'fungus face' to fellows with beards like that and he thought it very apt.

If Amanda would allow it and the tenants didn't mind, he'd place some much better-quality hidden CCTV cameras around the units and see whether they could grab a more recognisable image of him. He was quite sure Murad and Vicki would be interested to see that.

If the guy was Carla's ex, he'd surely come back another night.

Would she still stay here if she thought he'd found her, though, or would she flee again?

He hoped she'd stay. And not just so that he could catch her prowler and free her from the rat. He'd really like to get to know her better. She had a shy, hesitant smile like a flower opening up. He was surprised at himself being so poetical. It wasn't something he was normally noted for. But she was . . . well, special somehow.

From their few conversations, it sounded to him as if she hadn't had much to smile at in the past year or two, and he didn't like the thought of her being hounded like this. It'd be good to give this nasty oik a good thumping, see how he liked a bit of his own medicine, Rob thought. He looked down to see his hands had curled into fists at that thought.

Unfortunately he had various problems in his working life preventing him from behaving normally after meeting a woman he fancied. He'd have to deal with them before he could move on from this sort of work and see how the two of them got on long-term.

He'd planned to change his life even before he met Carla because he'd had enough of dealing with criminals, some of them very violent, and wanted a more peaceful time. Trouble was, he didn't like to leave a job half done.

The ongoing hassles in her life needed sorting out quickly, if he was to keep her safe, so he'd bring Murad and Vicki in on that. He wasn't giving this sod even half a chance of murdering her as he had that other woman.

On that thought, he contacted the two detectives to tell them what had happened and this time he identified himself properly.

'Someone was prowling round the car park at the units last night.'

'What? Did you see who it was?'

'No.' He told them about the guy's size and beard, then sent them the actual footage. They said they'd go and check out the tracer visually too.

He sighed as he broke the connection. There were distinct disadvantages to doing undercover work but this was the worst time to be in the thick of a case.

He smiled ruefully. He was fairly sure she was as attracted to him as he was to her. You could usually tell that sort of thing.

When he saw signs that the others were up, Rob knocked on their doors and asked them to meet him at Amanda's cottage in fifteen minutes to discuss an intruder.

They were shocked to think someone had been spying on them and agreed at once.

Carla's first reaction after agreeing was to go and check her escape bag. She sat on the bed with it hugged in her arms for a couple of minutes before she forced herself to put it down and check her appearance.

The face that stared solemnly back at her from the mirror looked so frightened it surprised her and she felt ashamed. Nothing had happened yet! Was she such a coward now that she was afraid of shadows? She stiffened and straightened up. She had to find out what was going on and face up to it this time, not flee like a helpless, terrified child.

She glanced at her watch and stood up, locking up carefully behind her. She would have been the last to get there except that Brett had been waiting outside for her.

'I thought I'd walk across with you to the cottage, Carla.'

How did he know she'd welcome his support? Young as he was, he was a wonderful person. She wished he was her brother or cousin, that they had some sort of real family connection. She'd be so proud to be related to him.

When he fell into place beside her and winked at her, there was something just plain *decent* about him that she felt better at once.

As they started to walk slowly across the garden, he started telling her about a book he was reading, a whodunit. It was lovely to see how happy it made him to be able to read a story easily.

He stopped moving and gave her an anxious look. 'I hope you don't mind but I wanted to ask you something before we join the others: am I wasting my time reading books like that? Only, it's really exciting and I think I know who the murderer is. Ought I only to be reading the sort of books people call classics, so that I can catch up on my education?'

'I doubt it matters much what you read as long as you read something. I heard Amanda say that you need to become more skilled at taking in written information of all sorts.' She grimaced and couldn't help adding, 'And actually, Brett, I didn't enjoy the classics I had to read at school nearly as much as I enjoy detective stories or family stories, which are what I mostly choose to read now. I like to see happy endings and the two Dickens stories we read at school were utterly miserable. In one of them the hero got guillotined. That gave me nightmares for a few weeks.'

'I'm glad you said that. I read the beginning of a Dickens book online and it didn't tempt me at all. Life is too short to be miserable on purpose, don't you think?'

She felt it only fair to say, 'I agree with you. But some people do actually enjoy the classics.'

He grinned and started walking again. 'I don't think I'm going to be one of them.'

She chuckled as he gestured to her to lead the way into the cottage. 'That's how I feel too, Brett.'

'Thanks for your advice.'

The warden's cottage always seemed very welcoming and today was no different. She felt her anxiety subside a little the minute she walked inside.

They were the last to arrive and as soon as they'd sat down, Amanda gestured to Rob to start. He looked so solemn that Carla knew something bad must have happened even before he started speaking and anxiety began churning in her stomach again.

He was wearing his working overalls as usual but he had a serious expression and an air of authority today. He told them about the prowler he'd seen the previous night and the tracer that the guy had left on Matthew's car.

'I hope you took it straight off again,' Matthew said at once.

'I didn't but if you want me to, I will. The trouble is, Matthew, if I destroy it, he'll know. I'm assuming this was your stalker, Carla.'

Everyone turned to stare at her and she couldn't for the life of her think what to say or do. Part of her wanted to set off running this very minute and not stop until she was as far away from here as she could get.

Another part of her wanted to stay here with these people who already felt like true friends. It had been ages since she'd had people to turn to, people she trusted. Frank had seen to that and made such a big fuss about finding a lovely house that she hadn't realised till they'd moved into it that they were now quite a long way away from everyone she knew.

She realised that Rob had stopped talking and was looking at her as if he understood exactly how she was feeling.

'You all right, Carla?'

'Yes. Sorry. Go on.'

He continued speaking in that deep, gentle voice she loved. 'The police who dealt with that earlier case are still very keen to find the man who killed the poor woman a few years ago in Bristol so that he can't hurt anyone else. It was . . . a rather nasty crime.'

He looked at Matthew, who was frowning now, as if still worrying what to do.

'You're sure that if we leave the tracer on my car we'll get a warning if this sod comes back, Rob?'

'Very sure once I've added a gadget or two of my own to the parking area.'

'And you'll be nearby all the time until it's sorted out?' Carla asked.

'Near enough to get back in a couple of minutes,' Rob said. 'How do you feel about that, Carla? You are his prime target, after all.'

They all turned to look at her and she told them the truth. 'I'm torn every which way.'

'The bottom line is that Carla should not go anywhere unless there are people around or one of us is with her,' Rob said. 'She's definitely in danger.'

Matthew nodded. 'I agree. We'll try not to leave her on her own but I'm afraid Brett has a couple of appointments booked, today and tomorrow. Important ones that we can't miss.'

'I can simply stay at home if everyone is going out,' she said.

Rob gave her an approving glance then turned to Brett. 'Do you want to help me install my gadgets now?'

He beamed at Rob. 'I'd love to.'

That lad was like a sponge, Carla thought. Absolutely soaking up information and skills of all sorts.

And she was like a limp lettuce. She had to pull herself together.

Chapter Twenty-Nine

Grant wrote an urgent message to his uncle's next-door neighbours and shoved it through their letter box. He then went to the nearest police station, trying to find out who had dealt with his uncle and the arson case.

The desk sergeant wasn't aware of the details, having been away on holiday, like a lot of people at this time of year. But after Grant had produced his passport and driving license as proof of who he was, the sergeant found a constable who remembered the case clearly and was able to give them the name of the hospital to which Grant's uncle had been taken.

He tried phoning them but they told him frostily that they never gave out patient information over the phone and he should bring irrefutable photo ID with him and call at the hospital in person if he wished to pursue this matter.

He groaned in frustration as he put the phone down but slipped his passport and driving license into his inner pocket before enduring an hour's drive along busy roads to the hospital.

After nearly half an hour of waiting around, he was allowed to prove who he was once again and was then informed that Mr Woodley had been sent to a rehab unit, and yes, Grant would need to front up there in person as well, with the same sort of ID. Talk about being given the run-around!

'Can't you confirm who I am if I phone them now?'

'I'm afraid that's against our rules, sir.'

Grant walked outside, wondering whether to abandon the hunt, for today at least, but decided to give it one more chance before he found somewhere to spend the night.

He was glad he'd done that because the rehab people did know where his uncle had been taken.

The person he spoke to would only give him a phone number and first name, though, refusing point blank to give him the actual address. Luckily for him, she was called out of the office in the middle of their conversation. He could hear her talking to someone outside, so seized the moment to go to her desk and check the file she'd been consulting.

He scribbled down the name of this trust and the address of the units they were providing for people in temporary trouble about accommodation and was back in his seat before the woman returned. It was a good thing he had done that because she continued to refuse point blank to give him any more details.

Given that he'd provided identification, this was a level of so-called security he found as ridiculous as it was unnecessary and so he told her before striding out.

Soon after he settled in a modest motel, he received a phone call from the lawyer handling the transfer of funds from the sale of his business venture.

'The sale has gone through, Mr Woodley, and the money has been paid into your bank account.'

'Does that mean I can now access it?'

'I'm afraid not but it is sitting there and will be cleared and available in three working days.'

Nothing, it seemed, could be done in a hurry.

He found a takeaway Indian restaurant nearby and since he was feeling exhausted, he brought a meal back to his motel room. It was excellent, which cheered him up a bit.

As soon as he'd finished eating, he got ready for bed and if that wasn't good for the digestion, too bad. He lay for a moment looking round the cramped little space and sighed. He wasn't looking forward to spending nearly a week here.

He'd thought carefully about the situation and could only conclude that his uncle must have thought Grant had cheated him out of his money so had cut off all avenues of communication.

As if he'd try to cheat anyone!

But he had behaved stupidly and had nearly lost his uncle's investment, so he did feel guilty. Surely the amount of money he had earned for them both would make up for all the problems and misunderstandings. He just wished he'd been there to help Matthew when the house got burnt down.

As Grant tried in vain to get comfortable in the lumpy bed, he sighed. He was itching to get into his own home, but couldn't do that until the tenants had left it. Fortunately these were short-term tenants on one week's notice, in return for which he'd reduced the rent, but he still had several days to wait before he could get his home back.

Oh, to hell with caution! He was desperate to see his uncle and set the record straight about why he'd been incommunicado. He was going to use his waiting time to drive to Wiltshire, find these units and explain the situation to his uncle in person.

That evening Matthew invited everyone round for a drink and asked Carla if she'd like to spend the night in his small spare bedroom.

She declined, not wanting to inconvenience anyone. 'Thank you, but I'll be all right in my own place. After all, I can call for help if necessary or ring the alarm.' She looked at her neighbour and added, 'And you shouldn't go rushing out if you think you hear someone prowling around, Matthew. You're past fighting age and my ex is a big bully of a fellow.'

He sighed. 'I don't always feel old, especially when I see someone in trouble. But I must admit I have no experience of actual physical fighting.'

Rob clapped him on the shoulder. 'She's right, you know. Leave it to me. I'll be keeping watch from just across the garden during the daytime and I waken very quickly if there's trouble at night, believe me. I don't think any of you should come rushing out. Murad and Vicki will be available to help me, if necessary, and they're only just across the park from here on Hawthorn Close. Let's all put them on speed dial on our phones.'

Though they did that, Carla still felt vulnerable, but the night passed, she got some intermittent sleep and there was no sign of a prowler.

She knew Frank would be coming after her at some stage, though she didn't say that. She was planning to take each day as it came from now on. And to keep a very careful watch on the world around her.

As long as she stayed near other people, she'd be all right, surely?

The next morning, Matthew had to take Brett for another check-up at the optometrist's. He said they'd only be an hour or so, and Carla told them she'd stay home and not answer the door to any strangers.

But the hour passed and there was no sign of them returning and after she'd fiddled around for another half hour, she was feeling so twitchy, she decided she needed some fresh air as well as fresh milk. When she looked out there were several groups of people walking about in the park, so she decided it'd be safe to go across it and along Hawthorn Close to the little corner shop on Larch Tree Lane.

She set off, nodding greetings to others whether she knew them or not and enjoying the fresh air hugely.

But just as she was about to stroll along the narrow snicket that led to Hawthorn Close, someone whistled nearby, a type of whistle she recognised: Frank. She stopped dead, her stomach lurching with fear, and looked sideways, barely stopping herself from screaming.

He was there. Frank. She recognised him at once in spite of the beard. He was standing further along the perimeter path of the park and even as she watched, he began strolling towards her, smiling, confident . . . terrifying.

And suddenly there didn't seem to be any people nearby, except for a few moving away towards the far side of the park. She didn't hesitate but ran along the snicket, glancing over her shoulder as she got to the end. To her relief a man came towards her and walked along it.

There was no sign of Frank at the far end now. But she'd definitely seen him. She hadn't been imagining that. He'd be waiting for the man to go past. What was he planning to do then?

And today of all days there was no one else turning in to Hawthorn Close. What was she going to do? She'd not dare go back along the snicket because *he* would be waiting for her at the end in the park, she was sure. She'd have to make for Larch Tree Lane. He couldn't hurt her with people nearby and there were bound to be some.

As she hurried along the street, she suddenly remembered that the two detectives were renting a house there and paused to glance back towards the snicket before turning in at their gate.

There had been no further sign of Frank, just the man walking away across the park. Had she been mistaken? No, definitely not. She'd recognise her ex anywhere, even semi-bald and with grey hair. Ugh, he'd looked like a much older, uglier version of himself, more like a monster from a horror film. How had she ever thought him attractive? Or had he grown uglier looking as he became more unhinged?

She went round to the back door of the detectives' house and hammered on it, waited a few moments then hammered again. But there was no response.

Oh dear, this was a mistake. They weren't in. What was she going to do? She couldn't stay here at the back of the house. She'd be far more vulnerable if Frank caught her on her own.

Then she heard footsteps coming along the side of the house towards her and froze. Too late! She clapped one hand to her mouth to stop herself screaming in terror and made sure she could reach the joke pen. It'd do no good to scream. There had been no one in the street to hear her.

She couldn't help remembering how, towards the end of the time they'd lived together, Frank had enjoyed hurting her, muffling her screams with one of his big, strong hands.

That had been one of the increasingly violent actions that had made her pluck up the courage to flee as soon as she got the chance, even if she lost all she owned by doing it.

She bent to snatch up a fancy rock from the edge of a flower bed and pressed her back against the wall, hiding the hand with the rock in it behind her and keeping the other hand on the mock pen.

And then Rob walked round the corner.

'Rob!' She felt dizzy with relief, dropped the makeshift weapon and flung herself into his arms, shuddering and clutching him. 'He's here. Frank's here. I just saw him in the park.'

Rob pulled her close and simply held her till she started to calm down a little, making shushing noises. Then he said quietly, 'Come and sit on this bench and tell me exactly what's happened. Has he hurt you already?'

She sat next to him, grateful for the arm round her shoulders and the hand still holding hers. Not only the strength of them but the gentleness too. There'd be no bruises after he'd held her close, she was quite sure.

He had to repeat his question before she could start speaking. 'What's the matter, Carla? Have you been attacked?'

'No. But I saw him in the park. And . . . and he smiled. Such a gloating smile.'

'Are you sure it was Frank?'

'Utterly certain, in spite of the beard. He can't hide his eyes, and his hair grows in a funny twist to one side of his forehead.' She sucked in a sobbing breath and continued, 'He was standing in the park, watching me and smiling like' – she couldn't hold back another shudder – 'a predator about to pounce and tear his prey to shreds. When he started moving towards me I ran, but luckily another man walked into the snicket.' Then she looked at him and frowned. 'Where did you come from?'

'I saw you from Amanda's roof. You were walking across the park on your own and most other people were moving away from you. I knew Matthew and Brett hadn't come back from the optometrist's, because the car wasn't there, so I got down quickly and came after you.'

'Thank goodness you did.' Another violent shudder racked her.

'Did he threaten you?'

'Not exactly. He just – smiled and started walking slowly towards me.' She grew angry at herself. 'How could I have been so stupid as to go out on my own? Only, I get so ashamed of needing help. I want to be an independent person again. And I needed fresh milk. I thought I'd be all right because there were quite a few people walking about in the park. And it's only a short way along the snicket to get to Hawthorn Close, then to that little corner shop just down Larch Tree Lane.'

He stared into space for a moment or two and before he could speak again, they heard a sound inside the house and saw Murad standing near the window. He was filling the kettle in the kitchen.

When he saw them, he looked surprised and set the kettle down to come hurrying out of the back door. 'Is something wrong?'

Carla explained what had happened.

Vicki had joined them and heard the tale as well. 'You

know what,' she said slowly, 'I'm tempted to set a trap for him.'

'What do you mean?' Murad asked.

'Well, there are three of us as well as Carla. We could position ourselves carefully. If this guy is still around and she starts walking slowly along Hawthorn Close towards the main road on her own, he might be tempted to grab her.'

'No!' Rob said at once. 'We're not setting her up to be attacked.'

Vicki ignored that. 'I could go along the little path behind the back gardens and wait at the Larch Tree Lane end of the street for her. It's not a long street. Murad could walk out via the next-door neighbour's path and hide behind the hedge, then move in behind your ex after he's passed, and Rob could simply walk across the street towards the apartment complex on the other side as if he's heading there.'

She paused, then asked, 'You did say that Frank hasn't seen Murad, didn't you, Carla? Then you could walk out of our garden and stroll slowly along towards the lane, giving Frank time to get closer.'

'No!' Rob said again. 'It's too risky.'

Carla took a deep breath. 'I don't agree. I think it's a good idea. I'm desperate to stop him once and for all. And there will be three of you to protect me this time.'

Rob stared at her in shock.

'I can't go on like this, Rob, afraid to go out, afraid almost to breathe, in case he pounces. If he grabbed me and I screamed for help, you could arrest him and charge him with attacking me, surely? Then you could look into that other stuff from the past, see if you can find something more serious to accuse him of.'

'If the police had some evidence for that previous crime, they'd have pounced on him before now, surely?' Rob said.

'They did find some DNA,' Vicki said. 'But he got away and couldn't be found. If we got hold of him now, we could check his DNA. If there's a match to the traces of DNA on the dead woman, that's him done for.'

Carla gathered all her courage together. 'Let's do it.'

Rob still hesitated. 'Are you sure?'

'I'd give anything to be free of him. I've been living in fear for several months now, and before that living *with* fear till I managed to get away. I need it to stop.'

'He might not be hanging around there now,' Murad said quietly.

Rob relaxed a little. 'He probably won't be.'

'Let's do it quickly, then, in case he is still around,' Carla said.

Rob gave her hand a squeeze. 'You're a brave woman.'

'Being a cowardly one has got me nowhere, has it?'

'I'll go round the back and be waiting for you at the main road end of this street,' Vicki said.

Murad nodded. 'I'll go into the neighbour's garden and wait there till he passes.'

'And I'll walk across towards the other side of Hawthorn Close. I can duck behind a parked car or hide in the grounds of the retirement complex,' Rob said.

The two women looked at one another.

'I think you're right to do this, though we'll probably get reprimanded for putting you at risk.'

'I'll tell them I insisted on doing it if you get into trouble.'

Vicki moved towards the rear of the garden and let herself out into the little path that ran behind the houses.

Carla took two or three deep breaths then turned to go round the house and face her worst nightmare. Face it, not run away like a timid sheep!

'Pause at the garden gate and look around as if checking that he's not nearby,' Murad said. 'Then move slowly towards the lane. That'll give us two men time to get in place.'

'All right.'

As she walked along the side of the house, she suddenly remembered the joke pen full of vinegar. It was still in her pocket and might not be any use but it'd feel reassuring to hold it. So she took it out as she walked, moving it into the correct position for rapid use as she concealed it in her hand.

She wished she didn't have to do this. No, she didn't wish that exactly. What she desperately wanted was for their trap to succeed and free her from *him* once and for all.

She looked round, frowning. There suddenly seemed to be more people on the street. Was that good or bad?

* * *

When the man had walked into the park, Frank went partway along the thicket and waited behind a large shrub at one side. This natural look along one edge was very helpful. When a woman came along it from the park and hesitated, looking at him suspiciously, he glanced at his watch and said in a conversational voice, 'She's late.'

She didn't answer, just gave him a disbelieving look and speeded past him into the street.

Ugly old cow! he thought and crouched down behind the foliage of the shrub again, putting his hands into position as if tying a shoelace. He waited, keeping a careful watch on the garden in the street into which he'd seen Linda/Carla disappear before he'd had to duck back into the park. Did she have friends there or was she just hiding?

She probably knew the people in that house. It was taking longer than he'd expected for her to come out. Had she found refuge there? There had been no sign of movement in the house or garden.

A man was coming along the snicket now, slowing down to stare at him suspiciously so he felt it necessary to pat his shoelace, then stand up and start following him back towards the park. When he went out into the park, Frank paused, waited a moment then turned round and walked back to Hawthorn Close.

He saw no sign of her but she hadn't had time to come out of the garden and leave the street, he was sure. Even if she'd climbed into the back garden of another house, he'd still see her come back into the street.

Then, just as he was wondering if he'd missed her, he saw her come out of the same house so he ducked behind a bush again.

She stopped at the gate, peering along the street, first one way and then the other. She looked terrified. Nice to see that.

He smiled as he saw her take a deep breath before leaving the garden and moving out on the pavement, standing for a moment or two beneath one of those messy trees. Her face was registering sheer terror. Oh, he was going to enjoy this so much. If he took hold of her arm, she'd start trembling and be unable to speak. It had happened before. Terror did that to some people, as she'd already proved.

He laughed softly. He could always kiss her if she tried to scream for help. And hold her still as he did it, acting like an impatient lover.

Carla could see no sign of Frank. Had he given up and gone away for the time being? She didn't know whether to hope he had or to hope that he was still around while she had three people guarding her.

No, she definitely hoped he'd still be there. She had to get this finished.

She walked slowly along the street, forcing herself to pause and sniff a late-flowering shrub in the next garden. There were quite a few people around now, thank goodness, including a mother with a pram and a small child skipping along next to her.

And then Carla looked back again and froze as she saw Frank come out of the snicket and stroll towards her with *that* smile on his face. He was only a few houses away.

To her utter relief, she saw Rob come out from the garden of the retirement centre and start to cross the road towards her, staying slightly behind Frank.

Then a van turned in to the street just as the small child ran out onto the road chasing his ball. He bent to pick it up and the driver of the van, which was approaching quite fast, didn't even seem to notice him till the last minute.

The mother screamed and yelled, 'Dean! Come back this minute!' but the child took no notice. She shoved her pushchair into a woman's hands or it'd have rolled towards the street and turned to run towards her son.

She'd still have been too late if Rob hadn't changed direction to jump out onto the road and grab the little boy, hauling him back onto the pavement and barely saving him from being under the wheels of the van.

The driver screeched to a halt and the little boy struggled to get away, calling for his mother.

Other people who'd been going to try to grab the child crowded round, congratulating Rob.

At that moment someone grabbed Carla's arm and she looked sideways as her ex loomed above her and his fingers dug into the soft flesh of her upper arm.

She couldn't move for sheer panic, especially when he smiled that wolf's smile that said he was planning to hurt her and was enjoying her fear already.

When she heard running footsteps behind them, however, it broke the spell and jerked her out of her terror. Luckily the joke pen was in her free hand and she squirted the vinegar it contained at his eyes.

He yelled in shock and pain as the vinegar hit them and his hand slackened on her arm enough for her to drag it away and start running away from him up the street, yelling for help. Only there was no one to help her, because the people who had been nearby were still clustered round the child, who was wailing at the top of his voice. She couldn't see any sign of Vicki at the main road end, unless she was behind a group of people now standing chatting to one side.

A glance backwards showed Rob trying to push his way through the group, but it all seemed to be happening in slow motion and in spite of his pain, Frank caught hold of her again and tried to drag her back along towards the park.

'You'll pay for that, you bitch!' He swiped at his stinging eyes with the back of his free hand.

To her shuddering relief she saw Murad step round some women and move towards them.

'Police. Halt!' he called.

Again Frank let go of her with one hand, blinking furiously as he pulled something out of his pocket. The object flashed in the sun and Murad suddenly stumbled back, clutching his left arm. To her horror she saw the hilt of a knife sticking out of his upper arm and blood welled out between his fingers.

A passer-by watched in horror and jerked back away from them.

She tried to slow Frank down, wanting to give Rob a chance to catch him, but as usual he was too strong for her.

Then Vicki appeared beside them, yelling, 'You're under—!'

Before she could finish Frank punched her on the jaw hard enough to make her stumble backwards, trip over the edge of the footpath and fall.

He'd always moved quickly and before Vicki could get up, he let go of Carla's arm and began running towards Larch Tree Lane, running fast, still clearly as fit as he'd always claimed to be.

'I'll catch you another time, *darling*!' he yelled.

Carla moved to support Murad and they could only watch as Frank reached the end of the street.

They'd failed.

And he would come after her again. She knew he would. He always did.

Chapter Thirty

Frank reached the end of the street several yards ahead of Rob, who'd now got away from the group of people. Vicki jumped to her feet, threw an agonised glance at Murad and yelled, 'Someone call an ambulance and the police!'

A man detached himself from the group and took out his phone, waving one hand to show he was on to it.

The child had been restored to his mother, who was apologising profusely to the driver of the van.

The group of people were moving apart, about to get on with their lives till they saw the other crisis between them and the end of the street.

Vicki ran after Rob, upset at how wrong this had all gone, most upset of all about Murad, who was now being given first aid by a woman. She'd taken over in a way that said she knew what she was doing, thank goodness.

Frank speeded up, almost at the end of the street now and still rubbing his smarting eyes with his right hand, trying to clear his vision. He'd get away, he was sure, because he'd left his car parked just round the corner, unlocked and ready for him to jump into.

Then an old woman got in his way and he shoved her aside yelling angrily, but he didn't realise how close to the lane that had left him and his next steps took him right out onto the roadway itself just as a bus chugging down the hill began to gather speed and drive across the end of Hawthorn Close.

The driver yelled in horror and stamped hard on the brakes as a man ran out in front of his vehicle. But he couldn't stop in time and the man was knocked down and thrown underneath the front of the bus.

Rob reached the end of the street and stopped in disbelief as Frank ran into the path of the bus. He let out a yell that cut off abruptly as he vanished from sight.

He was dragged downwards beneath the huge vehicle and it was several yards before the bus came to a halt. There was no sign of Frank at the front of it now.

People who'd been walking along Larch Tree Lane stayed back but kept watching.

'He's a goner,' an old man muttered. 'Underneath it now, he is.'

'He just ran straight out in front of it,' a young woman exclaimed to her companion.

'How the hell did he not see it coming?' someone else asked the stranger next to her.

'His clothes must have caught on something, the way he got dragged right underneath that bus,' a middle-aged man said. 'There's no way you can make every vehicle safe against every accident. Poor sod.'

'Stupid sod,' another voice said.

The driver got out of the bus and leant against it, vomiting abruptly when he saw a blood-covered leg with a crushed foot sticking out from underneath the vehicle, just before the rear wheels.

Vicki went forward and took charge, yelling for someone to call for another ambulance, though when she bent down to peer underneath the bus, she felt sick herself and was quite sure they wouldn't be able to do anything for the accident victim, who wasn't showing any signs of life and had been mangled by the heavy vehicle.

Rob made no attempt to join the people gathering round the bus, but after one glance at the still body left Vicki to it and went back to Carla.

He put an arm round her and said quietly, 'He's dead.'

She could only gape at him.

'It's over. You've nothing else to fear from him.'

'But I didn't want it to end that way.'

'It wasn't your fault. He ran out in front of the bus.' He pulled her into both his arms and simply held her close as they waited for the ambulances and the traffic officers who dealt with serious incidents to arrive.

'Is she all right?'

He looked round to see Vicki standing next to them.

'Yes. Just . . . shocked.'

'We all are. He stabbed Murad. I saw that but I

wanted to get to Carla, in case he attacked her as well.'

'He'll never be able to attack anyone else, thank goodness.'

Carla said it again. 'I'd not have wanted it to end like that.'

'No one would. But he was violent to the end, wasn't he? He brought it upon himself,' Vicki said.

Carla made no attempt to move away from the comfort of Rob's arms.

He looked at the detective. 'Anything I need to do?'

Vicki shook her head. 'No. I just wanted to check that you two were all right. You look after Carla. I'll go back to crowd control. There's a first aider looking after Murad, thank goodness.'

As she walked back to the bus, there was the sound of an ambulance, followed soon afterwards by other sirens wailing and heralding the arrival of two police cars.

He tugged Carla away from the suddenly busy scene and told a young policewoman who tried to stop him leaving that he'd already spoken to the female detective. He pulled out his police ID card and she took one glance at it and let them leave.

As they walked slowly back across the park, Brett came running towards them. 'We only just got back. What's happened?'

'Bad accident. Man killed. We need to take Carla home and not clutter up the scene of the accident.'

'Yes. Right. Would a cup of tea be any help?'

Rob nodded. 'It'd be wonderful.'

Brett ran back ahead of them.

It seemed to take ages before they got back to the units and Brett's door was open so Carla let Rob guide her inside it.

'I'm all right now,' she said. 'Truly I am.'

Brett was putting the kettle on. 'Sit down.'

There was a knock on the door. Amanda and Matthew came in to join in.

Rob told them what had happened, then realised Carla was still clinging to him. 'Sit down. You're white.'

'Shock,' Amanda said.

Gradually Carla calmed down and later she even nibbled a sandwich from the plateful that Amanda had gone home to make and bring across. Rob nipped back to the scene of the accident then returned to report that the victim's body had been taken away and the crowd had dispersed. Murad had been taken to A&E and Vicki said she'd be round to talk to Carla the following morning.

'I'm staying the night with you,' he told Carla firmly. 'You shouldn't be left alone.'

She nodded. 'Thanks. I can't think of anyone I'd rather have with me than you.'

'Good.'

Amanda and Matthew exchanged quick nods of approval at that but didn't comment.

When the two of them went back to her unit, Carla sat beside Rob on the sofa and it seemed natural to put his arm round her. There was a blanket folded up on it, so he covered her with that.

The television was on but he couldn't have said what was being shown. In a surprisingly short time, Carla's breathing slowed down and he realised she was asleep.

So he sneaked part of the blanket, wriggled into a more comfortable position and closed his eyes. There was nothing they could do at the moment but recover from a very nasty incident. And he'd locked the entrance door as he came in.

He could get very used to cuddling her to sleep.

Chapter Thirty-One

The following day, Grant drove into Essington town centre and stopped his little car to ask his way to Magnolia Gardens.

'It's not a good time to go to the park,' the man told him. 'They've had a murderer on the rampage and there's police tape everywhere.'

'*What?*'

'Luckily the sod ran out in front of a bus and fate gave him his come-uppance,' he added with relish. 'Dead, he is now. Very dead.'

'Oh. Well, right.'

'But there are still police up there. Did you want to walk round the park or were you going to visit somebody?'

'I was told that my uncle has recently moved into a unit there.'

'Ah. Yes. Well, you don't need to go to the park to get to them new units, fortunately. You'll be able to turn off the lane before the scene of the accident.' He gave directions and stepped back.

Grant found his way there without any trouble, but when he got to the end of the curving street and saw the car park and the units, he slowed right down, feeling suddenly apprehensive. He hoped his uncle would understand. Surely he would? He'd done nothing wrong and he'd saved their money. It was all a misunderstanding, and they could get past that, couldn't they?

He drove the last few yards into the car park very slowly and stopped next to the other car. A man of about his own age came out of one of the four units.

'Were you looking for someone?'

'My uncle. Matthew Woodley.'

'Is he expecting you?'

'No. I've just got back from abroad.'

'Goodness.'

As they were speaking, the door of Number 3 opened and Matthew stood there, staring across at his nephew. 'You're the last person I'd expected to see here.'

Grant walked across to him but he didn't move out of the way. 'Aren't you going to invite me in?'

'Should I?'

'Yes. I think there may have been some misunderstanding because I've had trouble finding you.'

'Well, I suppose you'd better come in and explain, then.' Matthew turned and led the way in.

Rob watched the younger man follow him inside and the door close, then left them to it and went back into Carla's unit. He was still reluctant to leave her on her own. He'd stay with her all day but take her out to the pub for a meal that night. She should be able to face going out again by then.

Matthew led the way inside. 'Close the door. I suppose I'd better offer you a cup of tea, though I'm not sure whether you deserve it.'

He'd always been blunt but Grant had never heard him sound so frosty. 'I rather think I do, and if you'll let me explain, you may think so too.'

'Take a seat at the table, then.'

He did and watched his uncle move deftly to and fro in the kitchen area. He didn't try to make conversation, not till he had his companion's full attention.

When they were both sitting with mugs of tea in front of them, Matthew said, 'Go on. Tell me what's happened to my money.'

His expression was so sharp and suspicious that Grant was quite sure he'd guessed wrongly that it had been lost, so he changed what he'd been going to say first.

'What's happened is that I've saved your money and it'll be transferred to your bank account early next week.'

Matthew gaped at him.

'But there were a couple of glitches on the way and I had to rush off to Brazil to sort them out, which is why I disappeared.'

'Good heavens! *You were in Brazil?*'

'I have to confess that I rushed into these investments

too optimistically and things did get into a mess. So I let my house – I have a friend who's an estate agent – and flew to Brazil. I took over the management of the project and I don't think I've ever worked as hard in my life or had as little sleep. But I managed to pull things together and now I've sold the business as I always planned to do.' He waited and added slowly and clearly, 'At a profit too.'

His uncle was staring at him as if he was speaking a foreign language. 'Slow down, and start again at the beginning.'

So Grant confessed his sins and brought out the various summary figures from his briefcase, though he hadn't had time to finish them off. Then he sat back and waited as his uncle went through them.

Eventually Matthew looked up and said quietly, 'Well done.'

Grant smiled. 'I promise you I shall never rush into something so risky again, not as long as I live.'

'At least you retrieved the money.'

'Not just retrieved, doubled it.'

'What? Are you serious? *Doubled it?*'

'Yes. And when it's safely in your bank, we'll go out and celebrate.'

'I agree. But if it's in your bank now, it should be safe enough, so I apologise for thinking badly of you, Grant lad.'

'I deserved it. I'm going to set up my own little business now, as I planned, and work quietly and steadily. And

I'm not risking a single penny ever again.'

'Good. It's about time you found yourself a wife, then. Or are you intending to be the last of our branch of the Woodleys?'

His nephew blinked in surprise at this abrupt change of subject, then shrugged. 'I've been out with plenty of women but never met one I wanted to settle down with.'

'We'll have to start looking. In the meantime, I can put you up in my spare bedroom here. Where are you going to settle down and start this business of yours?'

'I haven't thought about that. It's online so I can live where I please.'

'Well, bear in mind that I'm intending to settle in this area. I really like Essington St Mary, and the people are very kind and friendly.'

'I'll – er – have a look round, but I'm going to sell my current house and rent somewhere cheap while I set up the business.'

'Good idea. Now, there's something else. I'd better introduce you to a lad I've taken under my wing. I've grown very fond of young Brett and I hope you will too.'

'Who is he?'

As Matthew explained about Brett, he didn't realise how his voice softened, but Grant did and was pleased by that. It showed that his uncle had moved on from losing his wife.

'I haven't asked him yet, mind, but I'm thinking of asking Brett to join the family. I'm sure you'll like him. He's a really nice person.'

'If you like him so much, I'm sure I will too. I'll look forward to meeting him.'

'You won't have to wait long, then. Stay there and I'll fetch him. He lives next door.'

Grant let out his breath in a few long slow exhalations as he waited. His uncle hadn't changed. Except perhaps to start recovering from his grief. But once he'd made his mind up, he still went straight to the point, both in words and deeds. Though he didn't often make mistakes about people.

He heard footsteps and turned to see Matthew come in, accompanied by a tall, bespectacled lad with an extremely nice smile.

Grant got up to shake hands. 'Pleased to meet you, Brett. I'm so glad my uncle found someone to look after him while I was overseas.' He waited and sure enough his uncle opened his mouth to protest and looked at him indignantly.

'I don't need looking after.'

Grant winked at Brett, who'd cottoned on to his teasing quickly and smiled back. 'I thought that'd get you going, Uncle Matthew.' That got him a smile.

'You're still a joker, I see. But I wish to make it clear that I'm not nearly old enough to need looking after, if you don't mind!'

Brett hovered near the door. 'It's nice to meet you but I should leave you two to catch up.'

Matthew went across, put an arm round Brett's shoulders and pulled him across to sit with them at the table. 'Don't do that. Come and join us, and join the family while you're at it, lad.'

'What do you mean?'

Grant smiled and added, 'He wants you to join what's left of the Woodley tribe. If you can stand us.' He'd never yet found a person his uncle liked to be anything but a good human being and this lad had a lovely smile.

'I meant that about joining the family literally,' Matthew said. 'Mind if I call you my nephew from now on?'

Brett caught his breath and stared from one man to the other, seeing both of them nod and smile.

'You'll have noticed by now that my uncle isn't exactly the tactful type,' Grant said. 'But if he wants you in the family, it's all right by me. Can you stand us?'

Brett turned to stare at Matthew, who pulled him to lean across into a quick hug.

Grant smiled at Brett and held out his hand, shaking the lad's hand gently. 'I gather you've done really well with your eyesight lately.'

'Yes. It's been . . . an interesting few days. And now this.'

'I accept your offer of a bed, Uncle, but let me invite you both out for tea tonight. I'm pining for a good hearty meal at an English pub. I'm sure there must be one or two places to eat in town. Meals have been a haphazard affair for the last few weeks.'

Matthew nodded. 'I thought you'd lost a bit of weight. A pub meal would be very nice. I was only going to get some frozen meals out. I warn you, though. Brett has a hearty appetite.'

'So do I.' Grant glanced at his watch. 'How about we go straight away? I don't care if we're their first customers.'

'Are you sure you two want me with you?' Brett asked hesitantly.

'Wouldn't have invited you otherwise,' Matthew said. 'Are you sure you want to join us?'

Brett's smile lit up the room. 'Very sure indeed. In every sense.'

Matthew cleared his throat, then turned to his nephew and gave him a big hug, after which he gave his nose a big honking blow into a crumpled handkerchief.

Grant nudged Brett. 'We'll lead the way outside and let him pull himself together before he follows us. He's been under a bit of financial stress and now everything is all right, hence the heavy emotion.'

'And he's pleased to see you.'

'Yes. And that, thank goodness.'

As they walked out, Grant said, 'Good thing we're all tall. We match nicely.'

'I'm still growing, actually.'

'Then I think you're going to be the tallest of us all.'

Was it that easy? Brett wondered, then gave a mental shrug. He thought they meant it about joining the family, and he certainly did. He could cope, though, however this ended. He'd always found ways to cope.

How strange life could be! But this might be the most

wonderful thing of all, after his glasses.

On that thought, he said it aloud: 'This is all amazing – but wonderful!'

Which won them another nose-blowing session from Matthew. No, his uncle Matthew now.

And a warm smile from Grant, who looked just like a younger version of his uncle.

Chapter Thirty-Two

The following morning, Riley from the university phoned and since he didn't manage to contact the lad directly, he spoke to Amanda and explained the situation.

When she put the phone down, she grabbed an umbrella and went straight across the garden to Brett's unit, knocking on Matthew's door then coming back to wait for Brett to respond.

'Good news!' she called when they both poked their heads out of their doors. 'Which unit shall we use for getting together?'

Brett couldn't hold back a yawn. 'Whose good news is it?'

'Yours, but it's partly Matthew's as well.'

'Then let's use my unit. And could we ask Grant and Carla to join us too?'

'Yes, of course.'

Brett put the kettle on and waited for them all to join him, still marvelling that he had somewhere to invite his friends – and the man who was far more than a friend now. That still seemed incredible to him but he was quite sure Matthew had meant it, and Grant had seemed to agree.

They'd had a good time at the pub, getting to know one another. Grant was rather like his uncle, same straightforward attitude to the world, same smile that brought out the resemblance between them.

He realised they were all sitting and waiting for him to pay attention and shut down his thoughts.

Amanda said, 'Riley phoned to ask if he could come over and speak to you.'

'Yes, of course. I'm always happy to see him. He's so interesting to talk to,' Brett said.

She got out her phone. 'I'll just let him know to come and join us. He's waiting in town.' When she put it away, she said, 'It's good news of some sort, I gather.'

'Do you have any idea what?'

'I'm afraid not.'

'We seem to have reached a stage of several bits of good news after some bad things happening,' Matthew said gravely. 'About time.'

'After Riley has finished, I need to speak to you about something, Carla,' said Amanda.

They were all on the alert at that.

'Not bad news?' Matthew asked.

'I'm not sure. I think you should hear it on your own, so that you can judge.'

'I don't mind them knowing, whatever it is,' Carla said. 'Tell us all now. We've been through a lot together.'

'Well, all right. The police want to see you, so I'm going to offer you my services as a lawyer if you need them. And don't worry. I won't be charging you for that but doing it pro bono as your friend.'

Carla looked worried. 'I haven't done anything wrong, surely?'

'Oh no, I'm sure you haven't. But it's always best to be careful when the police are dealing with the run-off from such a nasty situation. I'll give them a call and ask when and where they want to see you.'

She did that and ended the call quite quickly. 'As soon as possible. Can you be ready to leave in about half an hour?'

'Yes, of course.'

'Ah, here's Riley.'

He parked and came hurrying across the car park, beaming at Brett as he opened the door.

'We're all in here. Do come in.'

Grant was introduced and everyone stared expectantly at Riley.

'I've come with an offer for you. The university has a research fund for helping special-case students. I've mentioned your situation to them and they'd like to meet you and discuss how they might be able to help you.'

Brett stared at him in surprise. 'University? I haven't even had a proper schooling.'

'That's the beauty of it. These are cases where educational catch-up is tailored to an individual's needs, and we are particularly interested in how improving a person's vision can impact on their academic performance. Are you interested in them developing a set of educational programmes for you? You'd have to promise to work hard and there's no charge, but they'll want to document what happens and learn how to improve what they do on this programme from how you cope.'

Brett looked questioningly towards Matthew, who nodded encouragement, then at Amanda, who said, 'How wonderful for you!'

He turned back to Riley. 'I'm interested.'

'Good. Can you come to chat to them tomorrow? It happens to be the afternoon they meet.'

'Yes, I can do that. How do I get there?'

'I'll drive you there,' Amanda said at once.

'And Brett,' she continued, 'you remember that on your behalf I complained to the department of community services about your treatment at the various foster placements you had, especially the fact that no one took the trouble to check your eyesight properly? They have sent us a reply expressing their "profound apologies for your past treatment", and said that they are reviewing the whole way in which foster children are cared for so that a situation cannot occur again.'

'The usual bureaucratic flannel,' commented Matthew.

Then, Brett really did make everyone cups of tea, and if it was served in mugs that didn't match, no one cared as they spent a happy hour or two getting to know one another better and discussing life, the universe and everything.

'I see what you mean about Brett's lovely nature,' Grant whispered to his uncle at one stage.

'It's amazing, isn't it, that he's stayed so nice?'

'It is. His gentleness shows in his face.'

'He already feels like family.' Matthew sneaked a glance at his blood nephew.

Grant patted his shoulder. 'Stop worrying. As far as I'm concerned, he is. You've always been a superb judge of character.'

Amanda and Carla drove into town to the police station. They were shown into a waiting room where a police sergeant they'd never met before joined them, accompanied by a man in ordinary clothing.

She held out one hand. 'I'm Sergeant Pat Lennox and this is Peter Foxton. We need to talk to you about your ex, Carla.'

She shuddered. 'I don't even like to think about him.'

'Well, there are still a few things to clear up from his life, I'm afraid. Some of our people have gone through his house. They found a lot of women's clothing and some books with your name inside, other items of interest as well.'

'But I haven't lived there for months.'

'We wondered if the clothes are yours and you'd like to have them back. If you'd come there with us, we can go through everything else. If there are some more of your possessions, you should be able to get them back too.'

Carla stared at her in surprise. This was the last thing she'd expected to hear. 'I thought he'd have thrown everything of mine away.'

'On the contrary. There's a bedroom where what we think are your possessions are all neatly stored. It looks as if you're about to come back from an outing.'

Amanda seized the moment. 'What about my client's money?'

'What money?'

Carla explained about how he'd taken the money she'd inherited from her parents from their joint bank account.

'Can you prove that?'

'My parents' lawyer can and the bank will surely have records.' She gave the sergeant the lawyer's details and the necessary information about her own bank account.

'We'd like you to go back to his house again tomorrow afternoon and check things. Can you meet us there, Carla?'

'We'll both come and I'll drive you, Carla,' Amanda said, then remembered Brett. 'I'll get Matthew to take Brett to his meeting at the university. He won't mind and those people don't stand on ceremony, so he'll be all right.'

When they got back to the car, they sat for a moment, then Amanda asked gently, 'You all right going back there?'

'I'll manage. Especially if you're with me.' She looked at the older woman and added slowly, 'Actually I'll be more than all right going back if it means I can get my money back. Him stealing that was one of the things that upset me most.'

The following day, Brett went to the university with Matthew and Grant and they left him there with Riley, agreeing to come and pick him up when he phoned them.

He went into a comfortable sitting room, feeling nervous, as if this was going to be an interview. But once again he found himself relaxing and talking to the group of people who formed the casual committee overseeing this particular research program.

They talked about all sorts of things, and seemed particularly interested in his experiences since he'd received his special glasses.

Then they showed him round the department of optometry and to his delight let him try out some of the equipment.

When the tour was finished, he was taken back for an afternoon tea and they suggested he send for his friends to join them.

The food was excellent but best of all was when a man called for quiet. 'I should like to propose a toast.' He lifted his wine glass. 'Here's to the latest recipient of the Amata Award.'

Brett found they were all staring at him and raising their glasses to him and shot a puzzled glance at the proposer.

'I don't think I've ever found it easier to choose

someone who deserves to receive this award and the money that goes with it, money that will pay all your fees and costs of living, Brett, as well as the cost of putting together a special programme of classes to enable you to catch up on your studies.'

He couldn't find the words to reply, was too astonished to do anything but turn and look pleadingly at Matthew.

'I think I shall have to speak on behalf of my young friend,' he said. 'Brett is grateful for the award and promises he won't waste a minute of your time during the year to come. In fact I've never met anyone so eager to learn.' He raised his glass in a private toast to his young friend.

As they drove home, Brett sighed blissfully. 'My life has never been so good and a lot of it is thanks to you, Matthew.'

'It's mainly thanks to yourself and I'm sure you'll go far, with or without any help.'

It wasn't till Brett went to bed that he let loose the tears of joy that had been giving him a husky voice and a bit of a sniffly nose from time to time since he got the news.

He felt like the luckiest person on earth tonight and the future seemed to be glowing brightly ahead of him.

And best of all, he had Matthew and Grant to share it with. They were going to live in a house together, make a new home for themselves and had already agreed that it'd have to be near the university so that he could attend the classes, talks and lectures that were offered to him.

They said women were the ones to cry for happiness, but he could tell the world that men did that too.

That same afternoon, Carla asked Rob to go with her and Amanda to Frank's house. She was starting to feel that she could do anything if he was by her side and he was showing no sign of trying to avoid her company. On the contrary.

When they got there, he opened the car door for her but when she stayed where she was in the passenger seat and simply stared at the house where she'd been so unhappy, he glanced at Amanda, who was waiting in the driving seat and who simply shrugged and didn't try to hurry them.

In the end Carla found the courage to get out of the car, take hold of the hand Rob held out to her and move towards the house.

A uniformed police officer opened the front door before she got there and looked at Rob and Amanda, then back at her.

'My friend came with me, as well as my lawyer,' she said.

'That's fine. Do you two have ID?'

They showed him some, then he said, 'Come in, everyone.'

Carla moved slowly and reluctantly forward. The house was the same as ever, painfully neat and smelling of his aftershave still. She had to force herself to go forward to meet the other police officer, an older woman.

It took several hours for them to go through the house, opening drawers and cupboards and letting her explain some things. The officers took it in turns to film what they found and did with things, as well as recording their comments.

What had been her bedroom – Frank hadn't liked actually sleeping with anyone – was as immaculate as the rest. She'd left it in a mess when she ran off, but after he recovered from his broken leg, he must have gone through it all and set it to rights again. Most of her clothes were still there and when she said she'd like to have them back, a young constable began putting them in cardboard removals boxes.

They found a pile of books and she picked hers out from them and they too were carefully packed.

They found his bank books and one account had a lot of money in it.

She didn't want to base any of this on lies and deceit, so said, 'That money isn't all mine.' She told them how much had been taken from her and they nodded.

'You'll get the money after it's been audited and approved of by a judge. It's being treated differently from your own possessions, which clearly didn't belong to him.'

'That's all right. I can wait.'

In the end they'd gone through every room and she was really glad when they said that was it and she could go home.

She sat in the car again, feeling boneless with exhaustion and stress. The boot was full of boxes.

She might be tired but her heart was feeling lighter, somehow. As if she was removing the last of her life from Frank's clutches as well as the last of her possessions.

On the way, Rob stopped at a pub. 'Let's buy a meal here. You've hardly eaten anything today.'

'Yes, let's.'

As the three of them got out, she smiled at him and Amanda. 'Thank you for enduring what must have been a very boring day for you.'

'It wasn't boring to see you regain your possessions. My goodness, you're not going to need to buy clothes for a while, are you?'

Amanda hesitated. 'It's not far from home. How about I leave you two here and you can get a taxi back? I think you should celebrate together and make plans. You can pick up your boxes from my cottage.'

Rob smiled and nodded. 'Good idea.'

Carla gave her a quick hug. 'Thank you, Amanda. It was good to have you there.'

'I'll keep an eye on the handover of the money for you.'

'I'd appreciate that.'

They waved goodbye and she drove off, then Rob took Carla's hand and they walked into the pub.

As she looked at the blackboard menu, she suddenly felt ravenous.

'What do you fancy?' he asked.

'A lot. Seafood starter, veal parmigiana with a side salad, and ice cream.'

'I'll have the same thing. Drinks?'

'Non-alcoholic cider.'

'I'll join you in that.'

They chatted quietly as they ate, and Carla found that even their silences felt good, because she felt so right with him.

By the time they got back to the unit, she was asleep in the passenger seat and he had to wake her up, which he did with a very satisfactory kiss.

'Come in with me,' she said. 'I'd like to fall asleep next to you in a proper bed.'

'I'd like that too.'

But it was a while before they slept.

Epilogue

When they heard nothing more about the money in Frank's bank accounts, Carla shrugged.

'You're not upset?' Rob asked. 'I have something to tell you tonight, but I want it to be a happy occasion, so I can wait if you still need time to get over anything.'

'I don't care desperately about money because I feel so happy with you.'

'What do you care about?'

She smiled and said softly, 'Don't you know?' She took the initiative. 'It's you I care about.'

'That's the correct answer. But there's just one more thing.'

He suddenly went down on one knee, took her hand and said with the sweetest smile she'd ever seen on a man, 'I've been planning to ask you to be my wife. Or partner. Or whatever you wish to call it. Will you?'

'I want to be your wife, Rob darling. I feel rather traditional about that with you, though I've never wanted to marry anyone before.'

'Never?'

'No. Frank brainwashed me about all sorts of things, but he could never persuade me to marry him. You're the only man I've ever wanted to marry, darling, and the sooner the better as far as I'm concerned.'

He stood up and swept her into his arms.

It was a moment or two before they realised that the sound they'd been only half hearing was the doorbell.

'Don't answer it,' she said.

'We don't know who it is. If someone bothers to ring the doorbell more than once I usually bother to answer it.' He grabbed her hand. 'But on this occasion we'll both answer it together.'

A man was standing with a special delivery package. 'Ms Carla Hewitt?'

'Yes.'

'Sign here please.'

He had driven away even before they got back inside.

She looked at the sender details on the slender parcel. 'It's from the police! I thought we'd done with them.'

'You'd better open it, then. It's a special delivery.'

She did that and opened the package inside, reading the brief letter and gasping aloud. 'I can't believe it. An independent judge has decided that I should have all the money in Frank's bank accounts since we'd been living together for nearly two years.'

She held it out to Rob and he read it quickly. 'Good heavens! Have you seen the amount?'

'Yes.'

'It's a lot.'

'Yes, but would you mind if I gave some of it to a charity?'

He guessed suddenly what she was going to say. 'Not at all.'

'I was thinking about a women's refuge?'

'Sounds a brilliant idea to me.'

'Thank you. But let's use some of it to treat the friends we've made here, and do it before Matthew and Brett move into their new home?'

'Good idea. But on one condition.'

'Oh?'

'That you consider me a special case and promise to give me a long lingering kiss every morning for the rest of our lives.'

'I shall need to practise that.'

He spread his arms wide as if helpless, but with his usual lovely smile. 'Go ahead. I'm happy to find out the sort of kiss we like best.'

She felt as if the whole world were shimmering with joy as she kissed him. And it wasn't the money that was causing it but the love she could see on his face.

This time she felt quite certain she was doing the right thing. So she pulled him towards her, kissed him then waltzed him round the room.

Then they went together to invite their friends to join them for a very special meal to celebrate their engagement.

ANNA JACOBS was born in Lancashire at the beginning of the Second World War. She has lived in different parts of England as well as Australia and has enjoyed setting her modern and historical novels in both countries. She is addicted to telling stories and recently celebrated the publication of her one hundredth novel, as well as sixty years of marriage. Anna has sold over four million copies of her books to date.

annajacobs.com